COCKY PLAYER

STACEY LYNN

ONE

Brenna

"STOP FIDGETING." Gina smacked my hand on the hem of my way too short and skintight white dress.

I loved fashion as much as the next girl, but I'd spent the last fifteen years at all-girls boarding schools and college. It was ingrained in me for my clothing choices to be more conservative than the strapless stretchy cloth Gina insisted was actually a dress.

"You've stuffed me into this thing like a sausage," I grumbled, smoothing it down again. Too many tugs to make the length longer risked exposing my breasts. How in the heck did she think I'd be comfortable in this? The more important question was probably why did I let her talk me into wearing this?

"Well, you're the prettiest sausage I've ever seen then. And the men will think so, too." She hip checked me playfully, sending me almost sprawling to the pavement in my four-inch death trap heels. I bought them years ago but never had the guts to wear them before.

Tonight was about jumping in with both feet to my new life. Free from curfews and overprotective parents. Free from rules and Resident Advisors who acted like keeping control of our dorm at Vanderwilde Women's College was akin to keeping inmates in a maximum-security prison in line.

And the biggie: freedom to finally lose my V-Card. Hence the dress and hair out to there and makeup thicker than anything I'd done before. Three hours at a beauty salon and I'd been plucked and lacquered and highlighted and tweezed until I walked out looking like I was preparing to step on stage at the Miss Universe pageant.

But it was for a good cause. The first choice I made after college graduation when I'd put my foot down with my parents. I would move into my own apartment, start my own life, and yes...I'd go to work in the marketing department for the Rough Riders football team, a job courtesy of my father, current owner of the organization. Nepotism was alive and well, but I'd take the helping hand when it suited me.

Yes, tonight was about finding someone for a one-night stand. He had to be attractive. He had to not come across like a serial killer or stalker. But he had to be the kind of guy who would get the job done so I could stop worrying about giving it up to someone I was dating, embarrassed that I was twenty-three years old and I'd spent so much of my life separated from guys and now men, that I'd rarely had the opportunity. I had it all planned out.

Thankfully, my best friend made an excellent wingman.

"Let's just hope this works," I said, clasping onto Gina's hand while we were shoved through the line entering Glitz.

"Please. You already know you look incredible. All you have to worry about is not backing out. Trust me, you'll have all the men falling over their feet to get you tonight." She tugged my hand and got my attention. Perfectly coiffed brown eyebrows furrowed and her brown eyes bore into me with concern. "Although, it *is* totally okay if you decide not to go through with this, right? Don't feel pressured."

This was why she was my best friend. Gina and I met freshman year, shoved together in a dorm room the size of a sardine can. She came from an uber-rich family who helped build aircraft for the military on the east coast. She encouraged my wild side and protected my introverted side equally. Always there to jump into whatever I suggested, and yet wrap her arm around me when my common sense kicked in and I held back.

I was tired of shoving my wild side to the back burner.

"I know," I assured her, almost bumping into the group of women in front of us. Mid-twenties, hair that smelled of hairspray and mousse when the breeze blew. "I'll be safe."

"I have no doubt about that."

We shuffled along and soon found ourselves at the front of the line, handing over our driver's licenses. It would've been easy to request a VIP table, but we nixed that idea as soon as Gina mentioned it. If I was going to find somebody, I didn't want my selection to be mostly confined to the small number of people in the VIP level.

It took a moment for my eyes to adjust to the darkness of the club. Chandeliers glittered from the high ceiling and above the bar on the right and a second one I could vaguely see at the back. The dance floor was already packed and lights shimmering to the beat of the music from the DJ booth made it difficult to see faces.

"This is wild!" Gina exclaimed, shouting into my ear. The noise was deafening and already my feet were tapping to the beat. If there were one thing I could do and even excel at, it was dancing. Twenty years of ballet and jazz and hip-hop, even taking classes in college when I once considered minoring in dance ensured that.

"Drinks!" I pointed my freshly manicured finger in the direction of the bar and pressed Gina in the direction.

"Excellent idea. First round is on me!"

Gina's long and curled chestnut-colored hair bounced as she slid through throngs of people. It was only ten o'clock on a Friday. I had no idea the bar would be so packed so early.

We finally made it and while we waited to gain one of the bartender's attention, I scanned the area around us.

Men. A hot one who didn't seem like a creep. It was harder to find one I was attracted to than I'd originally thought. Hot guys were everywhere, but some wore that glazed expression of a night that hinted that they'd been at Happy Hour and drinking for hours already.

Patience. I had hours. I also had forever so if tonight didn't work, I would return.

Holding onto my virginity had never been my idea. I wasn't waiting for a serious relationship or to be in love. I never planned on waiting for marriage, although that would have made both of my parents extremely thankful.

It was simply a matter of lack of opportunity, but now, that opportunity was mine for the taking.

A cold plastic cup was pressed into my hand.

"Found anyone yet?"

"No." I scanned the bar and lines of people waiting for drinks and demanding them again. I grinned at her over my shoulder and waggled my eyebrows. "Ready to dance?"

I could lose myself in the music, the rhythm of the bass, the sexual pull of bodies pressed together. It wasn't like I'd never been to bars or clubs before, but at Vanderwilde, we were required to be back in our rooms by midnight on the weekends.

That timeframe never hindered Gina from dating and guys and anything else she wanted to experience.

More than once I'd snuck her in a back stairwell well after curfew, or minutes before the doors unlocked in the morning.

Me? It took me years to be ready for something like that and then I was too worried about getting caught, upsetting my parents.

It was something I had to learn to let go of if I was truly going to make it on my own. My past and history with my parents made it too easy for them to cling to me in a way they hadn't with my siblings.

Although they were all also married with a half-dozen children between them. It was easy to loosen the strings on the children who hadn't terrified my parents for days.

I shoved the reminder down. It was so far in the past the lingering effects were usually minimal. The last place I wanted memories popping up was here. Not now.

Dance floor. I need to dance.

"Lead the way, hot stuff." Gina gestured with her own drink, vodka and club soda most likely.

We shoved our way through more crowds. More drunken men who swayed on their feet, sloppily hitting on girls in little black dresses left and right. It wasn't until we were ensconced on the dance floor, hips swaying and arms raised while singing along to lyrics when I finally understood why Gina insisted I wore white.

Everyone, almost everyone anyway, was dressed in black and silver and red dresses. My white dress shone like a beacon and I imagined my strawberry blonde hair further put a spotlight on me.

Yes.

With the techno beats pumping through my veins, I lost myself in the music, the rush of the crowd, the press of bodies as we gyrated our hips. Gina and I danced together, swirled to partners, to hands that reached out to my hips. Scents of cologne and sweat overpowered me, pushing me from one partner to another.

Gina kept a close eye on me, reaching out to grab me, twirl me to her and out again, other girls joined us, moved away.

It was there in the crowd, the electric sensations of so many bodies close together, all enjoying and losing ourselves in the crush of the music and crowd along with the weeks of stress evaporating into the shimmering and pulsing lights, where I felt it.

A chill skittered down my arms and to my toes until my body erupted in goose bumps. Hairs at the back of my neck stood on end. Someone was watching me.

I stopped moving so quickly I bumped into Gina and reached out to keep her from falling onto the dance floor.

"Sorry!" I called out, but I didn't look at her as she resettled to her feet.

My gaze was focused, skipping from the men on the dance floor to the outer circle of guys who stayed close, probably couldn't shimmy their hips to a beat if their life depended on it but enjoyed watching the show, to the stairs...the upper level.

Straight to *him*.

He was there. Hands curled around a silver railing. Buttoned up white shirt un-tucked from jeans and sleeves rolled to his elbows. Casual.

Commanding.

Long dark hair on top, swept to the side but long enough it could also fall into his eyes.

I simply felt his pull. *Felt him.* I stood still and raised my drink in his direction.

His response was a nod. So minuscule it was difficult to see from the distance but even then, I knew he was the one watching me.

And if he wanted to watch? I'd give him the show of his life.

Two men flanked him, one shoved his shoulder, the other crossed his arms over his massive chest. The men were *huge*.

Yes. That was going to be him.

If he could gain my attention with a look from a hundred feet away, he was definitely the kind of guy who could do other things to me even more intensely.

I twirled around and gave him my back, grinning at Gina.

Nodding my head toward the direction of the guy, I leaned closer to her and shouted in her ear. "That guy in the white still watching?"

"Oh yeah! Salivating is more like it! Let's make it good." She slid her arm around me, pressed her chest to my back and then we ground to an R&B beat I didn't know but was perfect.

TWO

Connor

ANGEL.

It was the only word that came to mind when I saw her. Innocent. Pristine and pure. It could have been her creamy pale skin. It could have been due to the dress she wore, bright white, a shining light on her that illuminated her out of the crowd of hundreds of dancers on the floor beneath me.

Too damn sweet for me. I saw her as soon as she started twisting and turning her way to the dance floor. In a sea of darkness, she was the only one I noticed. Long, light red hair that had to be professionally colored recently. It gleamed when the chandeliers and lights danced over her. It was impossible to take my eyes off her despite the fact I hadn't come to Glitz tonight for this.

For her.

There was no way in hell I was leaving without meeting her. Touching her. Tasting the sensitive skin at her neck, right behind her ear where she'd sigh and press her generous tits to my chest. From the distance between us, it was impossible to tell her size, but she was dwarfed by most of the men, taller than most of the women. In heels, most likely with pointed, spiky heels that would feel incredible digging into my ass as I rode her hard. Rough.

"Found one yet?" Kolby Jones, a teammate of mine, asked. Nice as hell, rarely one to hook up with someone from a bar.

He blamed it on having a daughter, raising her by himself with the help of his mom. Proclaimed he wanted to set a good example of what kind of man she should want in her future. I said the girl was five, oblivious to what her dad did when he wasn't home. No matter, the man had more morals in his pinky finger than I had in my entire body.

Beaux Hale, another teammate and one of my best friends stepped to my other side, crossing his arms. "The one in white," he said.

As he spoke, the girl who was indeed the one in white, faced us and lifted her drink. A challenge or an acknowledgment? It didn't matter to me.

Her friend slid behind her and wrapped her hand to the angel's stomach. They swayed and danced, a provocative move done to ensure my attention fixated on her.

It wasn't a guess.

She kept glancing at me over her shoulder, tucking hair behind her ear when she saw I was still watching her before glancing away.

"How'd you guess?"

"She's sexy enough to attract every man's attention in this place. But you never go for the sweet ones, probably because you'd leave them in tears."

He wasn't wrong.

"Not my fault they'll never get better than me." It was true.

I was damn good in bed. Damn good at giving women every-thing they wanted, leaving them breathless and exhausted. I imagined if I stuck around until morning they'd also tell me about their sore hips and stomach muscles. It wasn't arrogant bullshit, just the truth. I never went back though, and this girl already had me thinking of tomorrow. Which meant she wasn't only beautiful, but dangerous.

I kept my sexual nights to one-night encounters for a reason, and I learned it after trying to date my first few years playing pro football. By the time the few I knew found out who I was, that glimmer of sexual satisfaction turned to something much more vicious.

Jersey jumpers. The last thing I needed was that in my life, a woman who didn't want me for me but for what I could give them. A small amount of local fame, a glance here and there on television during a game or a photo op at a fellow teammate's fundraiser. Women somehow blew our fame out of proportion thinking it would give them something more than a few thou-sand followers on Instagram and they were wild with trying to attract it.

No, thank you. I had little use for drama and less desire to get caught up with a woman who thrived on it. I preferred things simple. We both got off, she loved it, I took what I needed to relieve the stress enough to keep my head in the game. We both left satisfied with a smile on our face and a lack of promises given.

And I didn't have to worry about getting caught up in the drama of a relationship that could easily fall sour when undoubtedly, I refused to show her the attention she craved because I was too damn focused on my career as a running back, the only thing I'd wanted since I could remember. Age three, to be exact, watching the Super Bowl on my grandpa's knee. Beer bottle in one of his hands, my baby blanket over his shoulder, bouncing me to keep me quiet and engaged in watching the Packers crush the Patriots...two of the greatest all-time teams with the best quarterbacks duking it out.

I never had the arm to throw the ball like Favre or Rodgers or Brady, but I had feet faster than anyone currently in the league.

So women? No, I didn't have time for them. Not past the few hours I needed them.

And the angel? She wasn't my type at all.

Too sweet. Too breakable.

Yet no one else had grabbed my attention all night.

Which meant it was her or no one—and it'd been awhile.

"Damn," Kolby said next to me. "She can move."

Hips swaying. Hands slid down her body to the curve of her hips. Head thrown back to her friend's shoulder. Men swarmed them and watched, two beautiful women who had to be close to my age, maybe a year or two younger, acting like they were screwing on the dance floor always did. They weren't the only two acting the same way, but they had the largest group of admirers.

"Wait too long and she'll be taken."

It was from Beaux. Why he encouraged my assholish behavior was anyone's guess. I'd say it was because he was married and his sex life had turned boring, but I'd met Paige. Hell, I heard them going at it at all times of day when we spent time together hanging out. More than once he'd left me during a game we were watching in the off-season only to return later after getting his wife off. Loudly. Paige could scream the walls down.

How loud would the angel scream? Or would she be quiet and reserved, whimpering through her orgasm as I ate her or biting her lips to not draw attention. I was dying to find out.

"What are you still doing here?" He hardly came out with

us single guys anymore. Tonight was different because the season was starting soon. It was one of our last nights and we were showing the new players, those drafted and traded, a good time before we left for training camp in a few weeks.

"Paige is having Shannon and some of the other wives and girlfriends over tonight. They're probably sloshed on wine and cheese boards or some stupid shit like that."

A drunk wife? "So what are you still doing here?" I teased.

He laughed, shaking his head. "Fuck off, Quinten. I'll get some later, don't you worry."

Fucking sounded like a great idea. I slapped them both on the shoulders and stepped back. "Enjoy your night."

"Don't get arrested," Kolby called back to me.

I hadn't yet, despite my love of getting off in public places. It made one-night stands that much more fun. I loved the thrill of being caught. My name and photo splashed on gossip sites. It'd get me suspended from something I craved and needed in my life, something I loved, but the risk of it was such a damn turn on, it made me hard thinking about it.

Along with her—the angel. I was headed straight to hell and I would take her along with me.

THERE WERE times in public when I kept my head down, avoiding the gaze of others, mostly male fans, so I went unrecognized. This wasn't one of those times and as eyes widened in recognition as I stalked past tables filled with empty beer bottles and downed pitchers with plastic glasses knocked over, I hoped like hell it wouldn't bite me in the ass.

Phones coming out and pics being taken or being surrounded by fans would be a pain in the ass. I didn't always mind, but there was also a time and a place, and a fucking bar when we were all drinking and I wanted to get laid wasn't the place.

Head up, shoulders back, I strolled through Glitz like I owned the fucking place, which wasn't far off...forty-five percent owner made it almost as good as mine. She hadn't moved from her spot on the dance floor, still dancing dead center, twirling her friend out with her arm extended by the time I made it to her.

I didn't hesitate. As their arms were extended, I plucked the angel's hand from her friend and pulled her to me. Beautiful, light green eyes popped in surprise as she slammed to my chest.

"You," she said, and I more saw her mouth the words than heard them.

I didn't keep my distance. My hand was already just above her ass at the back, my other hand still holding hers pressed between our chests. She was taller than I assumed originally, her head coming to my chin, but a quick glance told me she was definitely in heels. I leaned in close. Forget formalities and seducing. Her heart was already racing and she gripped my hand like she'd held it for years.

"You," I whispered against her ear. I breathed in her scent, pressed my lips against the hinge of her jaw, not in a kiss, but a tease. A promise for how gentle I could be when I wanted. "Did you enjoy making me hard while I watched you?"

This wasn't the time for sweet nothings. I wasn't here to seduce, but to *take*.

To prove what watching her did to me, I rolled my hips. My hard cock against her lower stomach.

"Oh," she gasped, lips still parted like she hadn't overcome her surprise. Eyelashes fluttered and a pink hue stained her cheeks.

Blushing? The angels always did.

"Hi," she whispered. "I'm Brenna."

"Connor." My teammates always used my last name. Most of the public did. My first name wasn't on my social media handles or anything. It helped keep fans confused if they thought they recognized me. To everyone, I was Quinten. Running back with the fastest sprint times in five years with the NFL. If she wasn't a fan, and most jersey jumpers weren't really, the name would slip by her.

The tip of her tongue darted out, slid along her bottom lip. She was almost *too* innocent and a brief second made me second-guess myself. Her friend was most likely more my style. More wild, uninhibited.

This angel probably needed to be taught and one-night stands weren't for teaching anything.

"Are you going to dance with me?" she asked, speaking so sweetly and teasingly into my ear. "Or just stand there and keep staring at me?"

"You're pretty to look at."

She threw her head back and laughed, tugging me farther into the throng of people. We danced, found our rhythm with her easily following my lead. She was a good dancer, probably trained, but she still submitted to the way my hips rolled and my hands held hers against me. I turned her, her back to my chest. My cock to the top of her ass sliding my hand to the front of her stomach, my other at her hip moved to the hem of her dress where my thumb ran along her inner thighs, brushing the soft skin of her where I'd have my hands and mouth later.

She shuddered against me. Goose bumps slid along her skin, making it not only obvious but enticing at how easily I could turn this girl on. Talk about an ego boost.

I dropped my head so I could press my lips to the side of her neck, trailed them down, open-mouthed, brushing along her skin as she writhed in front of me. And holy shit this was hot. Her body was liquid, her skin delicious, and every puff of breath she made as I tasted her was powerful, like her hand was already wrapped around my dick, squeezing me.

My hand at her thigh brushed forward, barely beneath the bottom of her short dress but as I swiped again, her body tensed. A minute flinch of her stomach beneath my hand and I paused.

"This okay?"

Her hand fell to mine beneath her dress, hot small palm on mine and I couldn't help but look down. Her skin was pale against my tanned skin, so small and thin.

"Yeah." She turned and I met her gaze. Her lip disappeared between her teeth and back out again. That small movement.

She hesitated.

I started pulling my hand out of her dress. I wasn't a man who would take what wasn't offered. Had I read her so wrong?

"Can we...can we go somewhere more private?"

Ah, so that was her hesitation. No problem.

"Of course," I murmured and leaned forward, my lips brushing over her lips, testing...tasting...she inhaled a quick breath before relaxing against me, turning more so I could kiss her mouth head-on and she gave me what I needed. Quiet consent with her movements.

I kissed her, kept it light, respecting her need for privacy but God, one taste of her was so different than the hurried, forceful movements of so many one-night stands where it was all about the function and urgency, not the details of the color of her skin, the scent of peaches, the purity that still screamed angel.

"Let's go," I whispered, pulling back, licking the last of her off my lips. I held her close to me, twisting her arm so both of ours were behind her back.

"Wait," she said and tugged her hand from mine. "Give me a minute?"

She pointed at the friend she'd been dancing with, the brunette was now surrounded by more than one guy with their hands on her hips, swaying and grinding against her.

"Go tell her," I said, understanding dawning.

I kept my gaze on her, glared at the men as she approached and eyed her like fresh meat, and hell...she so was.

Fresh. Something new. Something so vastly different than the women I usually went for who were more assertive, confident, less mystery.

I refused to waste time thinking *why* this girl grabbed my attention. It was chemical. Simple.

She returned, head bent slightly down, eyes peeking up at me through her lashes as she pushed hair behind her ear and came straight to me, taking my hand and resettling them behind her as I'd done before.

"Ready?"

"Yes." She grinned at me, sweetly. Good God. I could *destroy* this woman.

I guided her off the dance floor and pulled a key ring from my pocket as we headed toward the gray metal door with EXIT in red above.

"This private enough?" I asked, focusing on the key in my hand, her body next to me, so thin, so small, so fucking beautiful I still couldn't decide where I'd start first once I had her in the back.

Those wide green eyes came to me as she sucked in another breath. "Where are you taking me?"

THREE

Brenna

CONNOR HAD A KEY. Something unsettling rolled through me as he pulled the ring out of his pocket. Did he work here? Was this planned?

Had he chosen me for a reason other than making out with an unknown girl in a bar?

It was nerves, plain and simple...most likely...but still, this monstrous-sized man I allowed to haul me off the dance floor where the lights were dimmer and his features murkier had a key to a door that could take me anywhere he wanted to go.

All the scenes from horror movies I'd watched over the years while cowering beneath a blanket flashed before my eyes.

This is how the naïve virgin dies.

The thought was so startling, I jolted, pulling on his hand.

"I won't hurt you," he said, like the magician mind reader he might have been. "Unless you ask anyway. And this is as private as we can get."

Gulp. I didn't want that. The thought of being hurt made me flinch at the same time something even more unsettling pulsed heavier between my thighs. I *didn't* want that.

Did I?

I needed to focus. "Why do you have a key? Do you own this place?"

"Not all of it," he replied and the door was opened, a sliver of light appearing before us as his hand went to the door. "Are you coming?"

Like a lamb to slaughter. This was what I'd come here for. A stranger. A person I never had to see again who didn't even have to know what I was giving him, or what he'd soon be taking.

I stepped toward him, pressed my hand over his on the door and answered without words, opening the door farther.

The bright lights of the hallway were shocking and I blinked several times, clearing away the spots in my vision. But finally...finally I could see everything and sensed the man at my back as the door closed behind us. The flashing lights stopped and music was muted to a dull roar.

Goose bumps skittered down my arms and I rubbed the chill away. "What is this place?"

"Backroom for bands when we have live music. Storage. Restrooms. This way." He took my hand and pulled me behind him to another door that was opened. An office. Filled with file cases and a monstrous desk perfect for the man in front of me. And a black leather couch that at least looked new.

How many women had he brought back here? I shook the thought away along with my nerves.

Connor was watching me, waiting for me, while still holding my hand. In the brightness of the room, I could finally fully make out his features. A mop of dark black hair on top that fell to one side, sweat on his temples from the exertion of dancing. Rich, deep blue eyes rimmed with thick lashes darker than his hair. His nostrils flared like a predator scenting their next meal. Beneath his white dress shirt that clung to his chest like my dress clung to me, sticky from sweat and hormones and lust, his chest heaved with his racing breath.

He might have wanted this more than me and wasn't that a confidence-builder.

I swallowed, knew from the way I'd frozen I had to take that first step and once I did, he yanked me the rest of the way to him, mouths clashing, bodies moving until I was against a wall, his hand at my thigh, lifting and settling over his.

Yes. This...this was what we'd had on the floor. Passion. Lust. It was heady and I swam in it, closing my eyes and allowing the sweet taste of him to invade my mouth while his fingers worked at my dress. He lifted and tugged on it until I was spread before him, only his jeans and a sliver of my thong separating me from everything I'd wanted for so long. My fingers curled into his shirt and I yanked him closer. I clung to him as he bent his knees and rocked himself against me.

Oh my God. He felt huge. Hot. His dick pulsed against my throbbing center and my head hit the wall, my mouth opening to groan. "Yes. More."

He lifted me and my legs wrapped around him.

"Fuck, you're so damn sexy." Connor's mouth slid down my neck to my collarbone. He sucked and kissed, teased with his tongue like he was tasting me and devouring me in equal measure.

And then his fingers were there, at my sex, brushing along my clit through the satin of my drenched thong and *good Lord* this was already everything I'd imagined and fantasized and more.

So. Much. More.

My entire body felt *alive*. Buzzing with anticipation and I kicked back that tickle of fear and the voice inside of me that said *you're making a huge mistake, girlie.*

There was no place for a conscience tonight.

A whimper tore through me as he found my clit, his thumb pressed there through my panties and my body jerked. Thank the heavens he was so big. And apparently strong. He had no problem holding me as he continued working me, taking my mouth when my cries grew louder. My shoulder blades hit the wall as I arched into him and pulled back. The sensation so perfect and terrifying.

"Please. More." I didn't recognize my own voice.

Connor slammed his mouth against mine, shoved my panties to the side and before I knew it, pain like I had never experience sliced through me. "Oh!"

"You're so damn tight," he groaned like it was a good thing, like he couldn't wait to slide inside of me and then he added another finger even as I fought against the pain rolling through me.

A *pop* came from inside me. *Oh no.* My eyes widened even as I tightened from the pain. I'd been prepared mentally for it but didn't actually think it would happen until it was too late to turn back.

He stilled instantly. "What the fuck?"

Humiliation stained my cheeks and somehow the heat clawing up my throat evaporated the pain deep inside me where his fingers still were.

Dark blue eyes so close to navy opened and inspected me. "What the fuck?" he asked again.

Words wouldn't come. With his fingers still lodged inside of me, I knew exactly what he'd felt. What he *now knew.*

"It's okay," I whispered, but it wasn't. Already tears were threatening. He wasn't supposed to know and maybe had the room been dark I could have brushed it off but with the lights on in the office, there was no way he didn't see the emotions and the truth rushing to the surface.

My pussy clenched around him, as if reminding him he'd been mid-finger fuck and his jaw tightened.

"Stop," I said, pushing against him. This was no longer what I wanted and based on the anger beginning to tighten against him, not what he'd planned for.

He did immediately. Two fingers slid out of me and even through his tightened muscles and furious expression, he settled me gently to the floor.

"What the fuck were you thinking?" he snapped, and I turned to the wall, fixed my thong and shoved down my dress.

My mascara probably made me look like a creature of the night and my hair a habitat for birds but I didn't care. I shoved past the mountain of sexy man who clenched his fists at his sides and shoved open the office door, hurrying back toward the door he'd unlocked, praying it was still unlocked. When I threw myself against it and it flung open I was thankful, so damn thankful for the darkness of the dance floor and the flashing strobe lights that hid my tears and my embarrassment.

Goodness gracious. I couldn't get rid of my virginity even when I was that damn close.

I found Gina, dark hair swinging wildly in the air as she twirled and danced with two other men. She'd stayed exactly where she'd been before. I grabbed her arm to get her attention.

"Hey!" she shouted. Her eyes were wide and a smile even more so until a light skated across my face and she caught whatever mortification looked like. It had to be stamped on me. "I'm going to kill him."

"No!" I shouted back. "Let's go. I'll explain!"

"ARE YOU READY TO TALK?" Gina was quiet and comforting. She left me to my silent shame in the Uber we ordered, hiding down the block from Glitz in case Connor came looking for me. Not that he would.

Why would he care that I ran away from him? It was clear he didn't want to finish what we started as soon as he popped my hymen. And the anger on him...it was so...so much worse than anything I could have predicted.

Didn't most men have a fantasy of plowing a field where no other man's tractor had ridden?

Not Connor. I couldn't remember a time someone had been so angry with me they shook with it.

"I need to change," I muttered, kicking off my heels as soon as we entered our apartment. "And I need a drink or twelve."

"Hey." Her hand grabbed mine and squeezed. "He didn't hurt you, did he?"

Concern stamped her face and I shook my head. "No, he just figured it out before the good stuff got started."

Although what I experienced was better than any self-given good stuff I'd managed to do on my own.

"Okay," she sighed, softening her look. "As long as I don't need to have him arrested or sic Joe on him, I'll get you that drink. Go change."

Joe was Gina's brother. A hockey player currently working his way through the minors, he was all muscle and was one of the few men I knew whose bite was definitely worse than his bark when necessary. Fortunately for Joe, if I needed anyone to take care of a man on my behalf, I had two brothers and brother-in-law more than willing to step in.

I shuffled down the hallway, defeat and embarrassment heating my skin.

"Good grief," I muttered once I got to my room and yanked off the dress. It took all my dancing flexibility to get out of the tight thing and once freed, I sagged with relief as cool air rushed against my still heated skin. I dug through my drawers, found the loosest and most comfy pajama set I owned and shuffled to the bathroom. It was there, I saw it...

Blood. If I had specks of blood on my thighs, please...please God, tell me he didn't have it on his hands.

"Oh God," I moaned and dropped my hands to my face. My humiliation had no end but thankfully this was why I'd wanted a stranger. I could do this and be done with it and not have to have all those awkward conversations and have a guy feel like he had to do something impressive to make it special and beautiful and perfect for me.

My virginity had never been something I cherished or protected, it'd been a noose around me.

Could I even claim to be a virgin now that he'd broken that thin membrane?

Dropping my hands from my face, I found a washcloth in my bathroom closet and cleaned up. Once dressed, I finally faced myself in the mirror. "You so totally screwed that up, Brenna. Way to go."

Now what in the hell was I going to do?

FOUR

Connor

A VIRGIN. A fucking virgin.

I threw back a swallow of scotch and hissed through my teeth, relishing the smooth burn as the alcohol slid down my throat. It'd taken me what felt like forever to have all the pieces click into place. She hadn't seemed so damn innocent grinding against my crotch on the dance floor, only a hint of nerves leaving to go to the office with me, but that'd be understandable with any woman with a dose of common sense heading off somewhere with a strange man.

She was so tight when I pressed my first finger into her but so damn into it. Hell, still thinking about how tight she was had me fighting getting hard.

Instead, ruining her hymen and making her cry out in pain...fucking hurting her? That wasn't something I wanted. And Jesus fuck...did she know who I was? Was she protected? Had she tried to trick me so I could knock her up? Sell her virgin rape story to a headline and get millions? No fucking way any woman in their right mind would go out looking for a screw with a stranger if she'd never done such a thing.

She had to know who I was, and as that realization had come to me, a slash of her virgin blood drying on my fingers, I was so fucking pissed it took me a while to get back to the VIP lounge. Beaux was long gone. Kolby took one look at my face and backed off.

Probably because I looked like I had last year after we'd lost in the playoffs. The refs made such shitty calls even the television announcers deemed them the worst in NFL history.

Two days later, I was still pissed. Pissed at the girl who tried to play me. Pissed at myself for falling for it when I was usually smarter and more aware. Pissed at *Brenna* whose name I grunted when I came, seething in anger and yet still got hard thinking of her.

Fucking infuriated that every time I jerked off, which had been way more than my normal amount, I did it because I was still thinking of Brenna and her curves and her slick lying smile and eyes so huge they seemed to swallow me whole.

My phone alarm buzzed, reminding me I had somewhere to be and needed to get my ass in gear. I was sluggish, not from the scotch but from the workouts I'd been doing all week, doubling up on everything in the gym to ease my frustrations. Not that it helped at all. And now I had to go to the boss's house, shake hands with David and Kassy Kemper, owners of the Raleigh Rough Riders and play nice with their family and my teammates all while wanting to find that sexy strawberry blonde woman and throttle her until she told me what damn game she was playing.

Awesome. I was in a killing mood and that was always fun when I had to be around my coaches and the man who was in control of my paycheck. Even better, I needed to shower and get to his house, walk around his freaking mansion while acting like I had morals and manners, two things my grandpa never bothered to teach me outside of his consistent teachings on how to treat women.

Somehow, I'd gone and messed all those up, too.

"Shit." I shoved off the couch, careful not to spill the rest of my drink, and headed upstairs to shower and dress.

An hour later, I pulled into the curved drive of the Kemper's house. It wasn't only enormous, but it was one of the oldest homes in Raleigh. I would have thought a man with his money and stature would move to the 'burbs, gate his land so no one could enter unless invited, and hide away from all the attention he received. David and Kassy weren't like that though. Admittedly, I admired the hell out of the man who had married his high school sweetheart right out of college, worked his ass off as a sports agent and then agency owner before purchasing the Rough Riders seven years ago to the tune of an amount I couldn't comprehend having in my lifetime. They were decent folks, had a family with more kids and grandkids than I could remember, and they lived in the heart of the city, remodeling an old-time mansion that now sat on the historical society.

David had also redone the entire organization over the years, taking us from an "almost making it to the playoffs" team to a team who now had a Super Bowl win and then loss under their belts, plus last year's fiasco of losing in the Division Championship before getting our shot at a second ring.

We were thirsty for it this year, intent and starved on proving our team wasn't a one-hit-wonder. Thanks to drafting some excellent new rookies in the off-season plus our seasoned veterans thirsting for another championship ring before retirement came calling, it was our do or die season.

I tugged on the lapels of my suit coat and headed toward

the house, ignoring the fact it was a ball-sweating one hundred degrees outside. As soon as I entered, a glass of scotch was in my hand courtesy of the roaming servers dressed in all white with silver trays and black cloth towels draped over their forearms.

Fancy fucking shit for what was supposed to be a kickoff party to our pre-season training that had already started. But we headed to training camp in three weeks and then straight into pre-season games. In just over one month, I'd be officially back on the turf, grinding it up with my cleats and my team, racing for touchdowns and dodging and diving over opponents.

The thrill of thinking about it made my blood race. Unfortunately, a sexy as sin strawberry blonde temptress popped into my mind, making my blood race for a totally different reason.

"Shit," I grunted and drained my drink. One more glass and I'd cut myself off but this was good shit, even smoother than what I usually bought.

Kemper might be down-home people, but he knew where to throw his money, and he was definitely a scotch aficionado.

"Hey, man! Glad you could make it." Oliver Powell, team captain and tight end superstar, slapped my shoulder as I walked through the house headed toward most of the noise near the back.

"I'm not late, right?"

The house was packed and the driveway filled with cars. I didn't expect to be the last person to show.

"Not late at all. Just in time actually. David and Kassy are getting ready to do their annual cheer pep talk."

Not what I needed, but as the murmurs of players and coaches and their families grew louder, so did the buzz in my adrenaline. We did this same song and dance every year, and it never failed. Despite the fact we were already practicing in the mornings and focusing on team and individualized workout plans, this bash was the season kick-off, and David was one hell of a motivator.

We reached the congregated group right outside the back door. Canopies were draped over his back porch, cutting off some of the sun and beneath his large covered patio, ceiling fans were on at full strength. Two bars were set up, crowded with my fellow teammates and brothers grabbing drinks. Music played through speakers at a volume low enough we could talk over it and at the far end past the pool was a makeshift stage David used every year. He came out, announced the new players to the team via drafts and trades. Then he brought out his family and kids and thanked them for their unfailing support. The numbers seemed to grow every year as his children had their own. He'd end it with giving us a pep talk that left everyone whooping and hollering like we'd never heard the man speak before.

It really was awesome. There was something about the man, knowing how much he loved his family and loved not only the players, but this organization just as much, that lit a fire under me. It was impossible not to want to exceed David's expectations.

In five years of being with the organization, Kemper and his wife were more of a family to me than my own parents. That probably had to due with the fact my parents were young and stupid, unable to care for a child, so they dropped me off at my mom's dad's house one day and took off to lands unknown to this day.

I searched the crowd and found Kolby, his mom and daughter nowhere in sight. They were probably inside playing somewhere with the rest of the kids. I headed in his direction.

Soon, Beaux flanked my other side and bumped my shoulder. "So, haven't heard from you since you took forever with that chick the other night. You finally come up for air with her or what?"

"Based on the volcanic expression on his face afterward, I assumed things didn't work out so well for him." Kolby. The asshole. It was like he'd been waiting all week to give me shit for that night.

"Seriously?" Beaux asked, brows raised and bottle of beer frozen at his mouth. His shoulders started shaking. "You get shut down or what?"

"Long story." And not one I was sharing. Ever. I took a sip of scotch as David and Kassy took the stage. Behind them, followed his family. Two sons and a daughter I knew well from years on the team along with their spouses and grandchildren, and at the rear of the line of family members was someone else, slightly hidden behind the sisters...

No. No fucking way.

Strawberry blonde hair I'd seen only days ago and fantasized about since. Curled and draped over one shoulder, I'd recognize it anywhere. She was barely visible, but there was no way I was wrong about this. That pull I felt toward her at the bar was back and equally strong if not more forceful due to the sudden rush of *what in the ever-loving fuck is going on* rolling through me.

A growl tore from my throat.

"Oh fuck," Kolby said, bent over, laughing quietly but in a way it was clear I wasn't the only one who saw her.

Next to me, Beaux struggled to contain his own laughter while falling into me, throwing an arm over his shoulder. "Oh shit. You fucked the boss's daughter. You are so screwed."

I hadn't fucked her. She'd left me with a lingering case of blue balls, but I couldn't stop staring at her now. And fucking hell, my cock hardened at the sight of her.

But screwed? Yeah. I was most definitely screwed.

"Shut up," I gritted out, teeth hurting so much from the shock and trying not to shove Beaux off me and make a scene. Not now. "The last thing I need is this getting out."

"What's going on?" Powell asked, taking his stance next to his brother-in-law, Beaux. Powell had married Beaux's older sister, Shannon, more than two years ago.

On both sides of me, Kolby and Beaux almost collapsed with laughter. I barely noticed. Everything was rushing through me, the sound of ocean hitting shore, muting and blurring everything around me until David announced, "And my youngest, who has recently graduated from Vanderwilde Women's College and is taking a position with the organization..."

Oh God. I was going to puke. I had to get out of there. She and I needed to talk, but it wasn't going to be when I was still fighting against going hard at the mere sight of her while my stomach rolled with expensive scotch.

I turned and pushed my way through the crowd, getting the hell out of there before I did something stupid like jump the stage and shake the living shit out of Brenna Kemper.

FIVE

Brenna

I LOVED my family to death. My father especially. Given the hell I'd gone through as a child, I always understood his need to protect me. Did I want to spend most of my life protected in boarding schools away from my siblings and nieces and nephews? No, however the seclusion, particularly in my earlier years went a long way in helping me heal.

But that time was over, and while there were lingering effects I would always battle from my abduction when I was waiting at a bus stop, I craved nothing but normalcy. A normal life. A normal relationship.

Trying to chuck my V-Card out the window at a bar to a stranger might not have been *normal* per se, but was it really all that different from college-aged one-night stands or high schoolers who gave it up to peer pressure? I doubted it.

What I despised though, more than anything, was being

paraded onto a stage. I'd refused to go every year my parents hosted the Rough Riders football team and their spouses and children. Fortunately for me, I was usually at college, attending summer classes. I couldn't get out of it now that I'd be working with these players and the staff surrounding the stage as my father made our introductions as well as commenced his welcome and team morale boosting speech.

I hated the limelight. My preference was fading into the background in my uniformed attire that made me look like everyone else, but I was curious. Ever since I hit the stage that prickle at the back of my neck, the one I had a few nights ago at Glitz, reappeared. Which meant as my father spoke, my eyes scanned the crowd, stopping on and recognizing some of the coaches I met over the years and the few players I recognized. I wasn't a football follower really, despite my father owning the team and loving the sport. My experience had been confined to watching games from the owner's boxes during playoffs when they didn't interfere with my studies.

It was a surprise to see so many people so focused on my dad as he spoke, intently watching and agreeing. I knew they liked my dad and respected him, but the feelings I felt from the crowd went far beyond mutual respect. They *adored* him, and a pulse fluttered wildly against my skin as I took it in. Inhaled the excitement dancing through the air.

Until I saw something—someone—who looked so familiar I fought against my jaw dropping to the stage. A man who was taller than almost everyone else pushed his way through the crowd, heading the opposite direction.

It couldn't be him. That hair. That body, it was so familiar, for a moment I wondered if that was why my pulse went so erratic.

It couldn't be Connor. It was my lingering imagination and humiliation as to how everything went so poorly last weekend.

Not that I'd been able to stop thinking about it. Or imagining what it'd be like had he finished. Had he shoved down his jeans, freed himself, slid himself into me still propped against the wall.

I replayed the fantasies several times over the last few days and came to one, severely disappointing conclusion.

After having a small taste of the real thing, I could no longer do the job as well as him. And wasn't that a massive bummer? Awesome bonus: I was craving him more in a way that had made me start fearing for my mental health.

I'd become sex-starved, desperate to experience everything. I wanted all the messy scenarios I'd imagined over the years—helped in part by my large collection of erotic romance novels.

Now that my first attempt had gone so horribly, disastrously wrong, I was trying to figure out how to gather the courage to go after what I wanted. Which meant my mind was definitely playing tricks on me when I saw the mess of dark hair disappear. I had to have imagined the similarities.

A raucous round of applause blared through the air pulling me back to the moment.

Oh God. I was turned on. On stage with my family. Did my embarrassment and self-respect know no bounds?

"I need a drink," I muttered to my sister Eva next to me. At twenty-eight, she spent most of the speech corralling her son, Kollin, while keeping her infant from grabbing at the neckline of her dress. I reached for Tomas as she laughed.

"You and me both, sister." She handed me my eight-month-old nephew and his hand immediately dove for my breast.

"Good grief, do you ever feed this guy?"

She shook her head and curled her hand over Kollin's shoulder before he dove off the stage. "Only every two hours and the monster ate right before we stepped up here."

He had. But my nephew always clung to my sister's nursing

breasts. She always laughed and told me it was a boy thing. Not that I'd know...or wanted to hear any part of her sex life. "Come on. Show's over. Let's get that drink."

"Gladly." I carried Tomas off the stage, followed by my siblings and family members, passing and smiling at the new members of the team, many of whom were my own age or younger as they waited to be welcomed into the fold. "Champagne?" I asked Eva over my shoulder right as Tomas made another open-mouth dive toward my dress top, small hands clinging to my Carolina-blue colored dress.

I might have graduated from an all-girls college on the coast, but I was a UNC girl through-and-through.

Eva took Tomas from me as he cried out, frustrated I didn't supply what he wanted. "I'll meet you there later. Let me get him taken care of and with the nanny inside."

"I'll grab a drink for you," I said, disappointed. I saw my family so little I was excited to be around them again. Now that I was home and living in Raleigh where most of my family lived, I couldn't wait to become the world's greatest aunt to all seven of my nieces and nephews. My family spawned like rabbits in spring, leaving me not only the youngest without kids and to be married, but an outsider to all of them.

No one understood how lonely I felt or how much I liked being alone. Trauma made me strange sometimes, desperately wanting to be around people and yet avoiding it and overwhelmed by it at the same time. Much like I was feeling now, being on stage, forced to say hello to dozens of women I didn't know along with men I barely recognized.

I craved people and my solitude. I desired physical touch without the risk of relationship drama. It was a dichotomy I fought through every day, but being surrounded by strangers all trying to say hello was overwhelming to my senses so much so that by the time I made it to one of the drink tables near the back and grabbed a glass of champagne, my hands were trembling and my heart was racing.

Other times, I was able to handle it perfectly fine, like the night at Glitz. The problem was I never knew when the trigger would hit, throwing me backward a hundred steps.

Keeping my back to the crowd, I inhaled several slow breaths and took a sip. I focused on the rose bushes and hydrangeas that led to the beautiful gardens. Behind the hydrangeas and on the other side of a large lilac hedge was a bench my father made for me years ago when I needed time alone.

I headed there now.

Just a few minutes. A few minutes of peace and solitude and I'd be okay for the afternoon.

It was quiet back there and I kicked off my heels as I reached the stone path. The champagne glass in my hand had stopped shaking the closer I got to the sweet-scented bushes and then I stepped inside the circular area. All around me I was hidden from sight, safely protected while still having freedom.

Goddamn, I was such a mess. Always, even when I thought I was doing better. Somehow freedom was restrictive and rules a safety net. I was a disaster waiting to happen, wanting my own space, missing the structure of school and required rules.

Another sip of champagne hit my lips and I savored the sweet bubbles. The bright blue sky dotted with popcorn clouds, the rush of leaves beyond and I took a deep breath.

Flowers. Freedom. I was okay and safe and loved.

A shadow fell over me, and my back straightened. On guard. I wasn't prepared for company and awareness spiked down my spine like ice picks.

"We need to talk."

That voice. *No.*

I spun and I wasn't sure what fell faster, my jaw or my champagne glass as it slipped from my fingers.

A hand reached out, grabbed the glass as it fell, and cool alcohol splashed on my shins and toes.

"Oh shit," I gasped, for so many reasons. It *was* Connor. "What are you doing here?"

"Funny." He didn't sound amused. His jaw was strained and his grip was so strong on my champagne glass I feared he'd shattered it as he held it out to me. My hand shook as I took it from him. "I was going to ask you the same thing."

"My dad owns—" Oh. Oh no. Oh absolutely freaking no. Reality slowly clicked into place with a viciously loud snap. "You're a player?" I stepped back. As if my humiliation couldn't increase. Leave it to me to test the limits.

"Connor Quinten, running back. Five years on the team. And there's no fucking way you didn't know that." His jaw ticked as his mouth slammed shut. Narrowed eyes rimmed with lashes I still remembered so vividly.

Oh God. He was angry. So angry. My heart jackhammered against my ribcage and my gaze darted for the exit but he was blocking it.

My hand went to my chest and I took another step back. Distance. Space. Air. It enfolded on me and darkened my vision. This wasn't right.

Or okay.

"I didn't. I didn't know."

"You expect me to believe you came to a club I part-own, wanted me to fuck you when no man has done that to you before, and you had no fucking clue I was on the team? With your dad being the owner? Do you think I'm that fucking stupid, Brenna? Your dad owns my ass and you have no idea the position you put me in."

"I had no idea. I don't follow—" God, I was so damn naïve and so stupid. I so desperately needed to get away from him. "I haven't even started my job there and I've been in school."

"Right." He scoffed. "What fucking game are you playing?"

"It wasn't a game." There was no way for him to understand. That I craved physical touch, but it had to be on my terms at the same time, I wanted decisions yanked from me. I was so damn screwed in the head. "It won't happen again," I muttered, taking another step back and to the side. If I could at least see the path toward the exit, my heart would slow.

It was only then I realized he hadn't moved. He wasn't looming closer to me. Connor was standing exactly where he'd been the entire time and it was me moving, backing up like prey, acting like a psycho.

"I'm sorry," I finally said, blinking harshly. Shaking my head, I closed my eyes until my heart rate slowed to normal levels and everything cleared.

Goddamn. I was on the verge of a panic attack and I'd already embarrassed myself enough around this man. "Let's just pretend it didn't happen. I won't say anything." I nodded toward the path behind him. "If you could let me through?"

"So you can run away again?"

"Yes. I think that'd be best." There was no point in denying I'd done that before.

A strange look flashed across his expression. "What if I want to talk about what happened?"

"I'd rather we didn't."

His hands went to his hips. I couldn't help but watch the movements. Those hands, so large and strong. The muscles I'd felt beneath his suit coat. With the way he shoved his unbuttoned coat to his hips, he opened the front, exposing his white dress shirt. So very similar to...

No. I wouldn't think about it.

"You're staring at me like you still want me."

If I wasn't mistaken, there was amusement in his tone. It'd been missing since he startled me. I wasn't sure I liked hearing it.

"I don't." My gaze jumped to the lilac bushes. In the spring, they bloomed vibrant purples and whites and pinks. They were now bare of flowers and all green, which only made the hydrangeas in front of them brighter in full bloom. But good Lord, I couldn't help myself. I still did. Was it the fear that made me want him? The riskiness of this?

Why was I so screwed up that when I was afraid, I wanted someone to touch me?

Normal. I wanted to be normal.

I shook my head, but it did nothing to stop the heat traveling to my lower stomach, the tops of my thighs. Oh God, this was what it'd been like when I first saw him. Intense and heady and my head swam as I realized he was still watching me.

"You should have told me," he said, and instinctively I knew we were no longer talking about my father or the team. His voice was low and deep. Husky. So much richer in the quiet open air than it'd been beneath strobe lights and blaring music. "If I would have known, I wouldn't have—"

"That's why I didn't say anything."

He scowled like that disgusted him. "If I hurt you—"

"You didn't."

"I did. Seriously, I have a right to know why you'd fucking target me for that. And I was there, Brenna. I heard when I hurt you, I felt it—"

"Please stop." I threw up my hand and cringed. Reliving it wouldn't help either of us.

"I didn't know it was you, or who you were." There was no way to explain without shame slithering through me. To him, I'd sound like a slut. Like there was something wrong with me and I was so tired of there being something wrong with me. "That I promise. But I don't want to talk about it further."

He stepped closer, one long stride almost moving in slow motion, yet he was in front of me before I could back up and get space. "I'm not a man who appreciates the idea of hurting a woman. You need to know that about me. But yes, considering who I am and who you are, I really think I deserve an explanation. If this was some game...some trick by someone..."

"It wasn't." He wouldn't let this go and once again, tears burned the backs of my eyes. "I'd like for you to step back." I stared at his shoulder. He couldn't see me again, not like this—crying and humiliated and running from him. But did he have a point?

I put myself in his shoes. He was a player for the Rough Riders. Of course...of course the one time I try to do something for myself I still screw it up epically. "I won't tell my dad. It wasn't...I wasn't trying to trick you, I wanted..."

I clamped my mouth shut.

"Wanted what? To throw away something special on a stranger? I've wracked my brain all weekend trying to figure this out. You fled with your blood on my fingers."

"Yes," I hissed. Blood boiling. He was too close. And that pulsing was increasing at my thighs. Goddamn, why did this turn me on? His fear of hurting me actually made me *want* it. "Okay? Yes. I wanted to lose my virginity to a stranger. Are you happy now?"

And could I crawl into a hole and die yet?

"Why?"

"Because it'd be my choice and over with it. That was why. Now if you'll excuse me, I need to go."

"To find another stranger to finish the job I started?" He spit it out with such venom, I attacked right back.

This man. I was never supposed to see him again. Still, he

listened and stepped to the side, giving me my opening, but not before leaving with a parting shot.

"Yeah. Probably. What difference does it make to you?"

SIX

Connor

THE NERVE OF HER. She was back and as I watched her prance through the main floor of Glitz from my view on the monitors, this time where I was in the office meeting with Malcom Lawrence, the majority owner in the bar, my blood boiled.

No more innocent angel for Brenna fucking Kemper. Learning who she was was still such a surprise it shamed the hell out of me that I hadn't been able to kick her out of my brain since the disaster at her parents' yard. At first, she'd looked so freaked out by me I almost left. But then, something else had happened. As she fought through her fear, it'd changed. Not to acceptance or awareness...but something else. My presence and her fear had turned her on in a way that made my dick jerk beneath my pants and iced my veins. It was equal parts scary and enticing. And her parting words to me? That she'd have no problems finding a stranger to finish what I started?

Hell no. Was that why she was back here? Red hair now pulled back into a sleek ponytail, vibrant red lips and a black dress even sexier than her angelic one. Was she trying to find me? Turning this into the game she originally denied or was she still on the hunt?

If this girl had a death wish it wasn't going to happen at my damn club. There was no way in hell I was having her assaulted here, not now when I knew who she was and what she claimed to be looking for.

Someone had to keep her safe from doing something stupid. I wasn't the man for the job. Not even close. But hell if I wasn't thinking about signing up for it.

"Who is that?" Malcom asked, peering over my shoulder as I zoomed in on her at the bar. Her friend wasn't close by this time like she'd been last time.

"Goddamn it," I grunted. She came here alone but now the question was if it was for me or someone—anyone—else.

"Know her, I take it?"

"Yeah." My eyes stayed glued to the screen as she ordered a drink. She waited, scanned the bar and her shoulder slumped in a way I only saw because I was so focused on her. Not once did she peer up at the VIP section though. She didn't behave in a way a woman usually did if she was even trying to get attention from someone.

No, she wasn't looking for me, but she wasn't leaving here with another man taking her either.

"I gotta go." I shoved back from the desk and the screen, eyeing her as she sipped her drink and scanned the dance floor. "We good?"

"Yup."

I was a silent partner in Glitz, which I'd demanded when Malcom originally came to me with his idea. I owned almost half of it but that was mostly because I was the one with the collateral to pull this off. Everything from the location to the design and decor was all Malcolm. When he first approached me for help, tail tucked between his legs, he'd started out his proposal with the statement, "I know friends make shitty business partners." I almost slapped him upside the head. We bonded before our freshman year of college ever started on the practice fields at Clemson and if it wasn't for him, I wasn't sure I would have survived the death of my grandpa after that first year of college. He was there for me every angry, pissed off, drunken step of the way to help get me back on the path to success. He might not have been good enough for the NFL, hell I wasn't even sure if he ever wanted to play professional football, but he was my rock. Saying yes to him was as easy as accepting my role on the Rough Riders. That didn't mean I wasn't smart when it came to doing business with him. I had my name buried so deep in paperwork and under an LLC corporation name my lawyers helped me with so no one ever knew Glitz was a part of me. Part of what I wanted so the bar didn't become rabid with frenzied fans. Partly because Malcom insisted if this place turned into a success, he wanted it all on him.

Hell, I never even told guys on the team I was part owner until two years in with the team even though we'd partied here frequently and Malcom always came and hung out. He'd slipped it accidentally one night over too many tequila shots and the guys had been pissed. Not because I owned half a bar, but because I kept it from them.

I was also definitely planning on keeping this trek to find Brenna to myself as well.

And on the way, determination grew.

Brenna wanted something and hell if her first time with some guy was going to drunken fumbling in a bathroom—or back office— again. Maybe she didn't care about giving something like that up, but if she was twenty-three and a virgin, there had to be a damn good reason she'd held onto it for so long.

She at least deserved to know it was going to be good for her.

Pleasuring women off the field rivaled my skills on the field. So that man Brenna so desperately wanted? It was going to be me.

Based on the way she responded when we'd argued at her parents' house, I doubted it'd be hard to convince her.

I DIDN'T BOTHER SNEAKING up to her when I found her at the bar. She was still in the same place where I saw her from the monitors and while her back was to me, I remembered that flash of panic she had when I found her in her parents' gardens. I didn't need her freaking out yet, so I slid through the crowd, careful of drinks sloshing to the floor as I weaved through customers until I approached her dead on.

Her soft red hair was pulled back into a severe ponytail, every strand yanked tight against her scalp and from her profile as her gaze roamed over the dancers on the floor, she was still the most beautiful woman to step foot into Glitz in months. More severe tonight than the other, more vixen than angel. My dick noticed the pout of her full lips painted a deep red. They'd look fantastic wrapped around my dick while she was on her knees in front of me.

Which was only one of the many fantasies I'd envisioned over the last week since first seeing her. My tanned skin tangled in her shimmering hair. Her mouth wide open as I gripped my dick with my other hand, outlining her lips with my pre-cum before sliding deep inside of her.

If she was a virgin, did she even know how to suck dick? How far did her inexperience go? Which only meant I was adding one more thing to what I wanted to teach her. The very idea made my dick harden further and as I moved around a group of women standing in a circle at the bar, sipping drinks with thin straws, I adjusted myself, shoving my hardening dick so I wasn't saluting her from my waist as I moved closer.

As if she sensed movement to her right, she pulled her drink, I assumed another gin and tonic, to her lips and turned, eyes widening as she caught me taking the final steps to her.

"Out trolling for strangers?" I asked, unable to hide the venom in my tone. This woman twisted me in ways I didn't understand and didn't want to dive too far into.

"No." She pressed her lips together. A twisted, wicked smile formed and she set her glass down on the bar. "I was actually looking for you."

"And you assumed I'd be here on a random Monday night?" Tuesdays were light practice days and off days during the season. I was always here on Mondays as long as we didn't have a Monday night game. There was no way she knew that unless she asked about me.

Her shoulder lifted and fell, one of them bare, the other one covered with a thick strap of black fabric that cut in an angle over her chest. The rest of her dress was as tight and short as her last one. For a virgin, she had sexual temptation down to an art form.

"Lucky guess."

I leaned forward, rested my arm next to her drink on the bar and dipped my head so my lips were at her ear. The music was loud, but we were far enough from the dance floor I didn't have to shout to be heard. Didn't mean I wanted anyone overhearing or recognizing me though. "Why? You want me to finish the job I started?" I nipped her lobe and a shiver rolled through her. Delivering herself up to me on a platter was more than I'd hoped for.

"Connor." She breathed my name on a sigh. My name on her lips, so innocent and sweet, shot straight down my spine. Hell yeah, this woman. So damn innocent...so damn tempting.

I teased her slowly, my lips to her ear, just beneath and along the column of her throat, flicking my tongue and gathering the taste of her scent, sweet like peaches. So enticing she made me dizzy.

"More," she gasped, the plea shooting straight to my balls like it'd done last week. Her small hand settled on my hip, fingertips dug into my shirt above my waistband. If she leaned closer, twisted and pressed her tits to my chest, she'd be greeted with my rock hard erection at her stomach.

"Fuck," I growled, pulling back. "Not here. Come home with me."

I met her eyes as they widened. Light green pools of fear and nerves flashed before she licked her lips. I craved the taste of her on my mouth again. She had me twisted in ways I wouldn't delve into further, but watching her lick her red lips was possibly one of the hottest things ever.

"Yes."

The most beautiful three letters in the English language. Before she could back out, I grabbed her hand, tucked her firmly to my side. "Follow me. I have a car out back."

"I was dropped off in a Lyft."

"Then I'll make sure you get home tomorrow."

"Tomorrow?"

"Angel, the things I have planned for you are going to take all night long."

SEVEN

Brenna

THIS WAS INSANE. If my father found out what I was doing, where I went, or *who* I met up with, he'd not only have my ass in a sling, most likely insisting I moved back home, but he could make life hell for Connor. Not to mention he could fire me.

I doubted that last one would happen. He enjoyed having a sense of control over me that went far beyond normal parenting. He was loving about it, we all knew why. When you couldn't find your daughter for days it tended to twist and ruin everyone, not only the victim. We spent hours in family counseling after that week from hell when I was eleven years old. I spent many more hours in counseling. I spent years seeing therapists when I was tucked away in private schools fashioned like prisons for the elite and rich while my dad stayed home and spun his thumbs, unable to know if I was safe save for my early set boundary of one weekly call only.

Otherwise he would have had me tailed with security and bodyguards and a tracker on my phone and calling eighteen times a day.

My dad might have commanded an entire NFL team but when it came to his youngest daughter, worry and fear weren't large enough words to eclipse what he felt around me.

Breaking out of that, seeking out Connor, could have been a stupid stunt to further defy and push the boundaries of my father's smothering love, but it was more than that.

There was something I felt around Connor that told me not only could I trust him with the darkest fantasies I had, but he'd enjoy them as well. After several days of unfulfilling moments with a few newly purchased vibrators, none of them were able to match the intensity of what I'd felt with Connor. On a whim, I came to Glitz, seeking him. Now that I knew the hint of how good it could be with someone, I wanted to see this through.

Fortunately, Connor was on the same page as he tucked me into a sleek black Mercedes sedan and zipped through the streets of Raleigh before ducking into an underground parking garage of a building at least ten stories high.

We barely spoke on the way to his place. Conversation could have pushed me away. His jaw had been tight the entire time along with his grip on the steering wheel. We were only a few minutes from Glitz, probably close enough we could have walked, so there hadn't been time anyway except for Connor opening the passenger door and asking, "You sure?"

I'd responded by sliding into the passenger seat, tucking the dress beneath my thighs as I moved so I didn't flash him.

Now, we were parked in a numbered spot, and he still gripped the steering wheel, keys in the ignition. As he silenced the heavy beat of the current song blasting from the radio, I was certain my thundering heart took its place.

"Nothing happens tonight you don't want, and we do need to talk when we get upstairs."

I wanted a stranger so I could avoid the conversation that would kill the mood and most likely any desire he had for me. I gripped the clutch on my lap that held my ID, cell phone, and credit card and reached for the door handle. "Talking. Awesome."

A large, warm hand settled firmly on my thigh, bare skin to bare skin, and an electric zip of interest sliced through me. Until Connor I didn't know it was possible to react to someone's touch so intensely.

"We will talk. I want to fuck you, Brenna, and I won't hide that fact." He gestured toward his lap where his erection was obvious. Straining against his thin dress pants, that part of him appeared as ominous and large as the rest of him. Fear sparked and I pushed it away as he continued, "There's a lot at risk here. Me. You. I want to make sure the air is clear before we go further."

"I understand." And I did, I merely didn't like it. Perhaps going back to him had been a mistake.

I opened my door and swung my legs to the side as he did the same. I was at the back of his car, his hand swallowing my smaller one as he pulled me toward a door. A swipe of his electric key, a beep of a lock and we were in a small enclosed room where he pressed the button for the elevator. Three of them lined a row and one promptly arrived. Thank goodness.

Air sucked from my lungs as I took that first step into the enclosed box. For once it wasn't my uncomfortableness with small spaces, but the heat from the man in front of me, prowling toward me until my hip hit the handle at the back and his hands went to the wall next to me.

Doors closed, taking my escape with me and a forceful breath rushed through me, reminding me to breathe. Lips parted, I tilted my head back as Connor lowered his. Our mouths so close, his warm breath wafted over my cheek, followed by the hint of his full lips I remembered so vividly at night in my dreams.

"Oh God," I gasped. My fingers clung to the bar at my back, solid metal quickly turned burning hot beneath my palms.

"I've fallen asleep for the last week to the memory of your mouth and the way you taste," he said. Our gazes were glued together. My breath came so fast my breasts strained against my clingy fabric. Why had I worn another restrictive dress that cut off my lung capacity?

Damn Gina and her closet filled with trendy clothes and my inability to say no to them.

He didn't wait for a response. His lips brushed over mine and he sucked my bottom lip in between his, tugging on it. A sting of pain sent a shockwave straight to my sex. Oh God. *Pain.* Somehow, in small amounts I liked it. It messed with my head and yet I found myself leaning into him, savoring that small biting ache and reaching for him.

"Keep your hands where they are," he whispered. "And take what I give you. Trust me, you'll have your time to give."

"Okay." I sank into his kiss, the flicker of his tongue against my lips before he crushed his mouth against mine and groaned, diving his tongue into my mouth and devouring me with a kiss so simple but demanding. With every swipe of his tongue over mine, my skin heated.

I was trembling against him and yet only his mouth touched me. This man...I had nothing to compare this to, but he had to be a master at seduction if my underwear could be soaked and he wasn't touching me.

The elevator dinged and the doors slid open and without breaking a single movement, his hand curled around my back, pulled me close to him and he backed out of the elevator, mouth still taking mine, guiding us down a hall.

"Neighbors," I gasped.

"I don't give a fuck."

My eyes flew open as he turned and my back hit another wall. There were four doors in this hallway, all closed, and as his mouth moved from mine to the curve of my shoulder, biting and nibbling and sucking as he pulled his keys out of his pocket, I considered what would happen if one of those doors opened. If someone stood in the doorway and watched as I ground my pelvis against Connor's. If someone paid attention to when he'd lifted my leg to his hips, spread me open in the office.

What would I have done had someone else seen me behave that way?

A delicious shiver wracked my body and Connor pulled back. Caught where my gaze was fixed to the doorway across from his and back to me. "You like the idea of being watched?"

I bit my lip and shook my head. I didn't. It was wrong. And yet... "I don't know."

A line furrowed between his brows and he pressed his lips to mine. "We'll talk about that later then," he said and opened his door, pushing it open and stood back, strong, muscular and massive arm extended. "Last chance to back out."

"Not interested," I declared and stepped around him on legs that trembled with nerves. His chuckle told me he saw and yet he closed the door, flipped a lock and turned on the lights.

His condo was nothing like I'd imagined. I expected a man who made millions to live in a home with landscapers and butlers, perhaps a housekeeper. Connor's home looked like it'd either been recently robbed or he was still a poor college student. Two faded brown couches. A massive television sat on a stand with piles of wires and various gaming systems. Empty glasses were littered on a coffee table and I was certain if they were moved, rings of dust showing how long they'd been there would appear.

He was a slob and I bit my lip again but this time to keep from smiling.

So very unexpected indeed.

"I'm messy, I know. Don't say shit. My room is clean, it's the living areas I don't care about."

I whipped my head around, surprised he could read my thoughts. "Not the first time it's been brought up?"

"No." He grinned and came toward me, smacking his lips to mine. "And if eighteen years of my grandpa on my ass didn't work to instill good cleaning habits, trust me, nothing you say tonight is going to change that. Want something to drink?"

"Is it safe?" I teased and this was new. Like he'd turned into some playful being instead of someone who wanted to crash his body against mine as soon as I stepped inside.

I ran my hands down my dress. I had one gin and tonic at the bar earlier but was nowhere near buzzed. Something with alcohol might help relax me. Not too much. I definitely wanted to remember this night. I had a feeling it'd be worth the memory. Probably seared into my brain.

I followed Connor into the kitchen, surprised again at the number of dishes in his sink and yet they were clean, rinsed and washed and drying neatly on a rack on his small U-shaped counter. Nothing about this place was extravagant and yet I'd done some digging. He was drafted to Rough Riders five years ago and this year was his last year on his original five-year contract. Slated to make over two million dollars base salary, he had the potential to earn eleven million dollars this year.

"Is this really your place?"

An amused grin stretched his face as he grabbed a bottle of red wine from a cupboard. "Yes. Why?"

"No reason." A million questions danced on the tip of my

tongue but the whole purpose of finding someone I didn't know to have sex with was to keep it casual and impersonal. Getting to know him wouldn't help anything.

Probably shouldn't have scanned his personnel file in the office earlier then. Oops.

"I'd love a glass of that wine, please."

"Figured you'd need it."

My fingers ran along the edge of his white counters. This building was older, not even recently renovated and my curiosity piqued as he handed me a glass of wine from a bottle I knew cost several hundred dollars and a wineglass that glistened like it was made of crystal.

Weird. All of this was weird, like he'd been plopped into a home that didn't quite fit him and spent his money on everything else. His car had to be crazy expensive, his clothes and shoes designer—yes, I'd noticed—even his glassware seemed he gave a shit and yet his apartment was straight middle class...

Nothing wrong with it at all, and I bit back the sudden bitter taste of judgment.

"So, you wanted to talk first?" Before we got to the good stuff. This had to hurry along. It'd been too long since he kissed me, but my body throbbed at the memory and taste of him. The way his body was so strong against mine last week. How good that pain had felt when he shoved his fingers deep inside me.

I took another drink.

"Yeah. What are you in this for?"

"Well, you don't beat around the bush, do you?"

"No." He crossed his arms over his chest. And I realized he'd only poured one glass of wine. Mine. Huh, again. "And I'll fill you in with more info. I will fuck you. I'll give you what you want and then some. Hell, I'll be your personal teacher if that's what you want, showing you everything that's been missing in your sex life, but I demand honesty. You could have found some asshole two-pump chump to get you off in the bathroom with a dick so small you would have left disappointed and instead you found me. And maybe it's because I not only know your dad, but I respect the hell out of him, but if you're coming to me for this, it's my way or no way."

Well, that was...wowzers. My head spun with desire.

"You'll teach me?" That croak came from me. A healthy swallow of wine washed away the dryness in my throat.

"If you'll tell me why...and what experience you actually have."

I bit down on the inside of my cheek. Arms no longer crossed over his chest, he splayed his hands on the counter across from me, arms straight, muscles bulged beneath the rolled-up sleeves of his gray shirt. His dick was hard and obvious, punching against his dress pants in a bulge so obvious my cheeks flamed bright hot.

Good Lord, this man was a *beast*.

I itched a scratch at the side of my nose unable to tear my eyes north of his belt. He was big everywhere and I hadn't seen all of him, but God...there was something thrilling about seeing how I affected him. He could probably have anyone he wanted, and probably took everyone he wanted. "Um. Experience?"

What'd we done the other night was about the gist of it. Somehow, I figured he knew.

"Yeah, Brenna. You want something from me, you're going to have to ask me for it. So tell me, you had a man slide his tongue into you? Taste you? Suck your nipples into his mouth and bite down so you cried out? I know no one's stuck their dick in you, but have you taken one anywhere else?"

"What?" Anywhere else, oh, he meant...

"Yeah. You ever sucked a guy? Wrapped those sexy as hell lips around another man's cock and taken him deep until you gagged?"

"Umm—"

"Or taken it in your ass?"

The room spun and I swear, that body part he mentioned clenched tightly. That was a no-go zone, right? Although women in books I read seemed to like it.

"No," I gasped and shook my head. I didn't want that. Right? And I'd never done the other. He moved slickly, the grace of a panther and the speed of a magician.

"No what?" He was in front of me, hand to my cheek, thumb at my chin tilting my head back and forcing me to meet his gaze. "No, you've never done that or you don't want it?"

The room had to be burning up. He had lit me on fire. Flames danced along my skin and sweat beaded down my spine. I sucked in a breath and blurted, "My experience is what we did."

I closed my eyes. God, out of all the things he'd said, that embarrassed me most.

"Why? And why are you in a hurry to do something that puts you in a vulnerable position?"

My lips pressed together solidly. This wasn't his business. But he'd said honesty. He wouldn't touch me until I gave him what he wanted. He wouldn't give me what I wanted until I caved.

Damn it.

"Because it'd be my decision. My choice."

The admission shocked him. His hand twitched at my cheek and his eyes narrowed, head tilted. "And that's important to you."

More than he'd ever know why. He saw too much. And around him, I felt too much. It was possible this was a bad decision. All of it. Perhaps joining the nunnery or a convent was better for me.

I couldn't bear to look at him. Very few people knew what

happened to me, not that it was difficult to find with a Google search.

He must have been waiting for a response but the words stuck in my throat like I'd swallowed cotton balls.

"Brenna," he said, and his voice was so rich, so slow... cautious. Who could blame him? "Has that choice been taken from you before?"

Not like he thought. Squeezing my eyes closed, I banished the memories and images that popped and flickered until all I saw was flashing lights behind my lids.

Pushing everything down I turned to him then, mask of health and innocence firmly in place. "I'm a twenty-three-year-old virgin who doesn't want to be a virgin anymore. Why does it have to be more complicated than that?"

I lashed out when cornered. It was the second time he saw it. Yet somehow, he smiled. Awesome. My anger amused him, like I was a cute little kitten.

"You're right. It doesn't. But if there was something...that could hurt you, I need to know that."

It was nothing like he was thinking. And absolutely nothing I had any intention of sharing.

"No one hurt me like that, Connor. I promise."

"Good."

And then his mouth slammed to mine, sucking my indignation and breath and any remaining sense right out of me.

EIGHT

Connor

SHE WAS HIDING SOMETHING. It was on the tip of her tongue but so well hidden, working it out of her would take time. Which was something I never considered investing in when it came to women.

There was an itch under my skin, an irritation that prickled when Brenna wouldn't look at me. She shouldn't mean so much to me. There was nothing specific about her that would make her different from any other woman, except for the fact I knew I'd been the only man to touch her.

That had to be this pull I felt to her. Some primitive male DNA embedded somewhere deep inside me that recognized her as *mine*. Had never been anyone else's.

She was also right. It was none of my business. Nothing except what she chose to give me was and right now, her mewls sliding into my mouth and shooting straight to my already hard dick was enough to make me say *fuck it*.

I didn't need her secrets to make her come.

I lifted her and carried her down the hall to my bedroom where she easily wrapped her legs around my hips and fused her mouth to mine.

Screw figuring out her secrets.

I made women come. A lot. Then I came. Then we went our separate ways. Brenna Kemper didn't have to be anyone different. As I had the thought, there was another spike of annoyance in my mind.

Possibly my subconscious warning me not to fuck over my boss's daughter.

Her attitude was in stark contrast to her actions. Sparking and burning bright white hot but fizzling as fast as a spring downpour. All of it done with blushing cheeks showing her purity at every corner. It was none of my damn business why the boss's daughter rarely made an appearance. I'd definitely remember if she had.

Perhaps that was why I was so damn curious. She had never been to a game I could remember. She'd never been at the annual fall kick-off. Another mystery to unravel on a day when she wasn't squeezing her thighs around my legs like a vise.

She tasted like honey, sweet with her mouth warmed from the wine and possibly lust and, hell, if it wasn't so damn sexy as she rocked her body against me. A hundred thoughts raced through my brain. Would her cunt taste the same? Sweeter?

I groaned, squeezing her tight and tangled my hand in her hair, angling her so I could shove my tongue deeper into her mouth.

She arched against me, her body pressed to me. It would take everything I had to take this slowly, to not hurt her again. And somehow, the idea of foreplay, driving her crazy with need, leaving her *craving* more when I was done with her tonight so I was all she thought about until our next time together, drove me frantic.

"Hold on," I said, pulling back, suckling at the soft skin next to her mouth, her jaw, the column of her alabaster white throat. There wasn't a mark on her. No freckles. She was so pale, her flesh looked as pure as the rest of her was.

I set her on her feet, my hands so large and her waist so tiny I could almost wrap them around her as I guided her back toward my bed. The white comforter was unwrinkled, but I was anxious to get her body on it, messing up my sheets and pillowcases, leaving her scent lingering long after this night ended.

My attraction to her made no sense. A smarter man might have questioned it, possibly denied it, but she had come to me for help before she truly asked that first night at Glitz.

Whatever the instant connection was between us, she was *mine*. Mine to touch. Mine to teach.

It was a rare beauty, a woman who could be so pure but strong, so beautiful yet innocent.

Something told me Brenna hid more than she shared and it was the hidden depths of her, the unknown places and desires I had the most illicit urge to unwrap.

She whispered my name, falling from her lips like a quiet plea, as if terrified of me...or to speak too loud to break whatever spell swirled around us when we were close.

I pulled back, skimmed my hands up the sides of her breasts, her shoulders, down her arms and to her hands. I caught every expression she showed me, every tiny little gasp or whimper, every tremble or wiggle when I slid close to sensitive places. Tonight wouldn't go as far as she wanted.

I was a man used to restraint when required, revelry in madness when acceptable. I was a man who knew my limits, thrived on pushing boundaries but lived by a set of standards.

That was all on the football field. The gym. My career or my schooling that helped get me to this place. I had never had to instate those practices to my sex life, but for Brenna, they were required.

With my hands holding hers, I brought them to my waist-band. "Take off my shirt, Brenna."

She blinked, a corner of her bottom lip disappeared between her teeth as her hands quivered. "Your shirt?"

"I want you to touch me. Get used to the feel of me."

It'd been so damn long since I'd *craved* the innocent, fumbling touch of a woman, but when her hands pressed to me, the pulse of hers racing with nerves and fear and indecision it all felt *new*.

I was wired with the electricity of it, as she tugged my shirt out of my waistband, shaking hands moving to the buttons. That lip of hers disappeared farther into her mouth with every button she undid and my grip tightened on her hips. Thumbs gently swirled around her hip bones. That soft flesh I knew hidden just inside of them. Her panted breaths were ragged, breasts heaved and fell as my shirt was undone and fell open.

"What now?" she asked, and it was the first time in several moments we'd spoken, the sound almost jarring, yet strangely erotic. Her lack of knowledge was the exact opposite of a turnoff.

I was hard as stone. I forced every muscle in my body to contract as I let go of her and slid my shirt off my shoulders, letting it drop to the floor like a feather as her eyes widened and that lip finally *popped* from her teeth.

"I don't know where to start."

My belt. My chest. My dick.

Her mouth. Her hands. Her *teeth*. I wanted all of it on me. "Wherever you're most comfortable, Brenna, but this is part of sex. The touching. The comfort with it."

A shiver rolled through her and even with the dim lighting, only a lamp flicked on from the hall with the bedroom door opened, I still watched her cheeks pinken as her shaking hand lifted, pressed to my chest right over my heart.

It seared me with a force of a flame I hadn't expected and I swayed back before collecting myself.

"Is this okay?"

There was nothing *okay* about her innocent and nervous touch.

"Perfect." I cleared my throat as she drifted to the other side, fingers brushing over my hair, a thumb swirling over my nipple shooting sparks straight to my balls.

"What do you want me to do?" I asked her, gritting my teeth so hard it was a wonder they didn't snap.

"I don't know what to ask for. You know what I want."

Sex. It wasn't happening. We were starting slow and yet it felt so damn fast. I brought my hand to her shoulder, trailing a single finger down her arm. "Does this feel good?"

"When you do that it feels like you're touching me everywhere."

A fucking finger on her arm had the same effect on her as her small, warm palm pressed to my chest as she brushed it down lower. I traced her movements. Sliding my hand to her stomach and where she touched me, I mirrored her own, touching harder, pinching her nipples through her dress until she gasped from the pleasure of it.

It was almost impossible to go slow after that beautiful, tortured little mewl echoed through the room even though she barely made a sound. My hands went to her back, her sides... searching until I found her zipper hidden in the seam.

I tugged it lightly, needing to see her body, not covered in cloth and hidden between my body and a wall or in a dark garden, but in my bed, where she was so pale it was possible she'd melt into my bed coverings and it'd take hours to find her.

Not that I'd complain at the search.

Based on everything else we'd done, I had the suspicion it would be more memorable than the best, hottest *fucking* I'd ever done.

"Is this okay?" I asked as I slid it down.

"Yeah, please." As she spoke, she began mirroring my movements, hands going to my belt, undoing it, she unbuckled it and popped open the button on my pants and had her hands on my zipper at the same time I finished her dress, shoving the strap off her shoulder, down her arm.

It slid to the floor and *holy fuck shit crap*...more spectacular than anything I could ever imagine was hidden beneath the confines of her dress.

It had bared everything while hiding everything that made her so uniquely her.

"You're beautiful," I whispered, and something thick lodged in my throat. My chest. I was not the guy who should be doing this with her. She should find a nice guy, one who'd be polite and slow and gentle. Someone who could take care of her after, whisper sweet words that weren't a part of my vocabulary. And yet she was here. *Mine.*

I ducked and kissed her before she saw my uncertainty, the strange emotions pummeling my chest. She wasn't mine because I was the only man to touch her. She was simply mine for now.

Someday, she'd find that gentle, polite man who wore khakis and polo shirts who could sit at her dad's table and actually belong. I was good for prepping her for that man.

As the thought rolled through me, my stomach flipped and I kissed her harder, sucked her tongue into my mouth, demanding. Forceful. I was unsettled, needed to regain my bearings and the only place I could figure out how to do that was by laying her down in my bed, spreading her out and getting lost in her body and sounds from her mouth and showing her what I liked instead of *thinking* so damn much.

I stepped toward Brenna, effectively forcing her to step back and kept moving toward the bed, my hands going to her waist and lifting her, holding her, adjusting her until she was lying on the bed and I was above her, pressing my knees in between her thighs and spreading her legs.

Her eyes were wide, lips parted as I drank in my fill of her, skimming her flesh with my palm, just touching her until she was squirming beneath me.

"Connor," she whispered. My name trembled on her tongue, her lips. It echoed into the room as much as I had to lean closer to hear her. "I don't know what to do."

So damn sweet I almost couldn't bear it. "Trust me to make this good for you."

She laughed quietly, lips ticking up at the corners of her luscious, swollen mouth with pale pink lips. "I'm more concerned about it being good for you."

If only she knew how good everything with her already was, and it made no sense.

I dropped to my elbow on one side of her, leaving space between us, and took her hand from my wrist. "Touch me. Wherever you'd like. Soft. Hard. Do whatever comes naturally." It would be impossible for me *not* to like the way she touched me. I pressed Brenna's hand to my chest, held it there and studied her. The shallow breaths forced her chest out, full breasts bobbed up and down. The thump of her pulse beating at the hollow of her throat.

She was glorious in her innocence and her bravery as she began to move her hand over the hair of my chest, down my abs, back up to my shoulders. I fought against shivering from her touch and the strain of staying still as she moved farther down, fingers playing at the hem of my boxers.

"Do you want these off?" I asked, brushing my hand to her cheek, back to her ear, cupping her neck.

Her fingers curled into the waistband and she nodded. Twice. I moved back, giving her what she desired, shoving them down my hips and kicking them off of my feet somewhere to the floor. Who gave a shit where they went?

I was unable to stare at anything but the creamy expanse of her skin.

Her swollen, glistening sex at the peak of her thighs.

"I don't want to hurt you," I admitted. "And yet I'm having a hard time moving slow."

"Do whatever you want," she whispered, her hand covering mine now, the innocent and the evil one, her taking control. She moved our hands to her inner thighs and upward until I was hovering right by her slit, her swollen clit already showing itself.

"God," I groaned as I took that first swipe over her, dropping my head so I could focus on her.

Her hips bucked.

And I continued, adjusting my body so I was close enough to see everything I was doing to her but so she could do the same thing to me.

"Get your hand on me," I gritted out, jaw tight. "I want to feel you on my dick."

Her first touch was tentative and her mouth fell into a perfect circle. "Oh." She brushed a finger over my length and around the tip.

"It won't break," I groaned and pressed my fingers against her sex. Her clit was swollen, her body already primed with wetness. "Wrap your hand around it. Tug. Pull. Get used to the feel of it. Pay attention to the head and don't forget my balls."

She took to my instruction like someone who wanted to go pro. Her hand moved up and down and I helped lubricate her with the juices from her own body, wetting myself with her before playing with her clit.

She gasped at my touch, bowed her back off the bed and while I worked on taking things slow, she picked up the act of a hand job like she'd studied it for years.

"That's good. So damn good," I grunted, thrusting my hips into her closed fist.

I rubbed my fingers against her, sank inside of her slowly, one finger at a time and stretched her while hooking my finger against the rigid flesh inside of her. Her free hand clawed at my arm as she panted and moaned pleas like *please* and *oh* and *so so good* and *yes*.

Her body trembled and her tight virgin pussy clenched around my fingers as I made her come. I wanted to kiss her. Wanted to watch. In the end, she made the decision for me as I came at the same time and her gaze was riveted to the creamy liquid spurting out of my dick onto her thigh, her stomach.

"Shit." I collapsed onto my side and pulled her to me, careful of the mess we'd made. She shook in my arms and slowly ran her hand down my arms.

"Was that okay?"

Okay? That simple hand job was the best thing I'd had done to me in months. Perhaps the last year.

I laughed and shoved my face into the crook of her neck, kissing her. "Yeah, angel. That was better than okay."

WE RESTED for a few moments before I rolled off her. "I'll be back. Let me go clean you up."

"Oh." Such a simple sound of surprise and she looked down her body. "Thank you."

I grabbed a washcloth and ran it under the sink. After I cleaned her up, I headed back to the bathroom and took a piss. Then took another minute to calm down.

This was the moment women went on their way with a gentle command from me that didn't allow room for anything else. It was the last thing I wanted to do.

I came out of the bathroom to see her back to me. She was no longer wrapped in my sheet, but sliding her dress down her body.

Something tight and hot squeezed into my chest at the sight of her. She was leaving. Seemingly unrushed, unhurried, but walking away from whatever in the hell it was we'd shared together.

"I thought you'd stay."

At my words, she jumped, head whipped around, all that glittering reddish-blonde hair a wave flowing behind her shoulder. "Hey. Well, yeah."

She was new to this. One-night stands and quick hook-ups and for a moment, I admired her bravery, the confidence in the straight line of her back and somehow, now, not fidgeting in the least.

I still wanted to throw her on the bed and cuff her to me so she couldn't go.

Forcing myself to adopt a casual stance, I leaned against the doorway, arms crossed, head tilted and plastered on a smirk. If she knew it was all fake, she didn't show it. "Perhaps I wasn't done with you yet."

I had been. But for the first time in as long as I could remember, I wanted to hold a woman in my arms. Cuddle her. Ensure she was okay after all we'd shared because I was rattled.

What in the hell *had* we just shared? A hand job. Kisses. I finger-banged like I'd done to my first girlfriend at the age of fourteen.

It was nothing in the giant realm of everything sexual. The basics.

There was nothing *basic* about the way Brenna moved and gasped and clung to me.

"Oh." She licked her lips. Hesitant. Her gaze slid to the doorway before coming back to me. Something about her nerves settled me. She wasn't leaving.

She was escaping. For tonight, I'd let her. It was probably for the best anyway.

"I was teasing, Brenna. You wore me out."

A brief smile. "Yeah?"

"Yeah," I drawled and pushed off the door and stepped toward her until my hand was at her cheek, brushing hair behind her ear. "You were exquisite. A natural, though."

"It wasn't, too, umm...elementary?"

Odd how I'd thought essentially the same thing. Yet now with my hand on her, it still felt anything but. "Perfect. I promise."

"Okay then." Another slide of her gaze to the door and I stepped back. If all this had shaken me so badly, I could only imagine how unsettled she possibly felt.

"Let me take you home?"

"I've already ordered a ride."

Of course. Innocent but self-sufficient. "Then let me get some clothes on and I'll walk you out."

It was late. The last thing she'd do was sit huddled on my doorstep like a girl I'd shagged and kicked out.

Before she could declare it unnecessary, I grabbed my boxers and pulled them on along with the pants she'd shoved off earlier. And then I was remembering...the push of her hands down my thighs. Her nails at my wrist while I slid my fingers through wetness no man but me had tasted, touched, reveled in.

Fuck. This was ridiculous. I shook the thought out of my head, steadied myself, and grabbed a T-shirt from my dresser on my way out the door where Brenna was already sliding back into her heels, shoving her phone into her purse.

And she was a liar. Her phone had been out here the whole time.

"You know," I started, pausing until my anger wouldn't come through in my tone. "Sometimes, men do actually like to be gentlemen when the night is over. Sometimes not, but lying is a sure way to start off on the wrong foot."

I gave myself quick applause for the playful but strained tone, and yet this time, Brenna's blush was fierce.

"I'm sorry, it's just...this is all, well, new. As you know." Her shrug was adorable as adorable could be.

"I know. But I did enjoy it." It fucking blew my mind and my body was still warm. *She* had blown my mind, her willingness, excitement, her nerves mixed with fortitude and the sounds she made when she came.

Goddamn it. What in the hell had I gotten myself into?

"And I'm looking for a repeat. Hand me your phone." I held out my hand and waited while she decided. If she didn't want my number, it'd be over. I'd have a beer or six and forget about how this girl, this innocent angelic creature, rocked me off my heels quicker than an opponent's safety.

She nibbled her bottom lip and pulled her phone back out of her purse. "I really liked what we did, too, you know."

"I'm pretty sure my neighbors know it as well," I teased. She laughed then and it was that mixture of sweet and sultry, making my dick take notice. Yeah. It was probably best she was leaving. I sent myself a text so I had her number and programmed my name along with my number and handed it back to her.

"Text or call when you're ready to learn more."

Ten minutes later, she was in a Lyft, I was back inside, drinking a beer, not getting a single hour of decent sleep because the scent of her definitely lingered along with the memories and images of Brenna's body.

NINE

Brenna

"BRENNA."

I jerked away from the blurry computer screen in front of me to find Shelly, newly promoted manager of the public relations department and my new boss, eyeing me warily. From the widened eyes and arched blonde brows peaked into points on her forehead, I assumed it wasn't the first time she called my name.

"Yes, Shelly. Sorry." I dipped my gaze down to the computer screen, only to see my screensaver with the Rough Riders Logo bouncing across the screen. "I was...um..."

"Daydreaming," she supplied and her lips pressed together like she was fighting a smile.

There was no point in denying. It was Friday, days since I'd been touched by Connor and he was still the first thing I thought of in the morning, the last thing I thought of at night, and invaded all the moments in between.

My cell phone had become my most hated possession. Obsessively checking to see if he texted me. Equally obsessively opening it while debating texting him. Yet other than my sisters and family and Gina, there were no other texts.

"I'm sorry, so so sorry." I pressed my hands to my desk and stood. My dad might have given me this job, one I was barely qualified for, but I was determined to do well at it. I had plans to move up, and move on. I'd taken this entry-level position as my father's only way to keep me close and protected, but I wanted to do such a good job that I could easily find employment someday of my own merits.

"It's okay," she said and pressed her palm to the high wall of my desk separating us. "It's Friday afternoon. A little bit of daydreaming is to be expected and you've had a long week."

It wasn't so much the weekend I was thinking of, but her upcoming appointment.

Connor Quinten was scheduled to be in any moment. And how was I supposed to react to him? Blasé wasn't in my repertoire, or at least it hadn't been before. Between the memories and the uncertainty of how to respond to him, my mind was a jumbled mess. How in the world was I supposed to hide the longing and desperate need for *more* I would surely feel when I saw him?

"Of course, Friday. Any plans?"

"My youngest has a football game tomorrow but other than that, just the usual."

"That sounds lovely." Her three boys were adorable. Her husband brought them in earlier in the week for lunch on his day off from a tech company. "Joey plays tackle?"

"Like a pro," she bragged with a gleam in her eyes that showed how proud she was of her kids.

"Well, I wish them all the luck. Was there something you needed from me? For your appointment with Mr. Quinten?"

She laughed softly, shaking her head. "You'll have to begin addressing these men as your equals, Brenna. Most of them come to us, groveling and needing assistance when they've done something stupid."

I didn't know what Connor's appointment with her was about. What had he done that he needed to meet her?

"Oh?" It tumbled out too curious before I could filter it and she grinned at me.

"Not Connor. We're here to work on some new promo opportunities I have for him, nothing serious, and no, I don't need your help with this...unless you'd like to sit in?"

And spend an hour confined in a room pretending I hadn't had my hand wrapped around his dick? I couldn't imagine how I'd behave.

"I'll pass if that's okay. I'm still getting used to the systems here, so I'll get some more online training done."

Shelly tapped her hand to the top of my desk and stepped back, waving. "Your call. When he arrives, send him directly back?"

"Yes, ma'am."

Her laugh followed her down the hall as she headed back toward her office, and I made a mental note to stop being so formal with everyone. It was a difficult habit to break after so many years at schools where manners and respect for teachers and professors was paramount.

I wiggled my mouse to clear the screensaver on my computer screen and opened up the training modules where I could spend the next two hours going through the scheduling programs as well as ordering apps we used for our promotional materials. All of it seemed so simple, but everyone knew I got this job because of who I was.

It was essential I got up to speed as soon as possible to prove I could handle it. Too bad the chances of me focusing on anything decreased with every tick of the clock. My vision blurred on the screen as the minutes ticked down.

Connor was going to be walking through that door any minute. What was the proper protocol when two adults got each other off with their hands only? Something told me blushing like a fumbling teenager when those things usually happened, wasn't the right response.

Plus there was the added bonus of my silent phone. Despite him telling me to text him, I figured he'd make the first move.

Maybe he didn't like what we did as much as I thought or he said? He was a man who was most likely not a stranger to having women drop to their knees at the quick snap of his fingers and his captivating gaze.

But me? I was just a girl who had no idea how to touch a man. God, perhaps going back to Glitz looking for him was a mistake. He probably had a grand time this week, laughing about getting off the clueless girl when he could be with women who knew what to do. My waffling thoughts were my nemesis, much like everything else I went back and forth between on in my life.

Confidence warred with nerves. Freedom conflicted with the comfort of safety.

"Damn it." Perhaps it was best to pretend that whatever happened with Connor was simply a one-time thing. We made no promises to one another. No further plans.

And besides, I wasn't even certain how to go about making more plans. *Hey there, want to make out again?*

How basic. And stupid.

"Well, hello there."

I jumped at the sound of his voice and whipped my head up.

"Connor," I sighed, and cringed. I sounded like a breathless girl with an obsessive crush. Not too far off the mark. "Um. Hi."

I was so lost inside in my head I hadn't heard him come in, or the elevator. I looked in that direction. Any possible chance I could rewind the last few seconds? Get my head in the game before he showed up so I was prepared for this? He was so large, broad-shouldered, casual in a T-shirt with the Rough Riders double-R logo over his heart, the only thing I could see from behind my desk.

He leaned forward with a cocky smirk I wanted to kiss off his face and rested his elbows almost where Shelly had done minutes ago. "Hello, Brenna. Good week?" He tapped his hands on the top, and I couldn't look away.

Was he taunting me with his fingers? The heat on my cheeks burned bright and I looked away, back to his eyes, which was almost worse.

He was so unsettling. So certain of everything and I was fumbling to find any word in my vocabulary.

"Yes. Yours?"

"Oh, I've been looking forward to this part of the week for several days now. Since Tuesday, maybe?"

"Oh, well..."

"You didn't text," he said and the grin of his evaporated replaced with a stern look. "I expected you to."

Something about the worry in his eyes slowed my racing heart at his presence. Had he been looking forward to it? Or concerned I'd become an overly compulsive girl at the first taste of something good?

I grabbed a pen and tapped it to my desk. "Neither did you."

"I thought about it, wanted to check in on you, but I also left that ball in your court." A slow arch of his brows put me in my place.

"I didn't know what to say."

"Thank you? Want some dinner? Want to hang out? Join me for a drink? All are perfectly acceptable options as well as '*Hey, thinking of you.*'"

I laughed softly. Perhaps I'd looked far more into this than he was. "I'm out of my element here, with you...with this." I circled my hand in the air in a gesture that made him grin. "Forgive me?"

"Only if I can see you tonight." He leaned closer, dropped his head and his voice to that beautiful, sexy low hum scrambling my brain.

"What?"

"It appears," Connor said, and damn him and his sexy lips that quirked up at one corner as his gaze traveled over my face, down to my breasts and back up, "I'm hungry for more of a taste of you and I don't like to be kept waiting."

A lump formed in my throat and I forced it down, slowly. "More?"

"Oh yes...*more*," he stressed, sliding his tongue over his bottom lip.

The area at the top of my thighs must have had a direct connection to that tongue of his because it spasmed, immediately grew wet at the visual and the very idea of what he was implying.

"I'd love too," I said, hesitating. This man might be too much for me. Perhaps I should jump ship, reattach training wheels and find someone younger. Someone...*less* in everything from confidence to body to whatever reaction I had with him. Someone who would have been okay with a one-and-done scenario.

"Great. Then it's settled."

"But I have dinner plans tonight. With my roommate, Gina."

His gaze flickered toward Shelly's office and back to me. A quick check at the clock said he was still a couple minutes early and who knows what was spinning in that mind of his. "Tomorrow then," he finally said, pushing off the desk. "And I'm not asking. I'm *taking*. I'll text you later, okay?"

I was already anxious with anticipation. "Yes. That sounds good."

"Wonderful." He stepped toward Shelly's office and as he put his back to me, my breath left in one giant rush, shoulders falling, tension melting. Dear God, the man was unsettling. Then he upended all of it by looking back over his shoulder. "And Brenna, you look beautiful today."

He turned with a chuckle. My gaze was glued to him until he disappeared into Shelly's office, finally giving me space to breathe.

~

"SPILL IT," Gina said. "You've been weird all night and not a good weird. What's going on? Work a pain in the butt?"

"Only in that I think I've found myself in a hole way bigger than I can dig myself out of."

"Well, that's clear as mud." She took a sip of her sake and I reached for mine. We were at our favorite hibachi and sushi restaurant, tucked into a quiet corner table for two instead of the louder hibachi tables on the other side. At the center of the table were rolls of sushi stacked delicately in a circular pattern and piled high like a pyramid.

"That man I went home from Glitz earlier this week?"

"Yes? He still on your mind, you dirty girl?" she teased and winked. Gina had been waiting up for me after I came home that night, almost two o'clock in the morning by the time I arrived, freaking out when I'd only replied to one of her texts saying I was on my way home. I'd been interrogated but spilled most of the humiliating details from the first night there and then finding someone else on Monday.

Protecting Connor's identity had been so important to me, but if I was seeing him again...would it be possible to keep it that way? At some point, surely he'd be recognized in public.

"I saw him today."

"What? Where?"

"Work." Her mouth fell open but before she could screech out another question, I continued. "He's a player."

"Did you know?"

"No, not the first time I saw him, but at my father's party..."

I dropped that bomb on her, that the man who'd sent me running from Glitz the first time was the same one I went home with the second time. "Gina, don't freak out. Please don't freak out."

"Holy cow, girl," she almost cried, throwing her head back and laughing. She slapped her hands on the table and garnered the attention of several nearby tables. "When you go naughty, you go all the way. So who is it? You have to tell me." She leaned in and whispered, flashing me a wink that gleamed with salaciousness in her eyes. "Every single tiny...or large...detail."

I sipped my sake and tried to gather my composure. My best friend was wild and crazy, and I usually loved her crazy antics, able to whisk me out of my shell when I wanted to tuck tightly into it. Tonight, we should have stayed at home, where I could pace the apartment, maybe compose a pros and cons list to this insane agreement Connor and I put in place.

"I need your discretion," I said. "Seriously, I don't really know what's going on or what will happen."

"You're right. You're right. I mean, what will your father say if he finds out?"

He'd most likely try to force me to move back home, wrap

me in bubble wrap, and lock me in my bedroom forever. It wasn't a risk I could take. And stupidly, I'd been so consumed with how Connor made me feel, I'd taken little time to consider the consequences.

But this was huge. And he wanted to do dinner tomorrow? It wasn't possible. There was no way.

"Have I made a huge mistake?" Oh God. I had. My fingertips burned with a sudden need to text Connor and call this whole thing off and that familiar flutter of panic edged into my senses.

"Hey, easy there." Gina's hand covered mine on my glass of sake. I hadn't realized I was shaking until she stilled my hand. "Tell me what's going on, and of course you know I'll be discreet. You can trust me with anything."

Of course I could. Gina might be the only woman I'd ever trusted with everything. She knew the horrific details of my life. I could only hide them for so long due to my occasional nightmares that would wake her because of my screams. The terror of being taken. Confined. Beaten but untouched sexually and scared for every moment of my life. The girls who didn't make it.

The heated stench of the shipping unit where we'd been cuffed, all of us stolen and stripped, starved and dehydrated so badly our cries produced no tears.

She knew it all. The only one outside therapists and family.

"Connor Quinten," I whispered his name, gaze darting to ensure no one was listening, but who would. We were two young cliché twenty-somethings, indulging on sushi. "And he's amazing, Gina. He...when he touches me...it's..."

I couldn't finish. My pulse raced at the memories and my body hummed with the pleasure of them. The sake fueled the heat rushing through me as Gina, across from me, no stranger to hot sex and no prude to not give out all the details, chuckled while I struggled to get everything out.

"He, well, he found me the second time I went back to Glitz, took me home with him. Then he said he'd... well..."

"Spit it out, silly," Gina teased.

I leaned across the table, took a roll from the sushi stack and quietly hissed, "He said he'd *teach* me everything."

"Oh damn." Her eyes popped, grin widened to her cheeks. "Good for you. So much better than the drunken fumbling and screwing around you anticipated."

"It's not good. It's horrible."

"Because his dick is small?" She propped her elbow on the table, dropped her chin into her hand and waggled her eyebrows. "Steroids, huh? It happens."

No, because it was glorious. "I like him, or I'm starting to, and there's nothing between us besides sex. And if my dad finds out. Gina..."

"Stop." She held out her hands. If she could grab my shoulders and shake me while I tumbled down the *what-if* rabbit hole, she would. She knew when to stop my rambling, my panic, my incessant need to have control while wanting to burn it to the ground. "It's okay, honey. It really is. You're twenty-three, you've already been through hell and back. You're *allowed* to find a hot guy and do whatever you want with him. You'll be careful because you're smart."

As she spoke, my anxiety flooded out of me with a heavy whoosh.

"And your dad loves you more than his own life," she continued. "You know he only wants what's best for you. He's fair and he respects his players, but you're an adult. You can't make decisions for your family anymore. You have to make the decisions to live for yourself, do what you want even if it's scary." She reached across the table and took my hand, squeezing it. "But promise me one thing?"

"What?"

"Protect your heart. Learn what you want. Take what you want, but a man like Quinten might not stick around. I don't want your first jump into self-discovery to end with you broken-hearted."

Tears burned the backs of my eyes and I blinked them away. "Thank you."

"And now honestly...tell me...how big is he?"

She was crazy, had me laughing despite my fear and nerves, but she'd done what she did best and the anxiety was a mere calm wrinkle beneath my skin. Barely physical.

I tossed back a swallow of sake and to Gina's absolute pleasure told her *everything*.

Gina was right. I could do this.

I just had to remember that the only thing I had to give and take from Connor was our bodies and orgasms. Our heart, especially mine, wasn't for the taking. To give it to him would be disastrous.

Holding on to it would protect us both.

TEN

Connor

I GRUNTED through my weighted squats, trying to keep my focus on my form, the weight on the bar, and the thump of music pummeling my ears. Next to the squat rack, Kolby rested a shoulder, waiting his turn, smirking at me. The giant asshole. He couldn't stop giving me shit and he was affecting my workout.

He also didn't care.

I stood and shoved the weights back into the hooks. "What?"

"You're playing with fire, you know that, right?"

An idiot wouldn't. I was no idiot.

"It's nothing," I said, shoving a towel to my face and breathing heavily into it. The lie thickened in my throat as I thought it. Brenna Kemper was *not* nothing. She was consuming me and it was unnatural.

Unwanted.

She was dangerous to me and yet turning my back on her before I had a full taste of her wasn't going to happen.

Kolby was giving me shit because he'd been next to me in the locker room at our training center before we began our early morning workout when her text came in.

Can't do dinner tonight.

That was all she sent and Kolby started giving me grief for being pissed about it. I didn't get pissed. I didn't get emotionally invested in anything other than the goal of winning another Super Bowl. My five-year contract was up at the end of the season and I had five more months to become the best to ensure my best chance at contract renewal.

Which meant walking away from Brenna now—especially when she was ready to break things off so easily with no explanation, no conversation—was the smartest thing I could do.

Apparently, I might be a slight idiot.

"Back off, Kolby. It's nothing. It's all in good fun anyway."

"And yet you're throwing weights around today and working out like you haven't been laid in a year. Too bad it's not regular season, you'd be a monster."

"I'm just prepping for training camp. That's all." Kolby might be a good guy, one of the best, but the less fodder I gave him to give me shit, the better. It wasn't natural for me to open up to people. "And it hasn't been a year," I grumbled.

Only weeks. A couple of months. But what I'd done with Brenna was more memorable than the last handful of women I'd taken to bed.

So no, she wasn't getting out of this without at least a conversation.

I dropped the towel and snagged my cell phone, opening it while Kolby started his squat set, ignoring the smirk on his face.

It's happening. We can order in at my place if that's easier for you.

Perhaps she had the same concerns I did. Being seen in public could be detrimental. In my most stalkerish moment, I spent a small amount of time looking into Brenna Kemper over the last week and hadn't been able to find anything. She had no social media accounts. Not even the standard LinkedIn profile every college grad had these days. All I saw were a few photos with her family at games over the years. It was no wonder why I hadn't recognized her until she stepped onto the stage. At my last appointment with David, she was only in one of the framed family photos he had in his office and even that one was hidden.

Like they were trying to hide her away.

The mystery surrounding her only made me more interested but perhaps that's all this was. She was a puzzle, a woman who made me chase for her, and maybe that's all that was so captivating about her. Perhaps once I finally had her and got to know her, the thrill of her would dissipate.

Unlikely. But I'd cling to the lie I told myself for as long as possible.

I switched back to the music app, shoved my noise-canceling headphones to my ears and moved to the other side of the weight room and lost myself in my workout until my legs and arms were burning, my abs sore, my body drenched in sweat. I didn't look at my screen again until I'd showered and dressed, hesitating when I saw her text.

Seven tonight. I'll be there.

I quickly texted back. **What do you want for dinner? And don't request dessert...I already have a plan for that.**

I imagined her receiving the text. Blushing as she read it. The tips of her ears turning pink in a way I'd only seen happen once or twice, when I really pushed her. Her hand would go to her hair, tucking a chunk behind her ear. She'd fidget, hands would tremble. Perhaps she'd drop the phone as she tried to come up with a response.

When her text came in while I walked to my car, it was me who almost dropped the phone.

And you will be mine. As far as food, I'm flexible.

My stomach flipped in an unknown, but not undesirable way, and I shoved my phone into my pocket. The last time she was at my place, it'd been a mess and I hadn't given a shit. We weren't going to spend time in the living area anyway.

Tonight, I wanted it to be different. Perfect.

Because tonight I was going to get my mouth on Brenna, on *all* of her. Fuck the consequences. I'd prove myself so worthy to the damn team and her father that even if he found out about us, it couldn't possibly damage my chances of staying in Raleigh.

IT WAS possible I went overboard on dinner based on the piles of to-go containers spread on my counter. Beaux gave me shit all the time when we went out to eat. When it came to food, I liked so much of it, it was difficult to decide what I wanted. The excess of food didn't bother me. I'd eat it all eventually. Next to a half-dozen containers of noodle and rice and curry dishes, there were burgers and fries delivered from Ride 'Em Rough bar where the team often went after nights we had late team meetings. It wasn't only close to the stadium and had the best fucking "man food" in the world, it was where Beaux met his now-wife, Paige.

My apartment was clean. The food cooling. And there was

a restlessness racing through me with the strength of a bear, the savagery of a lion.

I never cared before that I knew so little about the women I took to bed, but Brenna was different. When I thought of her, it was new in a way I didn't always appreciate but was losing the fight on exploring.

For whatever reason, I wanted Brenna. And she'd now tried running from me three times. People didn't *run* from me. They wanted something from me. My money. My dick. I kept my circle small for many of those reasons.

In a sense, Brenna was the same, but it was also part of her allure. She was upfront with what she wanted. She wanted me to teach her...she was willing to take what I gave her with no pretense, no manipulation.

A quiet tap rapped my door three quick times and I moved toward it, brushing down the simple navy colored shirt I wore and jeans, no socks, no shoes. Tonight would be causal. I wanted us comfortable. I wanted her relaxed so she'd spread those legs of hers and let me put my mouth between them.

Tonight, I'd teach the angel a host of wicked things she'd never get from any other man.

I swung open the door and arrested at the sight of her. Her strawberry-blonde hair was curled in large waves, pulled across her neck and draped over one shoulder. The black dress she had on was modest, except for the thin belt tied at her waist. I could tug on it and have it fall open in a second. Somehow, the simpleness of it was sexier than any dress she wore prior. I had a feeling this was the real Brenna. Not the person she pretended to be when she was at Glitz.

"Hey," I said. "Come on in."

I stepped back and she strolled in past me, grinning at me in a way that made me want to kiss her. It was so soft and shy. Yeah, this was Brenna without pretense and I liked it.

"Sorry I'm late." I took her purse from her hand and leaned in, kissing her cheek. "I think I was still debating about canceling."

"Not the best thing a guy wants to hear, angel." She shivered as I brushed my lips across her jaw, back to her cheek. "But I get it."

She was new to all of this. Hopefully dinner would loosen her up because right now even though she would melt at my touch, she was stiff as a board, showing her nerves.

"Food's in the kitchen, this way." I guided her there and dropped her purse on my kitchen counter.

A sound came from her, a half-snort half-laugh when she caught sight of the containers sprawled all over my countertops.

"Well." Her hand covered her mouth. I pulled it down. She didn't have to hide herself from me. "This was more than I expected."

"I didn't know what you'd like."

"So you bought something from every restaurant in Raleigh?"

She poked me in the ribs and I flinched. I was used to the jackass kind of ribbing men gave each other in locker rooms, not the playful teasing from women. "Something like that. Come on, help yourself. I'm starving."

I handed her a plate and as she scooped up some of the curry, I turned toward the liquor cabinet. In the fridge, I'd stocked it with tea and water and soft drinks, but I also had a couple wine bottles and beer. Everything stocked so she had her choice.

"Want something to drink?"

"Red wine would be great if you have it, otherwise water is good."

I poured her wine and grabbed a water from the fridge. I

wanted her relaxed, not drunk. Brenna slid into the chair where I put her drinks and grinned at me.

"This does all look really good. You outdid yourself."

How was it possible such a simple compliment felt so damn good? I grunted out a thanks, poured a glass of wine for me and settled at the table.

Slowly, we fell into conversation about work. Our week. Upcoming training camp where I'd be gone for almost two full weeks. It was jilted, maybe we both felt the tension. Her hesitancy. My craving for her. It mixed into a weird swirl between us, putting distance where I didn't want it.

But there was one thing I knew would definitely pull her out of her shell.

"What's your family really like?"

She laughed softly. "What do you mean?" She was twirling noodles around a fork and brought it to her mouth.

"Your dad's a great man. I respect the hell out of him and not what he's done for the team, but the way he always talks about his family. But I guess I'm curious what it was like for you, growing up in a house with so many siblings."

She chewed and swallowed, took a sip from her water bottle. I noticed she'd been alternating between the wine and water. "It was loud most of the time. The way my dad speaks to his team? That's the way he always was with us, our own personal booming cheerleader. And my brothers were older, you know? Aiden was thirteen years older than me, so he was always more like an uncle than a brother. I mean, he was dating when I was still in pre-school."

"Are you close with him?" Families confused me. Especially stable ones. I didn't know if I was hunting to know more about her or trying to figure out if they were all as perfectly happy and adjusted as they seemed to be.

"Aiden? Yeah, I'm close with all of them. In a sense, they all helped raise me just as much as my parents did."

A cloud of something dimmed her expression as she spoke. She grabbed her wine and took a hefty gulp. Like she was remembering being raised by them and wasn't quite so thrilled about it. It made me more curious. I didn't want to consider *why* it was so important to me.

I set down my burger and picked up my wine. Something didn't add up. "So tell me something?"

"What?" Her head tilted in curiosity.

"If you love your family so much and if you're so close to them, why did you spend so many years away from them at boarding schools?"

She reacted like I slapped her. Or kicked a puppy. Her face went ashen white and her spine shot up straight.

"What'd I say?" And what could I do to make it all better? And goddamn why was there a sudden pain in *my* chest?

Brenna shook her head, and in her hand, her wineglass trembled. So much for switching back and forth. She was clinging to the wine like it was a sudden lifeline. What the fuck?

"It was best for me," she finally said through a whisper that sounded like she was spitting nails.

"What does that mean?" The question came out like a bark and she jumped in her chair. "Shit, Brenna. I wasn't trying to scare you, but you get how odd that seems? I mean, there are dozens of pictures of your family, always together, and yet you're barely in any of them. For someone who claims to be so close to their family, you don't really seem to be a part of it."

That ashen white on her cheeks turned a furious shade of red. "I was studying. Going to school. That's all."

She'd been at a school no more than a few hours away. I'd

looked, because apparently, when it came to Brenna, I was losing my balls.

Still, her reply left no room to respond. Somehow, I'd pushed her into something that made her lash out. That wasn't at all what I wanted to happen.

Plus, there was something *more* running through me at breakneck speed that terrified me.

I was feeling too much. Wanting too much. This had to get reined in before we both lost our heads, and more importantly, before I gave away my heart to a woman who couldn't have it...a heart I'd just discovered was actually alive and well beyond the beating necessary for survival.

ELEVEN

Brenna

THIS WASN'T how I planned for the night to go. When I sent the text earlier this morning planning on canceling it was because I'd spent hours awake, thinking of Connor, my desires...the risks involved in getting caught.

It was a dangerous game I was playing. But wasn't it a game I'd wanted to have the confidence to play my whole life? The dichotomy paralyzed me with fear and yet it was my fear I insisted on trying to vanquish as forcefully as Daenerys with her dragons. If only I could be her when I grew up.

When I received Connor's text earlier, it took me hours to respond. I racked up a mental list of reasons why continuing to see him was a bad thing versus what I'd wanted. When I capitulated, I assumed tonight would go differently. That we wouldn't be sitting at his kitchen table, food spread out all over the place, conversation flowing as easily as the wine he always seemed to have on hand.

He didn't seem like a wine drinker, but like so much about what I'd been able to find out about Connor through conversations with Shelly as well as a quick Google search confirmed all my worst and most exciting ideas of him.

He was a man who didn't date, at least not publicly. He lived a quiet life with limited social media, only reposting photos on his Instagram where teammates or professional photographers tagged him, no caption of his own included. The same with Twitter. There was essentially no social media footprint or anything personal about him and it only increased my curiosity.

Who was this man who would risk his career for someone like me when he could most likely have any woman in his bed, with much less effort than it took to get me there?

And why was he the one taking it slow? He could have finished this nights ago, the first time we were together. He could have walked away as soon as he discovered who I was, as soon as there was a risk involved.

I hadn't expected dinner. Drinks. Him asking me about my family.

Or me craving to know so much about him in between bites of shrimp curry on a bed of noodles.

I sipped my wine and took another bite. Sitting so close to him scrambled all my thoughts, and I knew he caught how I'd tripped over why I'd been in boarding schools. He was right... the way I was treated was vastly different from the rest of my family.

He caught my hesitancy, the way I tried to change the subject, but now that the door of *getting to know you* was opened, I was leaping through it. So much for keeping the personal and my heart out of this.

I liked him. I wanted to know everything I could. Google was a poor substitute for the real thing.

"What about your family? They must have been really proud when you were recruited by Clemson."

"My grandfather was thrilled." Connor took a drink of his own wine and chewed another bite slowly. He went back to his meal like he was done with me asking about him.

There were several things wrong with his statement. The least of which being his abruptness. The lack of information on his part when he'd just tried to pry into my life, pushing when I hesitated.

"That's all you're going to say?" I twirled noodles around my fork and tried to appear nonchalant but inside, uncertainty swirled slowly but was growing.

"What else do you want to know?"

I speared him with a glare and brought the noodles to my mouth. "Are you always so obtuse and stubborn?"

He had to know I wanted more after what I shared with him.

Leaning back in his chair, he crossed his arms over his chest. One brow arched into a sharp point in the middle. Challenging me? Angry? I couldn't name what I saw on him but even as it increased my nerves, something else warmer...more beautiful...pulsed somewhere so much better.

"You can't expect me to answer all your questions and shut down when I return them."

"I can't?"

"Do you know how conversation works?"

"Maybe I wanted to know more about you, your past. That doesn't necessarily mean you're entitled to mine."

A sledgehammer couldn't have fallen more harshly against the table as his words did to me. Somehow, a switch was flipped. Here I was, thinking he was beginning to like me as much as I was falling for him.

How embarrassingly wrong I'd been again.

Perhaps that was my naivety. Just because he gave me orgasms didn't mean he wanted more from me. I knew that logically. Putting it in place emotionally was proving to be much more difficult.

"You're right," I said. I could play this his way, at least until I got what I wanted. If that's how he wanted it, his brutal responses and challenging, angry looks were enough to put me in my place. This, tonight, didn't have to be any different than the night I went to the bar.

So I had a crush on the first boy who got me off. *Welcome to high school, Brenna.*

I settled the rearranged pieces of how everything had changed so quickly, why he'd suddenly closed off, and ate my noodles. I lost my taste for them and the rest of the food he'd bought. So silly. But he'd done it for a purpose. To impress me?

It didn't matter now. He had no problems showing what he wanted from me and who I was to him. And I learned long ago that when someone showed you who they were, it was best to believe them.

I had two choices left...continue on with what I wanted from him, or leave and go finish my search somewhere else, with someone safer. Kinder. Gentler.

Screw it.

Something was happening between us. Sure, I was naïve to relationships and men, but I desperately wanted Connor to be the guy who gave me what I desired. I wanted to push him like he pushed me.

My stomach full, my food and nerves settling in it like boulders stacked on a shore, I shoved my plate away and refilled my wineglass.

"Are you done?" he asked as I took a large gulp.

How in the hell could I imagine seducing this man, who had seduced so many, so easily? Who probably didn't have to bother with seduction in the first place, just flashed his smirk and his scowl and flexed his muscles.

"I am." I couldn't look at him. This was it. If only I knew what I was doing. "And everything was delicious. Thank you."

"You have two choices tonight, Brenna."

Connor's voice was gritty, irritated. And possibly, by the way he'd slowed his words...his cock was hard beneath his jeans. I'd been with him enough to know what he sounded like when he was turned on. A fire in my belly ignited, hot enough to turn those boulders to dust.

"What are they?" I slid my gaze to him. He was sitting back in his chair, still visibly angry since I asked about his family.

Why?

It doesn't matter.

My inner back and forth was going to give me a headache.

Connor slid forward, grabbed his glass of wine and brought it to his mouth, eyes narrowed as he inspected me. "I've upset you and I won't apologize for that. Some things, no offense, aren't your business."

"If you don't want me prying into your personal life, then stay out of mine." He had, after all, started it, and when backed into a corner, I didn't hesitate to attack. It was only the sexual area of my life where I felt too ignorant to take control.

"Agreed." He set the glass on the table and pushed it back, brushing a hand over the table in front of him and clearing away the takeout containers. He was making space, but for what? "I think for what we both want out of this, that's probably for the best anyway, isn't it?"

After the way he reacted, reminding me of my place, it most definitely was.

"My choices?"

"You can leave." He arched a challenging brow, and at the same time slid his chair back, spreading his knees wide. My stomach flipped and flopped all over town. "Or you can come to me, sit on the table right here" —he gestured to the large area he'd just cleared— "and let me taste you. Eat you. Fuck you with my mouth and my fingers."

Which was really no choice at all. Connor knew exactly what I wanted, what I was there for. I only had to remember that this was *all* I needed—and wanted—from him.

No emotions. No entanglements. No public dates. Nothing more than this.

This would have to be enough.

I pushed back my chair. The brutal scratch of wood on tile floor a screech that blasted through his condo. For a moment, I hesitated, gave him time to wonder exactly what choice I would make and I waited...I would take what he gave, but I also had to learn to take what I wanted.

I wanted this. The wicked picture he painted with words was already seared into my brain and he hadn't yet touched me.

His shoulders slumped as I debated and as he shifted to stand, I stepped toward him. My hand went to the belt of my simple black wrap dress, chosen for easy access and wrinkle-free fabric in case it ended on a pile on the floor. As I moved, my hands went to the knot at my waist. I undid the bow as Connor settled back into his chair.

Even I could see he was more strained. Tense. Fighting against attacking and yet relieved I was staying.

He wanted me as much as I wanted him, and that knowledge slipped into me, settled my trembling fingers and boosted my own ego.

I stood in front of him, back to the table and pulled the belt from the dress, opened it without fanfare and tossed it off my shoulders. The cool air instantly caressed my body, whispered over my nipples, hardening the buds behind my lace bra until they ached for his touch...his mouth...the sting of pain as he pinched them.

"You're gorgeous," he murmured, tongue swiping over his bottom lip, heavy-lidded gaze dropping to my black lace thong and bra. With the same perfunctory motions of taking off my dress, I removed the bra, shoved my panties to the floor and climbed onto the table.

My gaze stayed on his and I was surely not mistaken when his eyes narrowed, a muscle jumped in his jaw. Lips pressed into a thin line, he said nothing else as I slid to the edge of the table. The heat in his annoyed glare settled on my pussy that was throbbing for his touch. For the promises he made.

He would deliver, of that I had no doubt, but the passion I thought we both felt so strongly?

That I would save for someone who deserved it.

My knees were wide and my sex on display for him. My arms shuddered from restraint as I curled my fingers around the edge of his ebony wood table, clutching it until the unfinished edges dug into my palms. Straightening my back, I thrust my breasts forward, but there was no way Connor noticed.

He hadn't yet taken his eyes off my pussy.

"You're so wet you're soaking," he commented so blasé we could have been discussing something mundane like the ripeness of fruit at the grocery store. "Getting naked and showing yourself to me turns you on."

There was no point in lying, but I could leave him curious. "A lot of things turn me on. I might be a virgin, but my fantasies are vivid. And frequent."

He jerked at my admission and I suppressed a grin. I'd

surprised him, and he hadn't expected it. If only he knew. He wouldn't now.

"Was this one of them? A man, focused solely on you, desperately wanting to touch you, to taste you, to slide his tongue inside of you until you scream so loud the neighbors hear?"

Yes. One of the more mundane ones. My chest heaved with a heavy, thick need for him. I was breathless as I replied, "I believe you just drew the line of sharing personal information."

It wasn't meant to be a slap, but he flinched. "Very well then."

He scooted his chair forward, hands curled around the armrests as he settled himself close to me. To my sex. A warm shiver of expectation rolled down my spine. My fingers dug more harshly into the wood as his hands raised, pressed to my knees, my inner thighs, spreading me open until my hips ached.

"Wider. As wide as possible."

Oh God. It was a simple touch. A command. And my thighs were spread so wide I was now sitting on my hands, bound, but free. My hips arched toward him at the first touch, his jaw tight and whether that was from his desire for me or annoyance at his own words thrown back to him, didn't matter.

This...this was what I'd wanted to experience for so long and if passion had to be delayed, so be it.

He teased me with his hands, his gaze so focused on his task he never once looked up as his fingers pressed closer, eliciting goose bumps and a sensation so deep inside of me it was terrifying. One of his hands stayed on my inner thigh, warm and firm but gentle pressure as he slid a finger from his other hand through my wetness. The slick sound of me, the brutal tenderness of his touch as he teased, circled my clit, ran his fingers through my slit and back up forced the memories of the other night to the forefront. Of his body on me, naked and bared, the passion involved.

Everything was so different and yet still I whimpered, pressed closer to him until the pressure of his palm on my thigh increased, stilling me.

"Stay still and *take*," he demanded, blue eyes lifting to mine for only a moment. His jaw was taut, features so firmly in place they appeared etched onto him. He'd thrown up the block between us and was forcing it in place at all costs but it was costing him.

I understood why. It was for the best.

I still closed my eyes and tilted my head back, unable to meet the blankness on his face as his head dipped...grew closer.

"Oh," I groaned and my body shook with the pleasure of that first swipe of his tongue. So hard. So wet. So warm. He dove against my clit, circling it with his tongue the same way he did with his fingers and it was so different, so vastly *more* in the intensity of it that I was crying out, bucking my hips closer to him despite his demands.

He could draw an orgasm from me that would be so great he could break through the faux wall I was trying to keep in place.

"Connor," I cried, my voice distant through the rush of beauty running through my ears and I was in danger of losing everything.

I clamped my mouth closed and forced myself to focus. On his body. The softness and warmth of his mouth as he tasted me, fingers pressing into me and twisting.

My sounds became quieter, forced out between clamped teeth and a tight jaw.

I would give him my orgasm.

He couldn't have anything else.

As if he noticed the way I closed down, he stood abruptly,

ripped his shirt over his head and grabbed my chin with his hands. His thumb went to my mouth and he pressed it against my lips. "Suck."

I did as I was told, moaning around his flesh that carried the most intimate taste of me and met his gaze.

His midnight blue eyes were almost black. "Don't hide from me. Not with this."

I opened my mouth to challenge him and he kissed me, slammed his mouth to mine and shoved his fingers into my hair, leaning forward until my back met cold wood and the plates and glasses rattled.

"Connor." My voice had a warning to it.

"I know what I said damn it."

He kissed me again, one hand sliding down my body to my breast where he pinched and pulled on a nipple until I was arching into him, thrusting my sex against his denim-covered jeans, grabbing onto his arms, still trying to reply.

"You wanted this."

He pulled back abruptly, panting, and for a moment that wall he'd put up shattered to the tile floor at our feet. "I am giving you all I have to give."

And oh God, my heart hurt for him and a thousand questions erupted until he was moving, dropping to his knees, settling his mouth right back at my sex where he'd been before and this time everything was too much.

Hot blue flames skittered across my flesh and I reached down, grabbed his hair. To pull him away? Shove him closer? I had no idea what I needed or what I should do except I never, ever, ever wanted him to stop this magic.

When I came, I did it pressing my heels into his back, nails digging into his scalp. The remains of everything that was best to hold back from him went bursting into the air.

He left me breathless, pressing gentle and tame kisses to my inner thighs as I regained my breaths and scooted back to his knees, grabbing a hand and pulling me to sitting.

Before I could stop myself, I dropped to my knees. The cold tile stung my knees as I fell but I didn't care. I just wanted to give him what he'd given me.

My hands went to his belt and my gaze met his. "Your turn. Show me what you want."

TWELVE

Connor

SHOW ME WHAT YOU WANT.

The only thing in my life I'd ever wanted was a family and a career in football. The first was impossible. The second was all I had. If my teammates got pissed, I held myself back. I was able to defuse their frustration with me for being so distant with a smartass comment guys usually made about their dicks or losing their balls and all was forgotten.

If a woman wanted more, I showed her the door.

Brenna might have been talking about how I liked and wanted my dick sucked, but with her, the very thought of wanting more than a warm body in my bed for a few hours or a night was too terrifying.

But holding up something to separate us was nearly impossible. Whatever happened between us would end, it had to. It was better to end it before we burst into flames, with her father lighting my contract on fire, sending the only dream I ever had and was capable of keeping to glittering and vanishing ash.

"You don't have to do this."

But oh God…I wanted this. Her sweet innocent mouth wrapped around my dick had kept me hard for hours all week, anticipating this very moment. But when I imagined it, I imagined me on my back, her kneeling over me, that shining red hair a flowing curtain around her face.

Not her naked, still breathless from an orgasm I gave her on my fucking kitchen table, and on her knees on my tile floor.

"Please," she said and it was more of a hesitant command, not a plea or begging. So I stood, allowed her to unzip my jeans and shove them down my hips. I was too focused on her to notice anything other than the small peek of her tongue from the corner of her mouth as she focused on me. My dick.

She ran her hand over my boxers, the outline of my erection visible and oh God, when she cupped my balls through the thin, slick fabric, my hands curled into fists.

How was I supposed to talk and teach when she had me in her mouth? All I could think about was lodging myself deep and making her gag until I shot my load down her throat while she pulsed around me.

Fuck. This woman.

Warm fingertips curled into the waistband of my underwear and she tugged them down, popping me free. My dick jumped, the cool air hitting my balls, my dick, and I was impatient for more.

Reaching out, I cupped the back of her head with my hand and tilted her chin. Her eyes were glazed over with lust and desire, and her mouth parted. Ready for me.

Perfect for me. Shit. I kicked that thought far past the end zone.

"Go slow. Taste. Lick. Do what feels good and listen to me.

Use your hand and don't force all of me."

"Women can really do that? For you?"

Her question was so damn cute I barked out a laugh. "Some," I admitted. And it was fucking fantastic when I found one who could, but I wasn't expecting Brenna to.

Besides, a deep throat blow job didn't make it the best, it wasn't even always technique. A woman who lost herself, got off on getting *me* off was a bigger turn on.

"Wow," she breathed.

I shoved my boxer briefs the rest of the way down and kicked them off my feet, focusing on nothing but Brenna and how she seemed to admire my dick, her hand so small she barely wrapped around it. Light pink painted fingertips as innocent as the rest of her. She stroked me slowly, tightening her grip as she got to the tip like I'd told her to do the other night and the girl was a fucking *pro* because she'd learned how to give the best hand job in a night.

How quickly would she learn to use her mouth?

Hesitating, she leaned in closer and ran her tongue over her lips before pressing them to my tip.

"Fuck," I grunted at the first, hot and wet feel of her.

Her wide, green eyes peered up at me through her long lashes. I couldn't peel my eyes off them as she took me deeper. Her hand and mouth worked to find a rhythm that made me fight against rolling my eyes back into my head.

This was *insane.* Her inexperience was clear in her hesitant movements, the soft flicks of her tongue but goddamn I was at risk of blowing at any moment.

"Suck harder," I grunted, fighting against thrusting into her. "And don't forget my balls. Play with them, lick them."

She hummed around my thick dick where veins pulsed around my length. Good God, I'd never been so hard. So hot. So terrified at the thought that when I did come she could render me useless. I locked my knees and fought against shoving my dick all the way down her throat as she found the rhythm and *excelled*.

Holy shit this woman is a master at everything she touches.

"Yes. Like that." I didn't know if my words made sense and she'd long since closed her eyes, tears leaking out of the outer edges but then her movements increased, her mouth tightened, her suction so fabulous I put pressure on her scalp.

"Close, if you don't want…"

"I want," she muttered, pulling off and then taking me deep, so fucking deep I felt her gag against the head of my cock before she pulled back and Jesus Christ it was sexy.

Her gags. Her surprised whimper. The way her other hand slid down the front of her to her slit. Holy fuck. Gagging on my dick turned her on. Pleasure whipped through me, white hot in intensity and I pushed forward, gagging her again.

Her fingers moved on her clit faster, harder.

Her hand gripped me fiercely and then she sucked, took me deep, not all the way, but so damn deep, I couldn't fight it.

"Fuck, Brenna. Coming," I warned her. She swallowed deeper and then I blew down her throat. My orgasm barreled down on me so fast there was no hope of stopping it.

And through it, she worked herself, bringing herself to another orgasm with her fingers, moaning around my softening dick and sending a quick shot of pain and pleasure straight to my balls.

My knuckles ached as I untangled them from her hair before bending down and kissing her. I took her tongue into my mouth, ravaged her with a kiss until we were both kneeling on the floor, gripping and whimpering.

Nothing in my life had ever felt so damn right. My world spun around me.

How in the hell was I supposed to keep my distance when I

wanted her so damn badly?

"Come on," I said, gripping her waist as I stood and bringing her to me. "I need to lie down."

She laughed softly, warm breath skating across my shoulder as I swooped her into my arms and carried her to the couch. I laid us down, rolled to my side so she faced me. Grabbing a blanket from the back of the couch, I draped it over us.

"Rest, just for a moment." The urge to hold her, to comfort her and care for her after everything she'd done for me was so foreign I didn't even know if I was cuddling the correct way.

Unbelievable. I hadn't anticipated learning anything from her and yet there I was, uncertain.

"You're pretty amazing," she whispered, her hand at my chest, my shoulder. She traced my flesh with her fingertips, growing more comfortable and confident every time we were together.

I curled my arm around her, settled my hand on one of her ass cheeks and held her to me. We said little as we relaxed, my lips inevitably finding her forehead time and time again as she laughed and traced freckles on my chest, pretending to draw shapes. Animals. Constellations. Every brush of her skin brought a new design and the occasional tickle on my ribs.

It was more peaceful than any ending to a night of sex I'd ever had...and the irony, that we hadn't actually had sex yet wasn't lost on me.

So much for keeping passion out of what we had.

"I'm sorry I was an ass tonight," I whispered. She'd been so honest with me, so upfront on what she wanted and expected.

Her hand stilled and then wrapped around my bicep, squeezing. Tilting her head back, her smile turned playful. "Just because you're apologizing doesn't mean I'm telling you my fantasies."

Minx.

"I am sorry. I'm not...good with people. Or women outside of bed."

"But you're awfully talented on a kitchen table so you have that going for you." Her words were a tease, happily quipped, yet even I was smart enough to see the strain in her eyes, the caution and worry I'd placed there.

She was smart to have it, and it'd be wise to allow her to keep it.

"You make me laugh," I admitted, grinning as I pressed my lips to her upturned ones.

She returned it slowly, her muscles tense like she was holding back. I wanted nothing more than to spread her out again, take her slowly, yet the overwhelming emotion I felt would only muddle the waters further.

"Stay the night with me," I said instead, equally worse.

She pulled back from the kiss and if I wasn't mistaken, there was apology in her eyes. "I have plans tomorrow."

"What are they?"

Her lips pressed to the side and she shrugged. "I always go to the Farmer's Market on Sundays, and then to my parents' house for lunch afterward."

"Do they go to the market with you?"

"No," she laughed. "I go alone." Her hand drifted down my chest, her gaze following her movements. It was personal, the thing I'd told her we shouldn't cross. I didn't blame her for not opening up more now since I was the one who started it, sincere apology or not.

"Okay then." I groaned as I untangled my arm from beneath her and rolled, putting my body on top of hers and kissed her again, more slowly, tasting her lips before I took her mouth and my dick hardening against her as she pressed her svelte and warm body to me. "I should let you go then."

Her hand slid up my back, into my hair. She pressed her

head into the pillow beneath her and smiled. "Maybe in a few minutes?"

It was the best invitation I'd ever been given.

So I took what she offered, making her come again with my mouth and my fingers while she jerked me off, begging me to spill onto her stomach.

And it still wasn't sex. Not intercourse. But it ended up being the most intimate night I'd ever experienced.

ON ANY OTHER SUNDAY MORNING, I allowed myself one day to sleep in before heading to the gym for a cardio workout. I spent the day shopping, lounging around the condo in nothing but a pair of track pants, watching college football reruns on ESPN or playing video games. Maybe a dinner with a teammate who didn't have anything else going on, and the night was spent meal planning and prepping for the upcoming week. Or I swung by Glitz before it opened when Malcolm was there, hanging out with a drink, discussing any issues he was having which he never needed my help for. The man took to running a club like I took to the football field and soon, he'd have the savings to buy me out of our original deal.

So it made absolutely no sense that this particular Sunday, I was up before the sun, grabbing my car keys, wallet, and Clemson baseball cap and driving out to a nearby state park where I got my run in on trails through the woods until sweat dripped down my back and my legs and lungs burned. Eight miles later, I was back in my car, chugging water and throwing my hat to the passenger seat of my Mercedes.

"Shit." I shoved a hand down my face and grabbed a towel I kept in my back seat, drying myself off. It was hot as Hades out, humidity thick. The run should have exhausted me but it was still barely eight o'clock and my body was a live wire, electricity running through me in a way that had nothing to do with the run.

No, all the pent up energy I had had everything to do with Brenna Kemper.

A woman I should want nothing to do with and couldn't stop thinking about. Her laugh, her smile, the fire in her eyes when she was pissed and the glimmer in them when she was turned on. Her innocence mixed with her brave curiosity.

Perhaps most of all, the way she'd seductively drawled, *I might be a virgin but my fantasies are vivid. And frequent.*

And goddamn it. I'd spent hours awake, unable to get those words out of my brain after she left. Hours spent cursing myself for drawing that line where she refused to tell me. Hours more trying to figure out a way to get her to open up to me. I was honest as I could be with her. I didn't do well sharing personal shit. I was raised by a grandfather who watched football, drank Pabst beer before it became vintage and cool again. A man who worked in a factory assembly line with an eighth-grade education and the son of parents who were too stoned and drugged and young to want anything to do with their own kid.

While my grandfather was a good man, a strong one, he was silent and gruff. He spoke little and shared emotions even less.

Without further debate, I threw my car in gear, headed home, and less than two hours later, I was strolling through a fucking Farmer's Market of all places, the late morning sun now barreling down on the heated asphalt and cement and rows and rows of tent-covered proprietors selling their wares to throngs of people, chattering happily and sleepily in equal measure, sipping their coffee cups and grazing along, strolling through the packed streets.

How in the fuck was I going to find Brenna? And the larger

question, why was I even here?

Because you want her and can't stay away.

At some point in the last week, I'd lost my balls to someone who had only ever touched mine. And a part of me no longer gave a shit.

With a new black hat, the signature UA of the brand stamped in white tugged down low over my eyes, sunglasses that hid most of my face, I walked through the main streets, veering off to the side, and just when I thought all hope of finding her was lost and was debating counting the day a loss and heading back to my own place to get on with my day and find my balls, a pile of strawberry blonde hair on top of a woman's head snagged my attention.

I moved toward her without wavering, swerving in and around the pedestrians and strollers and almost tripped over a small ankle-biter type dog on my way until she turned, face almost fully hidden behind a large bouquet of bright colored flowers, my hand settling on her shoulders.

"Angel," I murmured and she spun around, jaw dropping, flowers falling to her side in surprise, the move so similar to the way she'd done it the night I surrounded her at her parents' house in the gardens, I reached for them instinctively, assuming she'd drop them like she had the champagne glass.

"Connor." Her gaze skipped around before landing back on mine and that beautiful smile of hers dimmed. "What are you doing here?"

My hand slid to her arm, bare because she was only wearing a thin, pale blue tank top with the words "Beach Hair Don't Care" written across the front. It hugged her plump tits perfectly.

I tugged her toward me, bending low and swirling my hat around so the bill was at the back and whispered, "I think we both know why I'm here, and who I wished to see."

THIRTEEN

Brenna

THE BRIGHT SUN had been heating me for hours, and I'd spent so much time wandering the Farmer's Market, gathering fresh fruit and flowers and even an incredibly adorable bracelet from Stamped, a store owned by one of the Rough Riders' wives, Shannon Powell. I'd been to her store often and loved every piece she made with her own hands and while we didn't speak frequently, the woman, several years older than me and the sister of Beaux Hale, the Rough Riders' quarterback, was always generous and friendly with everyone.

I was so hot I was preparing to head home and get ready for Sunday lunch at my family's house when Connor's hand swept down my arm and everything else around me melted in the background.

The loud chatter became a quiet hum in the distance. The sun somehow seemed less hot, due to the heat from Connor's touch on my arm and the richness in his voice as he pulled back. His eyes were hidden behind black sunglasses so dark I couldn't see them at all but I didn't need to in order to know they were fiercely heated.

"You came for me?"

"I wanted to see you."

This man couldn't be any more confusing. Gina always talked about how men hated it when women played games. They preferred straight-up honesty, not a back and forth pull on their attraction.

Connor was making me dizzy with his constantly changing antics.

"I see. And do you plan on talking today? Or just whisking me to a hidden corner somewhere and having your way with me?"

Smirking, most of his face still concealed, he slid his hand to my flowers, took them from me and then took my hand in his, lacing our fingers together. It was such a sweet gesture, I didn't realize he'd started walking until he tugged me forward and I almost tripped over my feet.

"What are we doing?" I hurried quickly to catch up until I was next to him. Walking side by side, strolling down the crowded street was the last thing I'd expected of him.

But it *was* a fantasy...a dream...I often imagined when I was here alone, creating stories of lovers who had done the same, wanting it with a man I would have fallen love with.

"What does it look like we're doing? We're friends, strolling through the Farmer's Market on a beautiful Sunday morning."

"Are we?" I asked, leaning into him. The fantasy was sweet. "Friends, I mean."

He smirked and stayed silent, and I fell into step with him easily, letting him guide me back down the way I'd come. He indulged me every time I pointed out my favorite shop or small family farm. He allowed me to graze at clothing tents and was patient while I flipped through baby outfits, onesies for Tomas I was debating between when another one caught my eye in a size large enough for Tomas.

I held it up and smiled at Connor. "Did you wear something like this?"

Future Ladies' Man, Current Mama's Boy

His lips twitched and tightened and between his teeth, I watched as he pressed his tongue to the front of his teeth. "No. Never."

How'd a stupid onesie make him mad? Ugh. He was frustrating. Whatever. It was cute and Evan would think it was hilarious. I paid for the onesie and turned back to Connor. He was looking away, gaze focused on who freaking knew and when I stepped up to him, I didn't bother holding his hand. "Ready to head home?"

Connor flipped from hot to cold faster than my kitchen faucet. He wasn't going to ruin one of my favorite days of the week.

There wasn't a single muscle on his body that moved when he said, "I didn't have a mom. Both my parents took off before I could sit up."

Oh. The wrapped onesie in my cloth tote bag grew heavy.

"I'm sorry."

His shoulders heaved and he reached down, taking my hand in his and started walking. "I don't like talking about it, obviously. Don't like thinking about it."

"I'm sorry, I didn't know."

"Few do," he stated so blankly I wanted to rewind our steps like hitting the back button on my remote and ignore that last tent.

He guided me down the street, only loosening his grip on my hand to settle it on my lower back. We were in one of my favorite areas of the market when I realized my mistake. We should have gone the other way.

Oh shit.

"Connor," I said quietly and turned my back to the upcoming tent. "We need to go." My hands curled around his biceps and I pushed us backward. "Turn around."

"What?" He glanced down at me, up straight ahead and swore. "Too late," he muttered right as Shannon Powell's voice rang through the air.

"Quinten! What are you doing here?"

"Fuck," he grumbled and looked down, lifting his sunglasses and peering down at me. It was the first time I'd seen his eyes all morning and they were stunningly beautiful in the bright sun. "I can't ignore her."

Obviously. She was the wife of the team's captain and tight end, Oliver Powell.

"Hand me my flowers and I'll see you later?"

"She's coming this way and is smiling so wide at me talking to you it'll look worse if you disappear."

"Shit. Okay. We just ran into each other, right? Said hello?"

He laughed softly and put his hand on my waist to turn me around. "We did just run into each other, remember?"

Yeah, but he'd come searching for me. Sort of different.

"Shannon," he said, right as I heard her come up to him and ask again, "What are you doing here?"

"Why wouldn't I be at the Farmer's Market? It's a beautiful day."

He smirked, and I almost laughed at his innocent expression. It didn't fit quite right on him, but nonetheless, he kept a straight face through it all.

"Uh-huh," Shannon replied. "Sure." She turned to me and brows arched on her forehead. "Brenna. Lovely to see you again."

She leaned in and kissed my cheek and I stepped away from Connor so I could return it. "Feels like I just saw you."

"About an hour ago." She winked at me and clapped her hands together. "I didn't know you two knew each other."

"Had a meeting with Shelly on Friday and met Brenna. Ran into her here." His tone had gone almost scolding, like he was implying Shannon was foolish for thinking anything else was going on. Of course he would, the hiding still made me conceal a flinch.

This was why being with him wasn't possible. Too much possibility of being seen.

"Uh-huh, sure," she said again, and our lie wasn't believable in the least. Possibly because Connor still had his hand on my back. I wiggled away from him and it didn't go unnoticed by Shannon who pressed her lips together to keep from laughing. "Well, I should get back to work then. Oliver's stopping by if you want to keep me company and wait for him? I'm sure he'd love to see you."

"I see enough of your grumpy husband during the week."

"The old asshole." She laughed and threw her head back. "I'm sure you do. Well, then, I'll see you both later? At a game maybe, Brenna?"

I would have to go to all of the home games now that I lived here and worked for the team. From the little I knew of Shannon, she preferred to watch from her own seats on the fifty-yard line but she occasionally joined my family in our suite. "I'm sure I'll be seeing you frequently at them."

"Wonderful." She squeezed my arm and then stepped back, waving to both of us. "I'll let you two get back to your day. We'll catch up later, Brenna, okay?"

"Any time."

As soon as she turned and headed back to her tent, I high-tailed it down the street, frantic. I didn't have my flowers, but it didn't matter, Connor was right on my heels, hissing my name so as not to gather too much attention to my completely panicked freak-out.

"Calm down," he said behind me, laughing. "It's nothing."

Calm down. Yeah, hasn't any man ever figured out that doesn't work?

I glared at him over my shoulder and kept hustling through the crowd, weaving around them much less polite than I normally would. Dodged a double stroller right before it rolled over my toes in cheap rubber flip-flops. "She didn't believe you for a minute."

"Probably because I was lying."

"You're not helping." I ducked around a tent onto a side-street. There were several shoppers and people walking by, but no tents or sellers so the crowd was much smaller.

"What do you want me to do, Brenna? Tell her I had my mouth on your cunt last night and couldn't stop thinking about you this morning? I figure the lie, even a bad one, would be better."

I gaped at him like a fish.

"Besides," he continued. "It wasn't a lie. I did run into you and I did meet you at Shelly's office on Friday." He shrugged. "She's not going to say anything."

"To anyone but Oliver? Or Paige? Or Beaux?"

"I'll handle it. It's fine, I swear, and by the way, Beaux was with me that first night at Glitz. He already knows and almost busted a nut laughing at me at your parents' house."

"What?!" I shrieked, my hands slapped my thighs. "You're kidding." My hands went to my hair and I groaned.

"Connor—"

"Brenna, we're going to run into each other. We're going to have to know each other. You work for the team. I play on the team. And your father has always insisted we behave like one big family."

He had a point. My nose scrunched. "Family?"

"What can I say, I *like* my family," he muttered, moving closer, not touching me but I matched him step for step until my back was against a brick wall, the hot brick digging into the bare skin at the sides of my tank top.

"We can't. Not here."

"No one will know who we are," he whispered, bending down. Tempting. So tempting.

He spun his hat around backward again. Why was that move so sexy? The flippant spin, his bared bicep flexing at the quick move and then I couldn't think of anything because his mouth was at the hinge of my jaw, tasting. Teasing.

Kissing and licking and nibbling my earlobe until I was clinging to his waist, my tote bag dropping to the ground at my feet.

"Connor."

"Someday, you're going to be saying my name just like that in my bed, *after* you stay the night and wake up next to me."

A shiver of delight skipped down my spine.

"And after you tell me those fantasies of yours, trusting me to make them come true for you in ways better than you could envision by yourself."

"They're not yours to have," I whispered back, unable to stop myself.

He grunted and rolled his hips against me, his cock hardening and obvious. "They will be."

And then he kissed me hungrily, like he'd been starving for me and oh what a beautiful fantasy that would be...

Where Connor Quinten, the only man to ever touch me, was falling for me like I was falling for him.

FOURTEEN

Brenna

"HELLO, MY BEAUTIFUL GIRL." My mom squeezed me to her tightly while around us, mayhem ensued. Her hugs were as warm as the sun, as comforting as a Thanksgiving meal. Mom's hugs always made me feel exactly like I should, regardless of location—like I was home.

"Hey, Mom." I squeezed her back and held on to her. Somehow, after the last twenty-four hours and the roller coaster Connor threw me on, I needed the comfort more than usual.

It'd been a long time since I clung to her like this and I forced myself to pull back before she grew concerned.

"Everything okay?" she asked, her hand pressed to my cheek. "You seem flushed."

I shook off her concern. "Everything's great, it must be the sun from the market this morning."

"Ah, what do you call it? Your new church?"

What can I say, wandering the indoor areas, as well as the outdoor streets, relaxed me.

"And I'm faithful to attend weekly. Unlike some people I know." I winked and skipped past her, her laugh following me.

"Someone has to take the time to cook a meal for all you ungrateful creatures," she called out, but I was already in the kitchen, pouring a glass of white wine and popping a small tomato into my mouth.

"Dinner looks amazing as always, as do you, Mom." She was nearing sixty but could pass for forty-something, and she didn't throw thousands into beauty treatments. I could only hope I aged as well as her.

"Aunny BeeBee!" The screech came right before two small chubby hands smacked the backs of my thighs. "Aunny Beebee here!"

"Well, hey munchkin." I squatted down and ruffled my nephew's hair. "And who are you?" I tapped my chin. "I don't think we've met."

"Me Mikey! Me Mikey!"

"Oh! So you are, that's right. And you're this many, right?" I held up four fingers.

He giggled and with his pudgy hands, he folded down one finger. "Thwee!"

Michael tended to speak in shouts or cries, a rough and tumble boy who *loved* women more than men. He'd climb into the lap of any woman he met and hid behind our legs when new men entered the room. It was the most bizarre and hilarious thing I'd ever seen. The onesie I bought for Tomas made me laugh.

It'd be more perfect for Michael.

"Well, how could I forget." I picked him up and smooshed my face to his cheeks, back and forth until he squealed with laughter and pushed against my chest. "I missed you, Mikey. And I have a present for you."

I made sure to grab lollipops for all my nieces and nephews when I came for Sunday dinners. After years of being gone more than I was home, I wasn't above bribery to get them to fall in love with me and fill my cupboard with mugs stamped with "Best Aunt in the World."

"Now, where's your dad and mom?" He shoved a finger in the direction of my parents' back yard patio and I leaned in, gripped his finger and nibbled on it. "Then show me the way, Mitchie."

"Mikey!" he shouted, legs already kicking for freedom.

"Oh, that's right. I'll remember next time." I gave him one last kiss and set him on his feet before pulling a lollipop from my purse. "Now don't eat this while you're running and ask Mommy first, okay?"

"Yes!" His final shout bounced off the walls as his feet thundered toward the back of the house.

I tossed another tomato into my mouth and grabbed my wine. "Need any help, Mom?"

The marble island countertop was already filled with salads and fruit, breads, and two incredible charcuterie boards.

My mom knew how to cook as well as entertain and she loved doing it most for her family.

"Of course not, go see the family."

Before she could rope me into polishing silver or slicing more vegetables, I took her advice and moved through their house, stepping over plastic cars and Barbie Dolls littered all over the hallways. They'd be cleaned up within minutes of everyone leaving, but when my mom was in grandma role, she never minded the mess.

A messy house means a well-loved house.

A clean house is a cared for house.

A time for everything and everything in its time.

She said it often through the years, laughing while we teased her allowance of messes and her fastidious need for cleanliness. Eventually, she just began tossing a cracker or chunk of cheese or what whatever was nearby when Dad started in on her.

I always inhaled a breath before walking into the melee that was my family. With four kids in the family, two incredibly still overprotective brothers and a sister who might even be worse, my family wasn't only full of love and occasionally restrictive in their love for me, they were loud. Boisterous. More than once a nearby neighbor called the cops on our family get-togethers for noise disturbance when we hung out in the back yard, my nieces and nephew splashing through the pool with Eva telling Sam to bugger off. My oldest brother Aiden sitting at the outdoor bar with a beer in his hand, still all over his wife, Becca, like they were newlyweds even though they'd been married for well over a decade. It was their boys, Maxon and Beckett who would get into screaming competitions, seeing who could jump higher and farther off the diving board while making the largest splash, causing their sister Sophie to screech, and Kollin or Mikey to demand they do it again and again.

My parents were beloved in North Carolina due to the winning team they produced and owned...but most likely despised by their neighbors who had to live around them. Who could blame them?

I stepped into the back yard and had a sudden rush of the last time I was there, the night I saw Connor again. It took me a moment to brush the thought out of my mind and head toward where my dad and Aiden were, as predicted, sitting near the covered outdoor bar area, drinking beer, and what else besides ESPN on the outdoor television.

"There's my princess!" my dad boomed, pushing to his feet. He wrapped me in a hug ten times fiercer than my mom's. He smelled like beer and his Old Spice cologne, something he never changed despite the money he made. He was a simple man, always would be, and his predictability was one of my favorite qualities in him. That and his hugs and kindness and pretty much everything else about him.

What can I say? My dad was the best man I've ever met.

"Hey, Dad. Cops called yet?"

"One time. It only happened the one time." He squeezed me one more time and let me go, only to find myself wrapped in Aiden's arms too as he kissed the top of my head.

"How's my best baby sister doing?"

"Not so much a baby anymore." I twisted my leg to the side and kicked the back of his thigh.

"Always will be, Brenna." He tugged me forward and I shrieked as he fisted his hand and proceeded to scrub the top of my head with his knuckles.

"Oh my God, you creep! Grow up, why don't you." I grabbed at his wrists and kicked out at his legs but he was quick, years of giving me and the rest of us noogies so often he'd mastered the ability to move out of our kicks and punches.

"Good luck with that," Becca laughed. She tugged me away from Aiden and shoved his chest. "Go away." She pointed toward the bar he'd left to come harass me.

"No," Aiden huffed and leaned in, kissing his wife. Her annoyance was a ruse as she pretended to ignore him lingering and turned to me. "I blame your mom for catering to him so much. He's a perpetual twelve-year-old."

She was kidding even if there was truth to her statement. Becca loved my mom almost as much as I did. She'd been a part of our family since they started dating when they were eighteen, exactly half of their lifetimes ago. Since I was thirteen years younger than both Aiden and Becca, she'd been in my life since I was five. I hardly had a memory that didn't include her.

"Ugh. Aren't all men, though?"

She gave me a side-eyed look and wiggled her brows. "Why, sweetie. You have some firsthand knowledge of that now?"

My cheeks erupted in a violent heat and I stumbled over my words. "No. No of course not, it's just ... you know...boys are gross." Ugh. *Boys are gross?*

They might have been...but men like Connor were anything but.

"Right," she whispered in my ear and hugged me. "We'll be talking later, you know that right?"

"Nothing to talk about unless you want to hear about the tattoo guy Gina went home with last week."

"Oh, I love me some Gina stories. Is she corrupting you yet? Please tell me yes. You have to live a little, you know? Now's your time." Becca had always been my cheerleader, my encourager in a happy, much less insane sense than Gina.

Too bad for both Becca and me she married the world's largest overprotective jerk.

"Her life is fine," Aiden grumbled, "and I don't want to know anything about men in her life or boys being gross."

"Dad!" Beckett, their five-year-old, yelled from the pool.

We all turned only to cover our mouths with our hands, my laugh immediately bubbling behind mine. "Oh wow. That's totally your kid."

The towhead blond was butt naked, standing at the edge of the pool with one hand cupping the front of him, the other hand at his back. He danced back and forth and shouted, "I have to take a crap!"

Becca and I lost it, bending over and laughing so hard I clasped my knees. Across the patio, Sam and Eva busted out into hysterics, Rachel collapsed into my brother Tanner's lap and Aiden cursed.

"No cops tonight huh, Dad?"

"One gosh darn time and you won't let me live that down." He took a swig of his beer and walked away, patting me on my shoulder and kissing my temple as he headed inside. Probably to make out with my mom in peace. "Good to have you home, darlin'."

After Aiden ushered Beckett into the pool's changing area to use the restroom, everything went back to normal, not like anything had paused at the five-year-old either cursing or shouting. I went and gave my love to Tanner and his wife Rachel. Then I snuggled up with my baby nephew, Tomas, pushed his hands away and pretended to nibble his fingers when he grabbed my boobs and spent a typical afternoon with my family.

Succeeding in, at least for a few hours, forgetting about Connor and I running into Shannon at the Farmer's Market and what that could possibly mean for us.

If there was an us.

FIFTEEN

Brenna

I HADN'T BEEN KIDDING when I told Becca that Gina had gone home with a guy from a tattoo shop last week. She found him on a Tuesday, came home with sex hair out to *there* and a glazed-over look in her eyes, declaring that night the best night of sex in her life.

It wasn't the first time she'd said it. I guaranteed it wouldn't be the last.

Not the visual I needed a day after my own night with Connor, and I'd left for work that morning wondering what sex with Connor would actually be like. I'd had years to imagine it, a couple weeks of experiencing it. In the quiet of my apartment, Gina out once again with the tattoo artist she refused to name—most likely because her men were never around long enough to remember them—it was all I could think about despite my efforts to push Connor out of my mind.

I had a glass of wine. A new book downloaded onto my

Kindle. Netflix pulled up. All my favorite distractions and yet I was staring at the television screen, thinking only of Connor and the text he sent me an hour ago.

Hey

Three letters. One word. How in the heck did I reply to it? A simple *hey* back? *What's up?*

Without context, my mind raced. Was it important he talk to me? Did he hear from Oliver? Did he want to talk? Was it a simple *thinking of you* kind of text?

Argh. Stupid, Brenna. Just text him back.

And say what? Hi? Hello? Whatzzzz upppp? With a crazy emoji throwing up devil horns like Gina and I shared.

Probably not the best idea. Ugh. Men were complicated, a non-relationship relationship with Connor had to be one of the worst. I needed lessons from Gina in getting your body involved and keeping your heart out of it because I was definitely failing with my first "just for sex" escapade.

The door opened to our apartment and I swung in the direction as Gina skipped in, same sex-hair she had the other morning, and yesterday, if I was remembering correctly. She dropped her keys and purse onto our kitchen table we used for everything but meals.

"Hey," I said and checked my watch. It was only eight at night. "You're home early."

"He had a late appointment, but if he's in the same condition I'm in, I have no idea how he's going to be able to concentrate on doing someone's ink tonight."

She winked and went to the kitchen where I heard the pop of a cork, the sound of a wineglass pulled from out under the cupboard glass holder. "And does *he* have a name? Or should I make up one for him since you're keeping it such a secret?"

"I'm not keeping his name a secret."

"So, it's..."

She appeared around the corner to our kitchen and shrugged. "Why do you need to know?"

She sipped her wine, nonchalant as could be but Gina wasn't mysterious and she had certainly never been *coy*...not with me.

I scrambled to my knees on the couch, careful not to spill my wine. "What's going on? What are you hiding?"

"I'm not hiding anything, Brenna. Maybe I just want to keep it private."

In the five years we've known each other, Gina had never felt the need to keep anything private...even her privates. She was the girl who'd waltz through the halls of our dorm to the bathroom butt naked, towel and shower caddy in her hand, not giving one single shit who saw her. Granted that was girls, but she was equally free with her thoughts and her affection and everything else in her life.

"You like him," I surmised, fighting a smile.

"Rubbish."

"And now you're British?"

She snorted and collapsed onto a chair, kicking her bare feet onto the coffee table. "I don't like him. Not like that."

"Just his dick?"

"Well, yeah, but he has these eyes...and ink. He has this scroll that goes down the side of his ribs. It's absolutely lickable..." She rambled on, and every description made my grin grow wider. She finally stopped talking, took a breath, and probably realized she was talking more to herself than me.

Realization covered her one single second at a time and her face made a hundred different reactions in those few seconds. "Crap. I like him."

I laughed and stood from the couch. "I'm getting a refill. Enlighten me why this is a bad thing?"

She sighed heavily, the overdramatic kind of sigh that

only Gina could make loud enough to be heard by our neighbors. While I refilled my wine, I did my best to encourage her.

"You know, this isn't the worst thing in the world, you liking a guy for *more* than sex alone. What's the harm....and what are you doing with my phone?"

I'd walked around the corner. No wonder why she went silent as I talked to the kitchen cupboards. Gina was no longer overcome with her own emotion, but she was grinning at me like a cat who'd had a taste of milk and craved more.

"Why do you have my phone?" I repeated, my steps slow.

"Oh, because some superstar football hottie just texted you and I was—" I snagged the phone from her as she finished — "curious."

"You are a brat. A major brat." I managed to set down my wineglass without spilling it despite my shaking hands. Gina could have already sexted the man, sent a shot of boobs from an old Tumblr account for all I knew.

"Gina," I groaned and opened up the text string. "You are so off my Christmas present list."

Hey. The one that was sent over an hour ago I hadn't responded to yet. But now there were more.

Home from dinner? How's your family?

And then Gina's response...

Oh hi there handsome man o' mine. Got some yummy dessert for me? I'm starving for something sweet. Maybe salty.

She had to be kidding me. "Are you for real right now?" I glared at her while she so innocently sipped her wine and shrugged. "I might hate you."

"You don't."

I didn't. I couldn't. But good grief, this girl. She'd do

anything to keep a conversation off herself even it meant throwing me under the bus.

Three dots appeared in the reply side and I hesitated, then debated, and quickly typed.

That was Gina. Ignore that insanity. Bitches be crazy.

The dots disappeared and I sank into the couch cushions, psychotically watched as three more appeared. Vanished. Re-appeared. Oh God. He had no idea what to say. My mind quickly whipped up a hundred more apologies that would make me seem neurotic.

Thank God. Finally showed up with an emoji of someone wiping sweat from their brow. **Thought you'd jumped straight to sexting and I wasn't sure how to proceed after thinking of you with your family.**

I chuckled and sipped my wine. Crisis averted.

"We'll finish this conversation with that nameless tattoo guy later," I told Gina, giving her a scolding look as I grabbed my phone and wine. "I'm going to continue this in private."

"I did it to help you since you hadn't responded to his first text and I figured you'd spent the last hour debating how to say *hi* back, you little nutcase."

I slammed the door on her and laughed. She knew me too well.

"That wasn't helping!" I shouted back through my door but she couldn't hear me. She was already blasting pop music from the music app on our television.

It took a few more seconds to decide. Texting I could do, but Connor's voice through the phone was like dark melted chocolate, smooth and rich.

I dialed his number and he answered almost immediately,

chuckling. "You know, it's pretty immature to blame someone else for your own texting faux pas."

"Shut up. I can't believe she did that."

"Gina seems...fun. She's your roommate, right? The girl you came to Glitz with?"

I shuffled the pillows against my headboard and settled against them, kicking my feet up and turned on the television in my room to drown out Taylor Swift's new album blasting from the living room.

"Yes, and best friend."

"Ah, the woman who had no problems dancing in a circle of men. Looked like she could handle herself."

"You have no idea." Gina was legendary at our girl's college, getting into more trouble than I could even remember, but mostly she kept her heart tightly fastened closed from men, always declaring it was because she needed to focus on school. She was starting law school at Duke in a couple of weeks, so I didn't blame her. Her hard work had paid off. She was the person the phrase *work hard play harder* was designed after.

This wrench in her plans had me more curious than ever. But with Connor on the phone, I didn't want to think about Gina.

"Sorry I missed your text earlier."

"Sorry it was so lame. I meant to send you another right away but got a phone call I had to take and just got off."

An hour long phone call? "Hope it was nothing bad."

"It was Oliver."

Shit. My wine settled in my stomach like a brick. "Yeah."

"Yeah, angel, and it was football-related. If Shannon said anything to him, he wouldn't have held back. Everything's fine."

I ignored the way my pulse kicked up every time he called me angel. I wasn't as pure as he thought, at least not in my personal thought life. Only in action maybe, and even then, he was divesting me of that quickly.

And I'm definitely not complaining.

"Well, that's good I suppose." He didn't offer more information, yet my mind was running wild. He was the one who insisted we kept it physical then he showed up at the market and sent me spinning all over again. I had no idea what Connor was thinking. What he really wanted. Or more importantly, what *I* wanted.

A low rumble came through the phone and there was a pause. Too long. "I thought we could talk about the conversation we were having before we ran into Shannon today."

If it was possible for hearts to melt with words, mine had just become a puddle. My grip tightened on the phone and I took a large swallow of wine.

"Your family?" My throat was dry. I knew exactly what he was talking about. Where we'd left off.

I didn't have a mom. Both of my parents took off...

I felt that pain acutely in my heart as I had earlier. Piercing. I couldn't fathom. My parents loved me to smithereens. Unconditionally. They would do anything for their children, and for me, they *had* one time.

"Yeah...they were young. Teenagers, really. Hooked on drugs. Dropped me off one day at my grandfather's house and took off."

"Oh Connor. I can't even imagine."

"Bet with a dad like yours, you can't."

It wasn't only that. It was being old enough to have been ripped away from my family. The fear of never seeing them again. Maybe not living. The ripples of my trauma swarmed around me, closing me in my bedroom.

I squeezed my eyes shut and pushed the thoughts back.

This was about him and he'd already said he never talked about it.

He was choosing me, though.

What does this mean?

"So yeah, anyway, my grandpa raised me. He wasn't exactly a family man but not a bad man. Just a simple man who liked his sports and his beer and worked."

His words were a fist to my heart. The darkness in his voice.

"He must be proud of you, then, I would imagine."

"He was, when I got a full ride to Clemson. He died after my freshman year of college."

Jesus. Tears beckoned and fell before I could sweep them away. "I don't know what to say, Connor."

"What can I say, angel. Life is shit sometimes, shittier more times for some people than others."

Now that, I related to in a vastly different way.

"I'm sorry you've had to live through that. Really I am, Connor. You should be proud of yourself though, for making it despite the odds, and I imagine your grandfather watches from wherever he is and is proud of you, too."

There was a long silence. "Maybe."

I was certain of it, but I wouldn't push. He'd shared so much already.

There was a rustling through the phone and I imagined him stretching on his bed, perhaps propping himself up on his pillows like I was sitting, biceps exposed, hand behind his head, giving anyone who walked into his room a deliciously incredible view of that body he'd have on display. Shorts only, most likely. Perhaps hard, thinking of me.

I muffled a moan but not quite fast enough.

"That's quite the sound you made, angel. Care to share?"

I set down my glass of wine. "Um. No, no, I would not." Oh

God. There was a heat at the apex of my thighs and I pressed them together. I should have been revolted, getting turned on after the saddening history Connor shared with me. And that wasn't what had done it.

"Angel," he murmured, and that voice with that tone sent my pulse skyrocketing. "Are you wet for me?"

"I was thinking of what you were wearing and if you were in bed."

He huffed a laugh. Perhaps thankful for the change of subject. This was where we excelled and sharing those things couldn't have been easy for him.

"I am in bed. If you were here with me, what would you do to me?"

Phone sex. It should have felt awkward, but I searched my mind for it and came up empty.

"I..."

"Don't get shy on me now," he teased and I closed my eyes, imagining my words making him hard. His hand moving down his stomach to his boxers, kicking them off, gripping himself.

"I would climb on top of you, taste you...your muscles on your stomach, your chest, your arms."

"My arms?"

I shrugged even though he couldn't see me. "They're sexy." He laughed softly and then groaned. "Are you touching yourself?"

"I am," he replied. "Thinking of you naked, climbing on top of me and straddling me. Pressing your cunt to my cock, sliding over me and getting me wet as I sucked your nipples into my mouth. Hard."

"Oh God." My hand moved on its own fruition. Sliding beneath the thin cotton pajama shorts I'd thrown on earlier until I was at my sex. And goodness, I was *drenched*.

"Are you wet? Wet for me, angel?"

"Soaking," I gasped as I slid my fingers over my clit. My hips bucked and I gasped again. "Please, keep talking. You're so much better at this than me."

He did. And it didn't take long at all before words were no longer necessary and the only thing coming through the phone lines were our pants and groans, our whispers and then my cries and his deep rumble as we came together.

I was still breathing heavily when Connor said, "You still haven't told me about dinner with your family."

"Another time, maybe. You've worn me out."

He laughed, sexily and sleepy, like he was after I'd been on my knees for him. Cuddly. I imagined sliding into his arms on his bed and letting him hold me close like he'd done on the couch.

"I should get to bed, Connor."

"Sleep well, angel."

I ended up having incredible dreams that night, but they were hardly angelic.

SIXTEEN

Connor

"WHAT'S PISSED YOU OFF? You were rough out there today."

I tossed my duffel bag over my shoulder and fell into step with Powell. He was right. I was pissed. Mostly because once again, I'd done something completely unnatural with any woman I'd been with—shared my life past— and I was blown off again.

Two days of waiting for Brenna to text or call had me on edge. If I didn't know how innocent she was, I would have assumed her a master game player.

She wasn't playing a game though. I had the very distinct assumption based on her behavior that she really did only want me for my dick. For the first time in my life, that really sucked. So yeah, I took it out on my teammates at practice, running harder, pushing everyone, grouchy as hell and still spent an hour in the weight room, pushing myself even harder than anyone else.

"It's nothing," I told Powell.

"A woman."

Powell wasn't our team captain for the sole reason he was the best tight end in the league and one of the best players on our team, save for me of course, but the man could obviously read minds, too.

I cursed and shoved open the door to the locker room. "Isn't it always?"

We walked down the hall toward the parking lot.

"Kemper's daughter," Oliver said quietly next to me.

I froze in my steps and dropped my duffel to my side. "You know."

"Shannon mentioned it. Figured I'd let you sort that on your own but if you're going to be taking out your teammates at practices then I can't stand by."

"It's nothing," I repeated. Oh thou who doth protest too much.

"Sure it isn't. Women can fuck our minds even more severely than they can fuck our cocks, Quinten. But this isn't a game you can play and expect to come out winning."

"It's not a game." Although the way Brenna had no problem avoiding me when we weren't talking about bodies or I wasn't teaching her how to have good sex, still made me doubt.

"Ah, so you like her. Can't blame you for that one. She is sweet."

The way he lingered on sweet made my teeth hurt. Powell was an ass to everyone. Had been an even bigger dick before he fell for Shannon.

"Speaking of sweet women. How's your wife?"

He shoved an elbow into my gut, and I doubled over from the force of it. He was kidding, but it still hurt. "Fucker," I growled and dropped my bag to the ground, shoving him play-fully against the wall.

"Yeah..." Oliver said, hands against the brick wall, raised in surrender, smirking at me. "Women, man, the ones we fall for the hardest always screw with us the worst, you know? My advice? Figure it out and soon. But you gotta know you have to be careful. Word is Kemper is very overprotective of his youngest daughter. She hasn't had the easiest life."

My hand was still at his chest. This was part of the mystery always lingering in her eyes or the walls she'd erect with a flick of her finger. I thought of the other night when I told her more than I'd ever willingly shared with anyone. She sat there and listened, cried for me, and gave me nothing of herself except the sounds she made when she came.

It hurt more than it should have even if it shouldn't have surprised me. After all, I'd chased her when she was willing to find someone else to have sex with her.

"What do you mean?"

His smirk grew. "So she's nothing, huh?"

I pressed him to the wall as he laughed and I stepped back. I shoved my hands through my hair and growled at the jerk who spoke only what I dared not think about. "You're an ass, Powell."

"Yeah." He laughed. "But not a wrong one."

I spun around and grabbed my bag. I threw it back over my shoulder and Powell stepped back up to me right as we reached a corner when a mass of strawberry blonde hair was the first thing I saw. She was moving too quick, and we were too close, talking with her father, so she didn't see us before her soft body ran straight into my chest, slamming into me and falling back with an, "Oomph!"

I reached out on instinct and grabbed onto her arms before she fell on her ass.

"Woah there," David said, placing his hand on Brenna's back to keep her from falling too.

"Oh!" She swiped hair from her face and over her shoulder before turning her wide, green eyes to me and repeated, "Ooh."

Next to me, Oliver chortled.

"David," he said, moving to the side and holding out his hand. "Sorry about that. We were messing around and didn't see y'all there."

"No worries," he said, shaking Powell's hand and looking to Brenna. "You all right, dear?"

"Oh, um. Yes." She slowly removed her hands from my chest and it took effort to unpeel my hands from her arms. The implication Oliver shared with me only moments ago, fresh in my mind, I caught the paling of her features as her gaze skirted to me and then her father, then Powell. She stepped back, rubbing her arms where I'd held her and cringed.

"Did I hurt you?" My words were tight, more forceful than intended.

"Um. No." She stepped back again, not glancing at me once and turned to her dad. "I'm fine. I promise."

David's brows pulled together and he stepped toward Brenna, concern stamped all over him.

What the hell was the concern? We hadn't injured her.

"Darlin'," David murmured and something else more fearful washed across his face. Brenna let her arms fall to her side.

Her hidden secrets. Oliver's warning pummeled my brain. And something else as her gaze turned to me.

The night she'd first come to my house and I asked her if she'd been hurt by someone.

It was the way she'd replied. *Not in the way you're thinking.*

"Brenna," I called her name quietly, unable to hide the depth of my worry for her and my confusion. "Are you okay?"

"Yes." She brushed her hand through her hair and smiled. It shook and wasn't anything like a smile she'd given me before. *Fake.* After all we'd shared, she was still hiding from me. "I'm okay, Connor. Just startled is all."

She blinked away her faux kindness and set her hand on her dad's arm. "Come on, Dad, we should go."

He patted her hand absentmindedly and it was then I caught the way he was watching me. The concern for his daughter long gone, now something else was in his gaze. Something more inspecting and I fought the urge to crumble under it. I'd never taken a girl home to meet her father but the way he watched me was one I'd imagine of any father. What had Powell called him?

Overprotective.

But why? Why with Brenna specifically?

A hand came down and gripped my shoulder, shaking me. "What brings you here to the training center, David?"

"Oh. Right. We were watching the practice. Thought now that Brenna is working for us, she should get to know the players as much as possible."

"And what'd you think?" Powell asked. "Of the players today?"

"Oh, well..." Her cheeks turned a soft pink at his words. "You all did very well, honestly. I admit I'm not much of a football fan but I'm enjoying learning a lot."

"That's my girl," David said, hugging his daughter to his side. It was clear he adored his daughter, but Brenna was stiff, unyielding against him and slowly pushed away.

"We should go. I need to get back to Shelly anyway."

"Very well."

Her gaze stopped at both Powell and me. "Gentlemen, enjoy your day."

With a quick turn of her head, she and her dad moved off

toward the locker rooms and the underground walkway that would take them back to the official offices.

"Well, that was…" Oliver trailed off. As at a loss for words I was.

"Yeah," I muttered. "I'll see you later."

I took off before he followed me to avoid further conversation. I had a feeling we were at a loss for words for different reasons, and there was no way I could articulate what had stolen mine.

Except for the fact that there was an angel, who I suspected was slowly stealing my heart. Leaving me more confused than ever.

IT WAS LATE, and I was on my couch, feet kicked up on the coffee table in front of me.

I came home from practice and had the strangest urge to clean my condo, so I spent hours, digging my vacuum out of my closet, dusting, sweeping, and mopping floors along with scrubbing and dusting. Now my house smelled like lemon-scented Pledge and ammonia from the window cleaning solution, and strangely, it felt oddly good to be resting on my couch, protein smoothie in one hand, remote in the other, while I flipped through channels on cable, switching back and forth between a crime drama and a medical drama I couldn't give two shits about.

Good Lord, if losing my balls and becoming a tightened knot of *what in the hell should I do* was what happened when you lost your heart to a woman, I wasn't certain I wanted to see Brenna anymore, unless absolutely necessary.

I'd replayed the run-in with her father earlier multiple times, every time coming to different conclusions. She didn't seem embarrassed to see me, but she'd done a hell of a job pretending she didn't know me at all.

I didn't know what was worse. That she could so easily act like I meant nothing to her, or that I was still so damn hung up on figuring out who, or what, had hurt her.

My phone was close to me, lighting up occasionally with notifications and texts from teammates. I looked at each one and promptly ignored it so when I settled the television on a show about sharks and it started ringing, I was tempted to ignore it completely.

Until I saw the name.

Brenna

I grabbed it, my thumb pressing the answer button before I brought it to my ear. "Hello?"

"Hey there. How are you?"

Such a mundane question with so many complicated answers. None I was willing to give.

Before I could even find an answer, her sweet, almost too peppy voice continued, "So, I was wondering if I could see you? Tonight, maybe?"

I kicked my feet off the table and set them on the floor. "Tonight?" It was already nine o'clock. Not late, but it'd take her a half hour to get to me.

"Yeah, well, I'm sort of outside."

"You are?" I was on my feet, moving to the front door where I had a security switch to open the doors on a panel by the door. "What are you doing here?"

"Hoping to see you. I thought after today we should talk."

Talk. Of course. She was most likely freaked.

So was I.

I doubted for the same reasons.

No, mine wholeheartedly dealt with the strange heat in my

chest and the flip-flopping of my stomach at Brenna's voice on the line and the fact she'd come here for me.

"I'll buzz you up."

I pressed the button and waited on the line with her until she was inside and at the elevator. "I'll unlock the door. Come on in when you get here, okay?"

"Yeah. Thanks, Connor."

I hung up the phone. It'd disconnect in the elevator anyway. Then I hurried to my bedroom in order to throw a shirt on. A brief stop in the restroom, I took a piss and brushed my teeth and was heading back out down the hallway when I heard her call my name, softly. Almost hesitantly.

"Coming," I called back and met her in the living room, her gaze sliding over my living room.

"You cleaned," she teased, grinning at me and facing me. "Looks good."

"Thanks."

For the first time in my life, I wasn't sure how to behave. It should have been so simple. Screw the heart-to-heart chats I gave her last night, things I wanted to give her, and just grab her. Fuck her.

It was our agreement, and I was the dumbass who started liking someone when it was supposed to be just physical.

Like any of the girls I'd dated had done to me, I knew how this ended when someone crossed the unwanted line.

Shit. "So," I drawled slowly and settled my hands on my hips. "Have a good day at work?"

"It was, well weird, I guess."

That made two of us.

"I, um, well, I felt like things were weird when my dad and I ran into you and I guess, I was thinking about you, wanting to make sure you're okay."

I stepped toward her. She was definitely nervous. I'd

learned that from the way she fidgeted with her hair or nibbled on her bottom lip. She did both now and turned to the kitchen. "Do you mind if I have a drink? Some wine or something?"

"Sure." I followed Brenna to the kitchen, unable to not only admire her small curves, but the seductive sway of her hips and her perfect heart-shaped ass. Her long, lean legs on bare feet. She'd already kicked off her shoes and for some reason, I smiled at that. Would she kick off her shoes and get a drink if she planned on leaving quickly?

It was too bad I didn't find my balls when I cleaned earlier. I could probably use them.

She helped herself to my wine, grabbed a wineglass, already familiar with my small kitchen and I liked that idea. Of her familiar with my things, my space, *me* that she'd make herself at home whenever she came over.

Settling against the counter, I curled my hands around the countertop behind me, crossed my feet, and waited.

"You drove all the way across town to make sure I was okay with you literally running into me and getting to see you during the day?"

Her green eyes widened. "You were okay with that?"

"Seeing you? Yeah...especially since I went to bed last night with the sound of you coming through the phone putting a smile on my face."

She laughed softly. This was where we had it easy. Sex talk. Flirting. It was everything else we were both virgins at...you know, things like *talking*.

"I didn't know if it'd worry you, with Powell there and Shannon. Suddenly in two days it feels like there's no way we can keep this a secret anymore."

The problem? The *this* she referred to was quickly becoming a blurred line. Tossing that conversation I wasn't prepared to have aside, I asked, "Is that what you want?"

I'd tell her about Powell already knowing about us when she didn't look three seconds away from Panic-ville.

"I thought that's what we agreed."

"Yeah, but I'm pretty sure me spilling all my secrets, things I've only ever told one person about besides you, weren't in the agreement either."

"Only one person?" Her voice went soft, awed, before an even softer smile kicked her lips at the corners.

"Malcolm. My college roommate and the guy who owns Glitz. Yeah."

"Oh." She looked into her wineglass. "I didn't know it was that private for you."

"Some guys on the team know. They know my grandpa raised me anyway, but in all honesty, guys don't really sit around talking about our feelings and shit."

She smiled at that and took another sip of wine. At this rate, she'd have the bottle drained over a few more awkward pauses.

I pushed off the counter and took the wine from her, setting it on the counter.

"What are you—"

"Why'd you come tonight, Brenna? Was it because you were thinking of my dick and wanting more of it? Or did you want something else? I'm happy to give you either, but if you want something from me, you have to ask for it."

She stammered for a moment and any other time, it'd be cute as hell. But something was pulsing in me, a need to get past the physical and give something of myself to a girl. Could I do it without getting more back from her as well?

Probably. I was a man who liked fucking and getting my dick sucked off, and now I could add Brenna's hand jobs as maybe my top three favorite things. The mechanics of it were easy. From the first time Brenna and I met though, we were way past mechanics and basic chemistry.

"I don't…I don't know what you mean. I thought we could talk, hang out."

"But you came over here to check on me."

"Yeah because I wanted to know if Powell said anything to you."

It physically hurt me to lie to her, hold back the truth from her. It was only temporary. "And what, worried your dad would find out you were making out with the resident team playboy?"

She flinched at that and fuck it stung. He'd said something to Brenna about me. Before we ran into each other? Or after?

"What'd he say, Brenna?" David saying shit about me made my stomach roll. He was the only man in my life I could look to as a father figure and a part of me wanted to think he respected me and liked me, too. My one-night activities with women, however, were hardly a secret from the team and since some men gossiped more than pre-teen girls, of course he'd heard.

He'd had a "be careful and a role model in public" speech with me more than once or a hundred times.

"He mentioned something."

"Had to be something concerning if it made you hop in your car to see me."

She licked her lips, and then grabbed her glass, took a large gulp. "He said he respects the hell out of you as a player, but as a man, he said you have some growing up left to do."

I laughed softly. It was the nicest way to warn her away from me and of course he'd be a nice guy about it.

"And what? You want my side? I don't think I have to remind you that you came to me for one thing, and my guess is you figured I'd be *good* at that one thing. Don't get that way without practice."

I was being glib. Kind of an asshole. Mostly because I still wasn't sure why she was here.

"You are good at it," she teased and whatever she thought of earlier was gone like a flash. "Maybe I don't care what my dad thinks or wants for me."

"No?"

She shook her head slowly, took a small step toward me until her hand pressed to my bicep and squeezed. Something warm smoldered in her gaze, darkening her green eyes and I knew without a doubt, if I leaned down, I could take her. I could probably pick her up, throw her on the kitchen counter, spread her legs and eat her for dessert. Or I could take her to my bed, prep her through one or two orgasms, getting her ready to take me. I could do *all* the physical things I wanted to do to her once the night we met.

First, I had a more important task.

"Do you know what I'm curious about, angel?"

"What?"

"Why was it when I touched you earlier today when you ran into me, you looked totally fucking freaked? And your dad looked terrified out of his goddamn mind?"

SEVENTEEN

Brenna

HE NOTICED. Of course Connor noticed. He seemed to know and understand things about me even I was yet aware of. Somehow, I was special enough to him to make him want to open up and share his past with me.

Like him, I'd talked to so few people about mine. I'd been required to tell my therapist, and Gina became a necessity once my nightmares woke her up.

To share this with a man who hadn't promised more than teaching me how to have sex with other men?

I'd given Connor more than I'd ever given anyone, but I didn't want him knowing. Not because I didn't trust him, or because I couldn't talk about it. I didn't want Connor to know because he'd look at me differently. He'd treat me differently. I could feel it. I'd had over a decade of experience with it from my entire family. By Connor's own admission he wasn't good with people so how could I know he'd handle my past with the understanding I craved?

I took my hand off Connor's arm and stepped back, running that same hand along the back of my neck. "I'm not sure what you mean?"

Dark, midnight navy eyes narrowed on me and his nostrils flared. "Yeah, you do. What are you hiding, angel?"

A roaring sound rushed through my ears, making him sound like he was talking from a tunnel. "Nothing."

"I don't think that's true. You said before that someone hurt you, maybe not in the way I was thinking, but I do think someone hurt you."

I struggled to regain my footing. The floor beneath my feet felt like it'd gone sideways, throwing me off course. So maybe I had come here because I was nervous about Powell seeing us together, the things my dad said about Connor afterward when he caught the deep concern in Connor's voice.

But mostly, I just missed him. I wanted to be with him. But this?

He was asking too much. "I'm not ready," I finally said. It was all I could give him. The small dose of honesty.

If he couldn't accept it, I had no idea what I'd do. I already had a feeling based on Gina's constant rambling about sex and one-night stands and how they could be good or a major flop, I would end up losing my virginity to someone who didn't know what they were doing.

We'd gone far past this being just about getting rid of my virginity. Even I knew that, at least for me. But the road ahead was murky and without a clear path, it wasn't really his business.

"I like you, Brenna," he said, stunning the *crap* out of me so much I took a step back, braced my hand on the counter for balance.

"What?"

"You heard me." His smile turned down, not quite a frown. Definitely not a smile. "And in all honesty, I don't remember the last time I've thought about a woman as much as I think about you."

He was saying all the right words. All the things I needed and wanted so desperately to hear, but I wasn't prepared for them.

"It's sex," I rasped. Denial rose up strong and abruptly inside of me, bursting from somewhere deep inside.

"Technically we haven't had sex, but I think we're both aware whatever connection we have goes far beyond the physical." His gaze met mine dead-on, and I squirmed under the weight of it.

I looked away, picked a spot on his bare cream wall and breathed deeply to calm my racing heart.

"At least, it is for me." He curled his lip and stepped back, reaching for the bottle of wine on the counter. He filled my glass and took a large swallow. "Maybe I was wrong."

He was so far from wrong it wasn't funny, but I panicked. I needed to process this. I needed to clear my head and consider this.

"What are you asking of me?"

"I'm pretty sure I'd take whatever you're willing to give me, but do I want honesty? Do I want to know you more beyond the sounds you make when you're in my bed? Yeah, Brenna, I want that."

I was Brenna. Not angel. Somehow that hurt.

"I'm not sure I can give you that yet."

He flinched like I'd slapped him. It hurt me to say it, but if he wanted honesty, he needed to give me time.

I chewed on my lip debating when he took another drink

and turned to face the counter, putting his back to me. "So what now?"

"I think now we say goodnight and I walk you to your car."

Obviously the night wasn't going to end the way I'd hoped, with me making the sounds he said he liked so much. He was within touching distance and yet making it clear his body was currently a no-hands zone.

"Okay."

Goodness. This night had gone vastly different than I'd hoped and I had no one to blame but myself. My constant, stupid desire to live wild and free along with my desperate need for safety and security.

A risk taker I wasn't, and handing more of me to Connor was the biggest risk I'd ever taken.

Was he worth it?

My gut said yes.

My brain screamed at me to slow down.

I left the kitchen, trudging along his tile and carpet floor like I was walking through mud. My mind and body warred against each other, whispering *turn around and tell him everything. Trust him* followed by *he won't get it. Everything will change.*

I needed time to think when I wasn't so thrown off course.

In the entryway, I slid into the Birkenstock sandals I'd kicked off when I entered and slid my purse strap over my forearm. "You don't have to walk me down."

"It's late."

I hadn't heard that tone in his voice since the night he caught me in my parents' garden, laced with anger and frustration. I didn't need to look at Connor to know his face would be etched like marble.

He reached around me, and I couldn't help but notice the strength of his muscles in his arms. The way his arm flexed as he pulled the door open and held it for me. On our way out, he grabbed his keys and fell into step next to me.

We reached the elevator and he punched the button to call for it like it'd personally offended him.

A thick wall of tension had grown between us with every step.

"I didn't mean to hurt you."

"You're not."

We stood next to each other like strangers. I was aware enough to know he was lying. Maybe I hadn't hurt him, but it also wasn't the first time I'd pushed him away due to my own fears. And I had a feeling if I did this, if I walked away from Connor tonight, the odds of him giving me another chance diminished greatly.

It took forever for the elevator to arrive and I jumped at the ding of its arrival. Stepping in, I turned and caught Connor's gaze on my backside before lifting and meeting mine.

"You have a nice ass," he smirked. "Can't help but look."

"I wasn't complaining."

Maybe there was hope after all.

The doors closed and as soon as the elevator began its descent, he shoved his hand through his hair and sighed, gripping the rail at his hip with his other hand. "I'm not mad at you. I don't want you to leave thinking that. But I am feeling like a fool for what I said, for pushing...for maybe reading too much into this. We can go back and keep this simple, you know. Forget the night ever happened."

It would never be possible for me to forget Connor telling me he liked me.

"I wasn't expecting to hear the things you said, and I don't do well with surprises. I just need some time to process everything, what you said, how you feel, how *I* feel."

Based on the curl of his lips and the way he focused on the panel next to the door it still wasn't the right thing to say.

"You asked for honesty," I reminded him softly.

"I did, and you're giving it. I can't fault you for that. Not really."

Yet he still looked like someone told him Santa Claus wasn't real.

With a heavy sigh, he shoved his hands to his hips and I counted the speckled dots on the carpeted elevator floor until we landed with a soft bump and the doors opened.

He walked me to my car, a hand on my lower back guiding me down the street and standing at the threshold like a gentleman who'd been raised with class and manners. Such a dichotomy to how he so often behaved, it made me smile as I reached my car.

"Thank you for walking me to my car."

He nodded. "I leave for training camp next Monday. Maybe we should take a couple weeks, give you the time you need. We can reconnect when I get back the following Friday."

"That's almost two weeks away."

"You asked for time and space Brenna and it occurs to me that maybe I've been pushing you too far too fast, in a lot of different ways. We'll step back. Give it a couple weeks, reevaluate then."

He sounded so final, so resigned I couldn't think to tell him I didn't need that much time. Or space.

I wanted him. Liked him...possibly way more than he'd admitted to liking me.

But it was terrifying at the same time. When I said I needed time, I meant the night. Or a day to settle my thoughts before racing into something so unknown.

Weeks?

His jaw jutted out, lips pressed into a tight line. He was

resolute in what he was asking and it didn't seem fair of me to request anything different.

"If that's what you want, Connor. I can give that to you."

He shoved his chin in the air. "Get home safe, Brenna."

~

I OPENED the door to my apartment, Gina's mouth dropping and her eyes going wide at the sight of me.

"Oh dear," she said. "This does not look like the face of a woman who finally rid herself of that pesky *maidenhood*."

A cough, followed by a choking sound came from the kitchen. I'd think about the maidenhood comment Gina said later.

"Seriously, Gina?"

"Oops. I forgot I had company."

"And now I feel so utterly welcome again." The door behind me slammed shut as the masculine voice, and the man who had used it, stepped out of the kitchen. If I was correct, he studiously avoided meeting my gaze.

And I didn't know which one of us was more surprised, me that Gina apparently invited over her man-who-was-still-name-less when she thought I was gone for the night, the tall and lean guy who looked nothing like a tattoo artist I'd ever seen, or Gina...either at my arrival home or for meeting her boytoy in such a way.

I came unstuck first and after dropping my purse and keys to the sideboard table at our entry, held out my hand to the guy. Clean cut, short spiky blond hair tinged with blue at the tips and wide blue eyes. He was well over six feet, and while there was a tattoo sleeve running down his arm, various brightly colored images, a hodgepodge of perhaps everything important to his life because it wasn't one design, he looked like you could throw him in a dress shirt and tie and he'd look like every other kind of uptight, businessman Gina dated.

"I feel like I should move us past this awkwardness and introduce myself as Brenna the virgin, but how about we stick to Brenna."

"Brandon," the guy said, shaking my hand and letting go.

My gaze slid to Gina. She rolled her eyes.

"Brandon, hmm," I sang. "How great to meet you. So what are you kids up to tonight?"

"Nothing," Gina quickly said. It might have been the first time in my life I saw her blush.

"Nothing?" Brandon repeated, arching a brow in a way that had I not been with Connor Quinten for the last two weeks might have made my knees wobble. Brandon was *pretty* with a capital P. "I don't think what we just finished up was nothing."

"Anddd...I've heard too much. You two kids just" —I flipped a hand in the air— "go back to doing *nothing,* but keep it quiet, please. I'm exhausted." I turned to Brandon. "Nice meeting you. I'm going to go crawl into a hole and die of embarrassment now."

He raised his glass of beer. "Cheers."

I scuttled off to my room but before I could close the door, Gina was there, blocking me from shutting it.

"What's going on? What happened?"

"I think I should be asking you that."

She shrugged. "So you were right and I like him. School doesn't start for weeks, so it's fun."

"And once school starts?"

"You know how insanely focused I get."

"But does Brandon know?"

She scrunched her face and stepped farther into my room, closing the door behind her. "Nooo, and he doesn't need to. Besides, he's busy too."

"Uh-huh. Okay."

She twirled a finger in the air at me. "What's that face for? And why do you look sad?"

"It's nothing." Just the ending, maybe, of hope I'd had for something more. I had thirty minutes in the car on the way home to mentally kick my ass for being such a terrified moron. I was skittish with reason. But somehow I knew, I could trust that to Connor. Why I had no idea. He was gruff and brash, bold and enormous. His size alone should have sent me running and yet it was that and the way he'd treated me gently that drew me to him. "Can we talk about it later? You have company waiting."

"He'll be fine. If you need me..."

"I don't need a babysitter, only some time to think."

"Ew. Thinking? That sounds dangerous."

"It'll be fine."

"Sure?"

"Yup."

"Are you lying to me?"

"Possibly." I shoved a finger toward the direction of the door. "Go. Get out of here. I'll figure this out."

"Okay, okay, but tell me one thing." She lowered her voice and concern washed over her. "Did he hurt you? You know..."

I hugged my crazy friend. "I love you, and no, he wouldn't do that."

"I love you, too. I'm always here for you, you know that, right?"

"Always, gingersnap."

She growled at the stupid nickname I'd heard her family call her once. She hated it, and in return, she nicknamed me something equally horrible.

"See you later, shortcake."

After Gina left, I grabbed my pajamas and ducked into the

hallway bathroom for a quick shower. The heat and steam did little to relax me or help me clear my mind.

I knew what I needed to do. What I should have done an hour ago. I shouldn't have hesitated and instead, the fear I worked so hard to move past for so long made everything topsy-turvy. That wasn't what I wanted at all.

Returning to my room, my wet hair was wrapped in a towel, and I'd barely taken the time to dry off before throwing on my tank top and short shorts that were now sticking to my back and thighs.

I could fix this. If only he'd let me explain.

I'm sorry about tonight. I texted to Connor before I could back down. **I like you too. I don't need two weeks.**

Then I fell asleep with my phone in my hand, waiting for a text that never came.

EIGHTEEN

Connor

BRENNA KEMPER MADE me as dizzy as an upside-down roller coaster. I spent my night replaying how everything went to shit, and so fucking mad at myself for throwing myself out there to look like a fool, only to realize that I'd pushed her too hard too fast.

Stepping back was best for both of us. Two weeks without her would have me forgetting all about her. Maybe then I'd be able to get into the mindset of continuing a physical relationship with her without my stupid heart getting involved, or we'd call it quits completely.

Regardless, I cared about Brenna enough, wanted to keep getting to know her enough, that I was willing to put the ball in her court.

When her text came in, I had no idea how to respond.

The strange smile I wore so frequently around her, more so than with anyone else, appeared and like an idiot, I had instantly opened up her text to reply **Get your ass back over here then.**

And paused.

She could change her mind in the morning after a night of sleep. So I'd wait. I'd give her the space she needed, and maybe more so, the space I needed to get my head together.

I barely knew this girl, and she, from the first moment I saw her, was the exact opposite of everything I ever wanted. Perhaps that was her draw, maybe that was *why* I liked her so much. It was because she was different.

She was someone who didn't give a shit about the game I played, the team I was on. She was a woman who grew up with money and most likely had her own trust fund to take care of herself for the rest of her life. She didn't need my money. She certainly didn't want notoriety from being with me.

What she wanted...*who she* wanted...was me, just as I came.

Talk about fucking mind-boggling. Until Brenna, and the few wives of teammates who were similar, every other woman I'd ever met had their own agenda.

Brenna was Brenna. And I wanted to know absolutely everything about her.

Still, I'd chucked my cell phone to the couch last night and shoved off to bed, leaving the phone in the living room so I wouldn't be tempted to text her back and send everything spiraling into another shitstorm.

I waited through the day, busted my ass in morning workouts and lost my freaking mind once I arrived at the training center. I fought against the urge to go track her down in the marketing department, take her into the break room, press her to the wall and resume what we'd started the very first night we met.

There'd be time for that.

Finally fucking Brenna wasn't my motivation. I had something more important I wanted from her than her virginity...I wanted *her*.

Her trust. Her heart. Her smiles and her kindness. I wanted to know what she wanted out of life and I wanted family dinners with her monstrous family.

It killed me to wait, to give her the day. The last thing I wanted to do was hurt her, ignore her text that came so late last night, but when we talked, I wanted us to have time to do it with clear minds.

So I plunked my ass in the seat in our team conference room, focused on the films we watched weekly after our practices. I joked around with Beaux and Kolby and Gage and the rest of the guys at lunch at Ride 'Em Rough Bar. And when I knew she'd finally be home after work, I took another shower, dressed in jeans and a simple white, short-sleeve polo shirt, and drove my ass across town to her apartment.

Nerves that assaulted me before every game hit me hard and fast. It felt like that moment before I lined up on the line for the first time, fingers tensed. Blood rushing through my veins. The thrill of the fight and the fear of failure warring and simmering in my veins. It was all there as I walked up the three floors to Brenna's apartment, her building so old and small there wasn't an elevator.

Then, I pushed all that down like I did right before the first snap. I fisted my hands, stretched out my fingers, exhaled one deep calming breath and focused.

Then I knocked on the door. Behind it was loud pop music so when the door didn't open, I knocked again, punching the door with my fist so it could be heard over the music blaring from the apartment.

It swung open and *what the holy fuck.*

A woman stood on the other side, hair wrapped up in a

towel and lime green goo all over her face. The pale blue eyes the only thing I could see was my only clue it wasn't Brenna, but her roommate.

"The hell?" I sputtered out. What in the hell was she doing?

"Wow." The girl grinned and bounced on her feet. "You are huge. And sexier up close." She cocked her head to the side. "And you're here to see Brenna? After she came home last night so upset, I'm not sure I want to allow that."

"You must be Gina."

"Her best friend. Her roommate. And her protector."

Seemed like Brenna had a lot of those. A tiny blob of green goo dropped from Gina's chin. "Let me guess, you turn into The Hulk when angry?"

"What?" She swiped a finger to her jaw and laughed. "Oh yeah, this probably looks weird."

"So you're going to be polite and let me in, get Brenna, and then go wash that off?"

"It's not time for another ten minutes." She didn't move from the door. Didn't open it farther. I could totally take the girl who barely came to my shoulder but that'd most likely not be the best first impression.

"And Brenna?"

Her blue eyes narrowed into slits. And good Lord. This was the weirdest conversation I'd ever had with a woman dripping in green slime. "Are you here to hurt her?"

"No."

"A man of few words," she said, grinning again. Around her lips, the goo was starting to dry, cracking as she smiled.

"Honest ones, too. Is she here?"

I already knew she was. Her car was parked on the street.

"Yup."

When she didn't move again, I grabbed my phone from my

back pocket. I'd text Brenna to get her ass to the door if I had to but I wasn't leaving and Gina's antics were frustrating as hell. Protective or not, I was over the interrogation from her slimy green fun-sized friend.

Right as I unlocked my phone, the miniature Hulk shouted, "Brenna! Someone's at the door for you!"

"Well, let them in!" Her voice rang from down the hall, barely audible over the music and then that went silent. "Who is it?"

"Oh," Gina sang, still grinning at me. She was bordering on creepy but so fucking harmless in towels and goo I laughed. "I think you'll like this surprise."

"Well, open the door." She was closer now and with the music off she wasn't shouting.

"As you wish," Gina said and looked over her shoulder. "I believe this stud muffin belongs to you?"

She shoved the door open and it bounced against the wall, slamming back. I slapped my hand out to keep it from closing and caught Brenna's jaw pop in surprise.

"Hey," I said, stepping into the apartment.

Gina slid into another room, kitchen based on the counters behind her, crossed her arms and kept grinning. I ignored her and faced Brenna. "Hey," I said again.

A public speaker I was definitely not.

Brenna was equally lost for words. "You're here."

"Thought I should respond to your text in person."

"Oh." She shuffled on her feet, played with her hair. I had one response in mind that would set her at ease. Ignoring the gooey friend to my left, I prowled toward Brenna, closing the distance in four long strides and then my hands were at her cheeks. I bent down and whispered, "I really liked getting that text last night. Did anything change for you today?"

Two small, warm palms of her hands pressed to my wrists. "No."

"Good." I kissed her, pressed my lips to hers and in the background, Gina sighed. I didn't give a shit.

If Brenna liked me too, I was going to kiss her whenever the fuck I felt like it, regardless of who watched.

She melted into the kiss but knowing there was a green monster watching, I kept our mouths closed and inhaled the sweet scent of her perfume, memorized the feel of her soft lips, and relished in the way she held onto my wrists, securing me to her. Her lips tasted fruity, like she'd just applied cherry or strawberry flavored lip gloss.

"We should probably talk," Brenna whispered against my lips.

"We'll get to that." I kissed her more, until my desire for her threatened to throw away my self-control.

Also, Gina cleared her throat, loudly and obnoxiously.

I pulled back from Brenna and smirked at Gina. "You might want to go to the doctor for that. Sounds deadly."

Brenna laughed quietly, her soft breath peppered my cheek.

Gina scowled and pointed a finger toward the hallway. "You're blocking my way to the restroom so I can finish getting beautified."

"Our bad." I stepped toward their living room, still holding Brenna, her matching me step for step until we'd clear the hallway.

"And give me a few minutes," Gina called out, already whipping the towel off her head. As long as she kept the one wrapped around her body on we were good. "I need to wash my face and get dressed and I'll get out of here for a while. I've got plans."

"With Brandon?" Brenna asked.

"None of your business!" she called back and then a door slammed.

"Brandon?"

"Her new boyfriend," Brenna said, curling her fingers around my wrists and tugging them from her cheeks. "But she doesn't want to admit it yet."

Oh, the irony. "Like someone else I know. Just how similar are you two?"

"I don't splatter my face with homemade face masks if that's what you're asking."

"It wouldn't stop me from kissing you. Or thinking you're beautiful." I slid my lips against hers again and this time, parted them with my tongue, tasting the sweetness of her. She matched me stroke for stroke, sigh for sigh until her body was plastered to mine and my hand was tangled in her hair, angling her head so I could take her mouth deeper.

I pulled back, breathless with my hard dick demanding release from the confines of my jeans. "About that talking."

NINETEEN

Brenna

I'D SPENT all day waiting for a text to appear from Connor that I'd been a mess at work. I screwed up three orders Shelly gave me for promotional materials we were ordering for the stadium. Life-size cutouts of Oliver Powell, Beaux Hale, wide receiver Gage Bryant, and one of Connor that almost gave me heart palpitations when I imagined the real version of him pressed into his tight football pants.

Man, bring on football season.

Yet as the day went on and I didn't hear from Connor, my mood soured further. He'd really meant it when he said a two-week break to step back and think about things and what we wanted. The problem was I didn't need it, but it was my hesitation that caused it in the first place. Around lunchtime, I vowed to myself that if I was given a shot again with him, I wouldn't hesitate. I'd throw it all out there on the table, cards face up, show him all the ugliness in my past and let the chips fall where they may.

I hadn't expected him to show up at my apartment unannounced, fling sass right back at Gina with missing a beat, and kiss me until I was senseless, swaying on my feet, barely able to keep my wits about me. Every cell in my body felt alive for the first time in my life, stronger than any sensation I'd ever felt, making me dizzy on my feet.

Stumbling to the couch, I collapsed into it and settled.

"You should sit for this," I said, and this time I watched as he hesitated. It was such an uncommon reaction from him. I was used to Connor being so sure of himself, directing every conversation we'd had from the beginning, pushing me to open up, to experience all the things I'd always desired and never had the guts to reach for, but I learned something valuable in the day I spent waiting for him to respond.

If I wanted a relationship to work with anyone, I had to give them all the parts of me, especially the ugliest and most traumatic pieces of me if there was any chance of them knowing me, why I reacted the way I did, why I fought against stability as much as wrapped myself in it.

"That bad, huh?" he joked, but there wasn't humor in his words.

I patted the couch next to me, curling my knee under my lap and facing him as he sat. "Worse than you can imagine."

He shook his head, drew his hand through his hair before letting his hand fall to his lap. "Brenna, you don't have to. I can wait."

"I think it's safe to say you know me a lot better, and in more intimate ways than anyone else in my life." I tried to smile. He did too. His looked as equally forced as one so I reached out, took his hand, and squeezed it, holding his hand against my lap while I inhaled a deep, preparatory breath.

"I was ten the day I was stolen from the bus stop."

He sucked in a breath, hand squeezed mine reflexively and jaw dropped. A trifecta of shocked reactions. "What? Brenna, stop."

"I can't. Please, let me get this out." Tears were already blurring my vision and I blinked rapidly trying to wash them away. Then his thumb was there, at my eyes, swiping beneath my eyelids.

"I've heard enough."

"I wasn't hurt." I sniffed. "Not sexually. But please? Let me talk about this? Besides my family, no one knows but Gina and my therapist and I think, if I want to be healthy in any way, I have to find a way to talk about this."

Was it selfish or wrong of me to use him as my sounding board?

He leaned forward and that hand at my eyes was now cupping my jaw, thumb running along my cheek, soothing me. I closed my eyes and inhaled the scent of him, all man, all strength and confidence somehow mixed with the soft scent of cedar or pine. "I told you last night, I think I'd be willing to give you anything you need. But I also feel like I've already pushed you too fast, I won't do it. Not with this."

"I want you to know."

He closed his eyes and moved closer, kissing me gently before pulling back. Then he adjusted us, settled me closer to him with his arm around my shoulders, holding me tight to his body. The warmth of him, cocooned in his embrace gave me all the strength I needed. Plus his lip at my temple, both of my hands holding one of his in my lap. It was easier to focus on the strength in his hand, the veins on the back, the small amounts of hair at his knuckles than it was to look at him and see his expression.

"He came out of nowhere," I continued. If I closed my eyes,

the memories would wash back too quickly and I didn't want to be living in them when I spoke. It helped if I could disassociate myself from them, even minutely. At least that was the large word Dr. Spanyard told me when I was little, too young to get it at the time. "He pulled up in a van, so typical, right? It'd been raining, so at first I thought it was a dad staying close until the bus came. He idled there and I ignored him, but he kept watching me and I started to feel that creepy crawling feeling, you know? The kind where it feels like pinpricks or ants?"

"I know, angel," Connor murmured. His grip on my shoulder tightened.

"I didn't know what to do. Sometimes there were other kids there, sometimes I was alone, but no one was at my house and I didn't want to miss the bus. My parents had already left for work and it wasn't like I had my own cell phone back then. So I stayed and he came so fast. Like he was waiting for me to get as scared as possible, or find the nerve to go home, but to do that I had to walk past his van anyway and when I did, he jumped out of the van, threw me in the back and I was shackled to a chain before I could think about kicking or screaming or doing anything to get away from him."

"It wasn't your fault."

"I know. But there were still a dozen decisions I could have made differently. Could I have gone to a house? The Johnson's mom stayed home. She would have been there. Or taken me to school. I could have gone home and called my mom. They would have understood. I could have bit his hand, scratched him."

"You were ten, Brenna."

"Yeah, but it wasn't like I hadn't had the stranger talk a million times with my parents, either." I shook off the lingering oily sensation that always covered me when I replayed this. The millions of decisions I could have made. The safer option.

The smarter one. Was it any wonder I was such a wreck and needed time to come to conclusions now?

"I wasn't the only girl he had." I sniffed and then screw it. My tears would fall whether or not I tried to stave them off. "He'd smack us around when we cried. Fed us once a day. We were all hooked to chains in a basement."

"Fucking Christ," Connor growled. His grip on my hands tightened so severely I flinched. "I don't know if I can hear anymore without wanting to find him and kill him myself."

It wasn't funny, but I chuckled. "You can't. He was killed three months into his prison sentence. Apparently felons and thieves and murderers draw the line at sex traffickers."

"Sex..."

"Yeah. Eventually he took us to a shipping container. I didn't know where we were going to be sent, but it was on the coast. Dark. Cold. We'd barely eaten, hadn't been cleaned in a week since I'd been there although some of the other girls were there much longer. We sat there, sniffing away our cries, waiting for death."

I crumbled then. Shoved my head into the crook of his neck and let him hold me while I cried, horrific, huge tears. I couldn't forget those memories no matter how often I tried. The cold salty air dried our skin even in the dark and our oatmeal turned to an occasional cheese stick, a bottle of water. The bare minimum to keep us alive and even then someone would be close by. When we screamed, we were beaten and kicked and it didn't matter who had started it. Once the men entered the container, we were all punished until one of them, a girl younger than me with two matted braids, stopped scream-ing, passed out, and never woke up again.

I took his embrace and his comfort and his quietly muttered curse words and wrapped in his strength and arms and comfort, I swore I could have conquered *anything* in my life.

It was when I was sniffing that another hand curled around the back of my neck. Much smaller, not nearly as warm, and then Gina's lips were at the top of my head. "You okay, honey?"

"Yeah."

"Be good to her," she whispered and I knew she was warning Connor.

He didn't flinch or growl as he replied, "Of course. You headed out?"

"I can stay," Gina said and this was why she was my best friend.

"No. Go. Don't stay home for me. Not anymore." I pushed off Connor and he untangled his arms from me enough so I could meet Gina's concerned expression.

"It's just a date."

"You've done it enough for me. No more. That's what we promised, right?"

I wasn't stupid. Gina found one-night stands and quick flings and would some nights not come home in college but they were rare. She didn't date more seriously or spend more time away because she wanted to be there for me, crawl into my tiny twin bunk bed when I woke up screaming, dripping in sweat and tears.

She was the best human on the planet.

"Okay. Love you, shortcake."

"Go away, gingersnap."

She laughed softly and gave me another quick squeeze before flashing a wink to Connor. "Later, hot stuff."

"See ya, Hulk."

She snorted and moments later the door was closed and I was through the worst of my tears and memories.

"She wasn't kidding when she said she was protective of you."

"Gina's the best." I exhaled harshly, shook off the tightness in my limbs and tried to regain some control. It was that strange feeling of a cathartic cry where I was exhausted and equally energized. "I have nightmares sometimes. Not often, but she was my roommate starting our junior year of high school. Then she insisted on attending Vanderwilde with me. She's spent a lot of time helping me."

I curled up off the couch with the excuse of space and needing water. Connor didn't take his eyes off me as I went to the kitchen, grabbed two bottles of water from the fridge and chugged one of them completely before sitting next to him on the couch.

"I was found, you know."

"I figured that."

"It was a huge production. FBI. SWAT. Police. I remember the helicopter hovering overhead, the whir of the motor blades. I have flashbacks from them sometimes. Or flashlights. Or that loud twang of something smashing metal."

"I'm not going anywhere, Brenna, if you're trying to scare me away."

"It's just...I'm a mess, you know, and I spent so many years being safe at all-girls schools that this whole *doing my own thing* is new and scary. And while I want it, I want all the normal things every girl in her twenties wants, you have to realize how utterly new at *living* I am."

He slid his hand through my hair, down the length of it, slowly brushing my hair and calming my runaway thoughts at the same time.

"Look at me," he finally said and his thumb was at my chin, tilting my head back until our gazes met. "I like you, Brenna. I liked everything I knew about you before today, even when you were backing away. I'm *here*. And I'm not going anywhere. Thank you...thank you for trusting me with this. I'm so, so sorry this happened to you, and so much more damn thankful you were found."

"Me too."

"Can I kiss you now?"

"I'd be upset if you didn't. Please...don't let your knowledge of this make you back off or change anything. You might think you're pushing me too fast, but I want it. I like it when you take control and get bossy. It gets me out of my head so I can enjoy everything we do and not overthink it."

"Then promise me one thing."

"Anything."

His eyes gleamed. "That's a large order."

I meant it with every fiber of my being. "What's the promise, Connor?"

"Be honest with me. Always. It's okay to second-guess yourself, it's okay to take time, it's okay to rush forward without thought of consequences. It's okay to live your life how you want on your terms. God knows I've been doing it for years, but if there's ever a moment you hesitate, need me to slow down... you need a break, you have to tell me."

It was possibly the easiest promise I could make. "I can do that."

"Good." That glimmer in his dark eyes burned brighter and he brushed his mouth over mine. "Now kiss me."

TWENTY

Connor

I MEANT to keep the kiss soft and warm. She'd thrown a lot on me and knowing the horror of what she'd lived through made me want to wrap her in my arms and ensure no one ever hurt her again. The raging need to protect someone was foreign, but with Brenna's lips on mine, her hands pressed to my chest and her sweet scent enveloping me, it felt like the most natural thing in the world.

She shuffled, scrambled to my lap and straddled me until the warmth of her center was pressed against me. A groan rumbled through me as I fought against getting hard.

Taking her after she shared so much and became so emotional wasn't on my radar but as she continued grinding against me, it was becoming harder to keep the pace.

"Brenna. Hey." I slid my hand to her cheek, through her hair and slowed the kiss. "Is this what you want?"

Hazy, soft green eyes landed on me and a pink bloomed on

her cheeks right before she shoved her face into my shoulder. "No." She laughed softly, the vibration slid across my skin. "I'm sorry."

"It's okay. You don't need to apologize for anything." I slid my hand through her hair, down her back.

She laughed harder and clung to me. "It's not because of *that*." Her voice lowered to a whisper. "I started my period this morning and forgot."

Oh. *Ohhh.* I hugged her tight. Spending so many years not getting close to women unless I was sleeping with them meant I didn't exactly have a lot of experience with this part of dating.

In theory, Brenna having her period didn't change how much I wanted her, but that'd be a first for both of us. And maybe after a night of emotional downloading wasn't the time to experiment.

"How about we order pizza, get some drinks and watch some television then?"

She relaxed against me and I could almost feel her relief at my reaction. Fuck it though. It was as natural as a man sporting a woody at the absolute wrong time. Nature happened. She didn't have anything to be embarrassed about.

"Or...we could go out to eat somewhere? There's a super cute Italian place around the corner."

Her eyes were so wide and hesitant I couldn't resist leaning in and kissing her nose.

"You ready for that?"

"Go big or go home, baby."

"Your wish, my command, m'lady." I shifted her off me and adjusted myself. A sexy woman on my lap for so long would make me hard regardless of the circumstance.

"Please." She slapped me playfully on the shoulder. "You could never pass for a gentlemanly old-time Lord of the Manor, let's not even pretend."

"Sure I could."

She moved to step around my legs and to prove it, I smacked her ass.

"Hey!" Her hands flew to her backside, her bottom lip between her teeth. As she rubbed her ass, I took in every inch of her perfect, plump and firm backside.

"Get moving, shortcake." I stood from the couch, tugged down my polo shirt, and made sure my wallet and phone were still in my back pocket.

"Don't you dare." She shoved a finger at me and glared. "That's Gina's."

"It fits."

"I like angel better." Damn straight. *Angel was definitely mine.*

"Yeah." I threw a hand around her back and yanked her to me, slamming her mouth to mine as she gasped. "I do too."

The Italian restaurant was close enough to walk to, so I let her guide me down the street.

We settled into chairs at a table for four, red and white checkered tablecloth covering it along with a small vase of three fake white flowers in the middle. It was cheesy but authentic and as we ordered, lasagna for me and a fettuccine alfredo for her, our conversation flowed more easily than I could have ever thought possible. We laughed as she told me stories of her childhood, growing up so much younger than her brothers. Her brother's wife who'd been around since she was five. The antics she and her sister used to get into, including hiding frogs beneath her brother Tanner's pillow when she knew he was sneaking girls into his bedroom at night when their parents were out late.

Despite the trauma she experienced, one she didn't mention at all after she unloaded it all onto me, she'd had the kind of childhood I could have only imagined and the only time conversation slowed was when she talked about going to boarding school. Her parents wanted her somewhere safe and away from the attention her abduction had received. They wanted her to heal and move on without the looks and stares she got when she tried to eventually return to her normal school.

They wanted her to have a fresh start and she was all for it. Through it all, my admiration for her grew until I was sitting there, tearing off chunks of garlic bread and stuffing my face because *damn, she was right. This place was incredible.*

But I totally understood her parents' desperate need to protect her. Every time she alluded to her kidnapping, a fierce white hot shot of fury rolled through me, reminding me I'd do the exact same.

Things being easy with Brenna shouldn't have continued to surprise me. She was different than anyone else I'd ever met, but she also made me feel different. And maybe that was it.

When you met the person you were falling for, everything about it was easy...natural. And strangely enough, I wasn't bothered by it at all.

I'd fallen for this woman without thought or issue, and now, I only had to hold out a few more days to show her exactly how much she meant to me.

I WOKE up in the morning before my alarm sounded, the sky still dark, but I was unable to sleep. I blamed part of that on my erection pressed against the soft cotton fabric of Brenna's pajama shorts. Shorts she'd nervously tugged on after she asked me to spend the night and *sleep, just sleep* beside her.

I wrapped her more firmly against me, smiling and peppering her shoulder with kisses while I remembered the way she'd stood in front of me, hesitant, her nerves more obvious over the simple act of sleeping than anything else we'd done. But I couldn't deny I was also feeling out of my element.

I might have been the teacher for sex, but somewhere along the way, the student became the teacher. She was teaching me how to open up to people. She reminded me I actually had a heart and it didn't just beat, I was starting to think it solely beat for her. It came alive when Brenna was around and I had a moment of feeling like a prick for all the times I gave my friends shit when they fell for their women.

Because somehow, when you met a woman who meant more to you than a simple orgasm or three, falling for them happened before you realized you'd done it.

Brenna's skin was warm as I kissed her. I wasn't trying to wake her, but God I wanted to take a few minutes to be with her, hold her, memorize the taste and feel of her soft feminine flesh before I had to shove out of her bed and get ready for my early morning workout. Gage Bryant would be calling me soon, asking me to grab him a cup of coffee on my way like he did every morning we met at the gym before seven. The man wasn't lazy, just declared the coffee shop by my condo better than the one near his house where he lived with his wife Elizabeth. And my local Ma and Pop coffee shop by morning and wine night slash open mic by night was a half-hour out of his way.

No problem for me but why the man always called instead of texting was beyond me.

I shoved thoughts of Gage and my plans for the rest of my day out of my mind as Brenna stirred, pressing her backside more firmly against my erection and let out a quiet, sleepy sigh.

I slid my hand down her stomach to beneath her thin white tank top, a tank top I remembered vividly as she pulled it on and then removed her bra. It was so thin her pebbled nipples were obvious and I wanted nothing more now than to brush my fingers over them, shove up her tank top, wake her with my mouth on her breasts, biting her pale nipples, sliding my fingers through her slit.

If only she was comfortable with it.

"Hey angel," I whispered in her ear. My memories of all the things I wanted to do to her were running away from me and now that I had a plan of action in mind, I had the urge to execute it perfectly. "Wake up."

I did what I first imagined and pushed the blankets down to her hips, exposing her stomach, my tanned and large hand against her trim, pale stomach and lifted her tank top as she arched closer to my touch.

Her eyes fluttered open, slowly awakening and when she caught me staring at her, she cupped my cheek and smiled. "Hey, good morning. What are you—" I brushed my thumb over her nipple. "Oohh...that's nice."

"It is nice, isn't it? I love your nipples, the way you gasp when I play with them. You like it a little bit rough don't you, angel?"

"Yeah," she gasped as I rolled one of them between my thumb and forefinger before shoving her shirt up so I could see her tits as I played with them.

My other hand played with the hem of her pajama shorts.

I propped myself up on my elbow and dropped my head, sliding my mouth to hers as she whimpered and moaned every time I tugged on her nipples, pinched them. Yeah, she might have been an angel but she was a wildcat in bed. Greedy for everything I gave her, always demanding more.

Brenna was hot as fuck and I couldn't get enough of her.

I took her mouth forcefully, showing her my need for her, how much her sounds and her body turned me on and slipped my hand beneath her shorts, giving her a moment to know my intention. Her body rocked into my hand but her hand curled around my wrist.

"Connor—"

"I just want to play with your clit. Make you come. That okay?"

"My tampon..." She looked so damn adorable. Blushing at the mention of it but I didn't give a shit.

"I don't mind if you don't." Slowly she peeled her hand off mine and buried her face into my chest.

"Please," she finally said, whimpering against my mouth. I was hard as a rock as I slid my fingers against her, pressing two fingers against her slit, finding that sweet spot and holy shit she bucked against me like she *needed* me.

Goddamn, she was perfect for me, so easily turned on, so responsive. It made me want to take her away for a weekend where we wouldn't have to do anything except fuck and rut and learn each other bodies as well, if not more than we knew our own.

My fingers went to work on her clit, rubbing circles, dipping down between her folds and gathering moisture before returning to her hardened bundle of nerves and I shifted on the bed so I could take her tit into my mouth.

She arched into me, both hands came to the back of my head as I sucked and played with her and by the whimpers she made, the tremble of her thighs against me, she was already close to coming.

"I want to feel you," she gasped, reaching for me.

I moved out of her way. "This morning is for you."

She humphed and then groaned as I pressed against her clit. She was going to go off quickly and I wasn't far behind.

"Shit. Connor," she gasped. "Yes. So close."

She was so damn wet my fingers easily slid against her. I pulled back from her breasts and watched as she bit down on her bottom lip, tried to keep quiet but her climax came too fast, too powerfully and she clung to my forearm, short pink nails dug into my skin in a way I knew they'd leave marks and I *fucking loved* that she wasn't afraid to be rough with me.

She came, her body quaking from the force of it and right as she opened her mouth, I slammed my mouth to hers and swallowed her cries as her orgasm rolled through. She twisted and turned to get away from me, but I kept at her, fingers rolling and pressing, pinching and pulling at her clit until her back bowed off the bed and she came again, hands clinging to me, mouth fused to mine.

"Wow," she breathed, dropping back to her pillow. Before I could move away from her, her hand was at my boxers, sliding beneath them and she had her hand wrapped around my cock, tugging firmly, the perfect amount of pressure I'd told her I liked.

Sweet hell and damnation she learned fast.

"I want you to finish."

"This was for you," I said, my jaw clenched from how good she felt.

Her eyes gleamed with something wicked and she nibbled on her lip before popping it free. "Then I want to watch you do it. On me."

The hell? "You want me to come on you, angel?" Mark her as mine? Fuck yeah. But the fact she asked...wanted it...*thought of it.* I couldn't help but tease her. "Is this one of your fantasies?"

She'd once told me they were none of my business. *Please let that have changed.*

She nodded and glanced down at her hand, drawling out a soft and quiet, "Yeah. I've always wondered..."

"Say no more." I wouldn't deny her anything.

I shoved off the rest of the covers and then pushed her shirt up, exposing both of her tits. She took over, whipping the shirt off of her and all that strawberry blonde hair of hers fluttered into the air before it settled around her shoulders. I climbed over her and smacked her hand off my pulsing dick. My balls were already drawn tight from her hand job.

This wouldn't take long and I wasn't embarrassed about that at all. Brenna beneath me, *wanting* this? So damn hot.

I kept my weight off of her, glued my gaze to hers as I tugged and pulled on my dick, stroked it like I meant it. Reaching behind me with one hand, I slid my fingers through her wetness and gathered it, used it as lubricant to make the friction even better and holy damn shit, her watching me, hands on my thighs, not doing anything except *looking* was such a damn turn on my blood boiled, pleasure raced down my spine, straight to my balls.

I cupped them, played with them, showed her exactly how I wanted it and her tongue darted out at the corner of her mouth like she couldn't wait to taste me.

"Shit, Brenna. You keep staring at my dick and I'm going to come in no time." I grunted the words, unashamed.

Her gaze flickered to mine for a brief second. "That's the point. I want to watch."

Jesus. So damn sweet, but she was showing me a naughty side of her we would definitely explore later.

My orgasm came fast and hard and it took all my strength to stay upright as I groaned, chanted *yeah, so close, fuck you're beautiful,* over and over until I couldn't hold back. I came on her stomach, her tits, unable to aim it but holy shit I came so hard and so much it was like I hadn't had sex in weeks. I watched it pool on her stomach, fascinated by the planes of her soft skin.

"Holy shit," I gasped, staring down at her. She hadn't taken her gaze off my dick for a second and I wasn't sure what was hotter...

Brenna staring at my cock like she needed it for survival, or when she ran a finger over her tit, gathered my cum and licked it off her finger.

All I knew was I was done for. Absolutely done for with this woman.

TWENTY-ONE

Brenna

THE WEEK FLEW by and by the time Friday afternoon rolled around again, I was once again distracted at work, but this time for an entirely different reason.

I was going on my first official date with Connor that night. In truth, it was my first official date *ever* and while I thought he knew that, I certainly wasn't going to be the person to spill that lovely cup of beans.

The week had flown by and every day I talked to Connor or saw him, once last night at his house for pizza and Netflix binge-watching of a courtroom drama, I shed my nerves like snakes lost their skin. It fell off me with every one of his touches, every time I made him laugh. He was as new to a relationship as I was but we were actually doing this.

The day after Connor left earlier in the week, Gina had caught me coming out of my bedroom with a wonky grin on her face as she sipped her coffee.

"Well, well, well," she'd sang. "You certainly appear to be in a better mood this morning. It doesn't have anything to do with the man who spent the night in your bed, does it?"

It'd been years since I turned hot with embarrassment around Gina but realizing she'd come home at some point, that she'd maybe *heard* us that morning, my cheeks burned hotter than a brush fire. "We're good," I'd muttered and slid around her to fill my own coffee. "How was Brandon?"

"He's good."

"That's all I'm going to get out of you?" God knew she'd begged enough to get more out of me.

"I like him. And yes, we're dating, but I don't want to lose focus on school is all. Law school's been the only dream I've had since I was a kid and we're so different."

"Because he's not a lawyer or doctor?" Besides Gina's father and two uncles building military aircraft, she also came from a long line of family members with multiple designations after their names. MD. Ph.D. DDS. LLM. JD. Esq. In a few short years, Gina would add a few of her own.

"No," she said, admonishment in her tone. "We're just *different*. For an artist, he's rather, I don't know...stable."

I snorted. "And stable is wrong?"

"It's different. He makes me think of settling down when all I've wanted to do is explore. When I'm with him, I have all these other common ideas."

She spit out *common* with the same disgusted look she'd had when she once caught me using a three-season's past Michael Kors bag.

"You poor thing." I wrapped my arm around her shoulder and hugged her against me. "Thinking of being a *normal* human being for once."

She reached up and patted my hand. "I'm so glad you understand."

I laughed and kissed her cheek. "We're quite a pair, huh? Is there anyone who is actually normal when it comes to relationships?"

"I don't know." She turned and stepped back, taking a sip of her coffee. "Connor seemed like he had everything under control when I left last night." She winked. "And when I heard you two this morning."

So she had heard.

And her bringing it up only made me think of it.

Not that I'd let that memory go for the rest of the week. Nope, the memory of that morning was now firmly cemented into my memory bank.

Connor jacking off onto me, painting my stomach as he came. It was one of the hottest things I'd ever witnessed. It was sexier than I'd ever imagined it could be from the scenes I'd read in my romance novels. It could have been because of the man, of how large he looked as he gripped himself, muscles bulging up his arm and bricks appearing on his stomach. Veins popping on his hands, slithering up his arm as he worked himself.

Every time I thought of it, I grew wet, and lucky me... tonight my period was gone and there was nothing holding us back from *finally* doing what I'd set out to do that very first time I saw him.

"Brenna!"

My head snapped up and back to the present at the sound of Shelly calling for me.

I pushed off the desk and hurried to her office where she was patiently sitting at her desk. She usually called me or paged me. Her shouting my name couldn't have been a great thing.

"Yes?"

"Do you have confirmation when the outdoor flags will

be in?"

"Company said ten more days. Cutting it close but we'll still be able to get them hung around the stadium for the FanFest night."

FanFest was a Friday night practice the team did for the public. It was the day after they came back from training camp and I was already feeling queasy at the thought of Connor being gone for most of the next two weeks. We were just getting started and finding our footing.

"And you've double-checked with PSE?"

Pro Sports Entertainment had several of our players signed with them. They provided jerseys and posters and helmets and miniature footballs for the players on their roster to sign. Before FanFest started, Beaux and Gage were expected to be there, signing items for the first one hundred fans who entered. Connor and Powell were scheduled to sign afterward.

I stepped into her office and took a seat at the chair across from her desk. I'd thought this was going to be quick but if Shelly was going to grill me on things she usually emailed or asked via private message, something was up and this could take a while.

"Yes. All of the jerseys are already here. And I've received shipping confirmation on the rest of the items."

"Good. Good." She crossed off items on a checklist in front of her and tapped her pen. "And the cutouts for the photos?"

I covered her paper with my hand. "What's going on? Everything will be handled."

"I'm nervous," she admitted and tossed the pen to her desk, falling back into her chair. "This is my first year being in charge of the pre-season parties and events and I want to make sure it's perfect." She'd been promoted to the manager of the marketing department last year after the season ended.

"It will be. You have an incredible staff who's been working non-stop since spring on this and you've thought of everything."

"You're right. Last minute jitters, I suppose."

It was only natural. I had my own set of nervous jitters dancing a jig in my stomach all day.

My first date.

I pressed my hands together to hide the fact they were shaking.

Whatever had shaken Shelly was put to the side and she smiled at me. "It's four o'clock. You can probably take off. Any plans for the night?"

"Oh. Well, yes, actually. I have a date."

"Oh goodness." She propped her elbow on the desk, her jaw into the palm of her hand. "A date? What are those like? It's been so long since Tim and I have had one I'm sure I've forgotten."

"I'm not really sure. It's our first."

"Oh. Even better. A new guy. You need to impress him then. Definitely go home. Get ready, and some advice?"

Anything. I'd take all of it like treasures. "What?"

"Have a glass of wine. Settle your nerves."

I nodded at her and stood. "Perhaps you should go home and follow your own advice."

"Oh, don't you worry." She laughed. "I've got my own date with wine and a bubble bath later tonight."

"Sounds incredible."

"Bet yours will be better. Have fun and be safe."

"Thanks, Shelly." She was so sweet. Sometimes so sweet I wondered if my dad increased her salary to keep an extra eye on me. "And let's hope so."

I left her office hoping I was able to help her out as much as she'd done for me. She was a patient boss, kind, and helpful along with the rest of the marketing department and like I'd hoped, I was settling into work quickly, figuring out the programs and ordering systems and her scheduling calendar with little difficulty.

Grabbing my purse, I shut down my computer and turned off my desk lamp and took off.

I had a *date* to get ready for. My first one.

With Connor Quinten with who I'd most likely be giving my virginity to by the end of the night.

I definitely needed that glass of wine Shelly suggested.

CONNOR CALLED when he was getting close to let me know he was almost to my apartment so instead of waiting upstairs for him, making him walk the three flights to my apartment to turn around and walk straight back down again, I met him outside, my jaw dropping as he pulled up to the curb in a massive matte black pick-up truck, wheels so large I hoped he had a stepladder for me to climb into it.

He'd texted earlier in the day. **I'm taking you to the country. Dress casual, angel.** The message spiked my already burgeoning curiosity about what a date with a man like this would be like, but I took it to heart, using the word *country* as a guide. I was wearing a short pair of denim cut-offs, the hem so frayed from frequent washing my butt cheeks almost peeked out from the back. The denim was soft and moldable though, making them some of my favorite shorts and on top I had on a pale blue tank top with the words "Be Bold Be Brave Be Kind" down the front, my favorite tan Birkenstock sandals on my feet. I'd debated if I was too casual but as Connor walked around the front of the truck, I was glad I did. He was dressed in similar sandals, nicely pressed navy shorts but a white T-shirt with the Rough Riders logo on the front, an unassuming Under Armour hat bent at the bill in the way men toyed with, tugged down low.

He had sunglasses on, but I still caught the way his gaze dipped low and slowly trailed up my legs and my body until he was close enough to me I felt his inspection like a caress against my skin, heating it from the inside out.

I went momentarily speechless at our size difference, the natural way I tilted my head back and he bent down to give me a kiss. I pointed at the behemoth of a truck idling at the curb.

"What is this?"

Connor placed his hand at my lower back and guided me toward the truck. "Where we're going, it's necessary."

"What like off-road driving the mountains?"

"Maybe next time, but that's not a bad idea."

I used to love going with my brothers. They'd strap me into my booster seat and take off the doors of their Wranglers. I'd scream for my life like I was on a roller coaster and then laugh until my stomach hurt. The last time I went was *before* every-thing happened but the idea of going again, with Connor?

Going mudding with my brothers used to be the highlight of my summer. I didn't doubt that going with Connor would be even better. "I'd be in. Aiden and Tanner used to take me all the time when I was younger."

"Something to consider then." He reached around me and swung open the truck door. I stared at the seat. It was easy to do considering it was at my eye-level and turned to Connor. "Uhm."

He laughed, low and beautiful. "Need some help?"

"I think I need it." Tossing my purse into the front seat, I grabbed onto the door handle as he gripped my waist, boosting me up until I was settled in the chair.

When I moved to close the door, Connor stepped in the way, his face still only inches below me. Damn, the man was so tall. Broad shoulders, sexy hair that flopped to one side with the perfect part and fade on the other. Connor Quinten was *scrumptious*. And all mine.

He tipped up his chin and I took his offer, kissing him. I meant for it to be a quick kiss but he took it deeper, sliding his tongue into my mouth and pressing our mouths together in a fast, but delicious way that left my lips tingling when he pulled back.

I pressed my fingertips there and caught his smirk as he rounded the front of his truck and once he was inside, he took that hand, tangled it with his and pressed them both to his thigh.

"So, are you not going to tell me where we're going?"

"Do you not like surprises?" Humor laced his tone.

It took me a moment to consider that. "I don't think anyone's ever surprised me before."

Outside of the typical surprises like what was wrapped beneath the ribbons and foil paper at Christmas time and my birthdays, it wasn't like I'd ever had a vast social calendar filled with copious amounts of friends and surprise birthday parties or anything of that sort.

Connor made a humming sound and squeezed my hand. "We'll see about changing that then."

He maneuvered the truck through Raleigh with ease and took us north on Highway One, earning a curious look from me before I decided to not only enjoy my time alone with Connor but maybe do a little bit of snooping.

I grabbed his phone. "Do you have a playlist we can listen to?"

"On my phone? Why not yours?"

"Because you can tell a lot about a man by the music he listens to."

"Have at it. Code is three eight three eight."

I snorted as I tapped it in. "Your jersey number?"

"It's not something I'll forget."

Laughing softly because I didn't know what to expect when it came to Connor, I pulled up his music app and went to his first playlist.

Game Mode. I pressed play and placed his phone back into the cupholder and was immediately blasted by a deep thundering bass and rap music that made me wish I was at the club.

"You listen to this to get into the mood for games?"

He shrugged. "It's a mix. Got some of that and rock and a bit of country on it, but they all get me focused."

We jammed out for the rest of the ride, talking about work, the upcoming FanFest Shelly was certainly freaking out about over the weekend when he pulled off the highway, following the signs to Raleigh Theater.

"A movie?" If curiosity killed the cat, I was on my sixth life, getting closer to dying of curiosity with every moment.

But I was in no way at all prepared for Connor to pull off into a dark two-lane road, a country road so simple there weren't painted lines down the middle. We drove in the dark for another mile before lights popped out of nowhere and suddenly we were surrounded by a parking lot of cars and an enormous screen at one end.

"A drive-in movie theater?"

Wow. I never would have considered it. My imagination ran away with me, the bed of his truck, making out like teenagers did, stealing gropes in the dark of night. Was this why he'd rented the truck?

He pulled into the line of cars, I assumed paying to get in and brought our hands to his mouth, kissing my knuckles.

"I can't believe we're at a drive-in." A giddiness inside of me leaped for joy.

"I was trying to figure out a place we could go, minimize the chance we'd be seen in public before we're ready to tell your family and it occurred to me from what you said earlier in the week that you probably haven't spent the time as a teenager making out in dark movie theaters."

He spoke about everything I'd shared with him with such ease, like he'd known about it for years and it was just a small thing. I appreciated it. "Uh. No, I can't say I did that."

"This drive-in only shows older movies, some of the most popular and it just so happens that the year you turned sixteen, *The Hunger Games* was the big blockbuster."

He'd looked into what year it was when I'd been sixteen. Wow. "You put some thought into this."

"Maybe I want to make sure you're given everything you lost or weren't ready for."

Double *wow*. I wasn't sure if it was that moment, or dozens of earlier, smaller ones he'd sprinkled around in our time together, but that was most definitely the moment it hit me.

I was falling in love with this man.

And I had not one single regret.

"This is really incredible," I said, my voice soft and awed. I leaned forward and brushed my lips over his, kissing him softly. It was a small kiss, but there was so much emotion inside of me, joy and happiness and for the first time in a long time *hope* I could be *normal* again, I wanted him to feel everything I was thinking. "Thank you so much."

TWENTY-TWO

Connor

GOD, she was gorgeous. Her tanned legs looked longer than normal in her short as hell shorts. She drove me to distraction as I helped her into the truck earlier, the curve of her ass cheeks peeking out below them. A dozen thoughts raced through my mind in that moment from wanting to squeeze her ass, slap it—playfully and maybe a bit more seriously—to biting it.

But when Brenna looked at me with stars in her eyes and pressed her lips to mine, I forgot all of it. I forgot the temptation she held inside of her along with the past she was trying to move on from. I forgot about the reasons why we *shouldn't* be together and resigned myself which didn't feel like resignation at all.

It felt a lot like love and protecting and caring for her and wanting to give her the best of everything.

Hopefully, I didn't fuck it up.

We pulled into our spot near the end of a long row of cars

and trucks already parked. We could have taken my Mercedes, but I rented the truck to give her the full drive-in experience. I hopped out and helped her down and flipped open the tailgate.

Her mouth fell open right before she threw her head back and laughed. It was the exact reaction I'd hoped for.

"You are too much," she teased, throwing her arms around my shoulders. "A bed in the back of a truck. You've thought of *everything*."

It was an air mattress and a fuck ton of pillows, not a bed, but yeah...I wanted us comfortable. I had more planned than simple movie watching.

"Need some help getting up there?" I was already moving my hands to her waist and she laughed again.

"I think you went to the car rental place and said, 'Give me the biggest and most manly truck on the lot.'"

"Some of the dealerships around town let us use cars for promo. Apparently a football player seen cruising around town in certain vehicles increases sales."

"Really?"

"Yup." It was a perk I didn't use often, but her enjoyment over everything made it worth it. "Now up." She braced her hands on the tailgate and with little effort I had her in the back of the truck, crawling onto the air mattress.

She patted the blankets to her. "Are you joining me?"

I held up a finger. "One more thing."

She eyed me curiously, cutely and sweetly, and all the other words I thought I'd never use to describe a woman I was with. I hurried to the back of the crew cab and grabbed the rest of our treats.

"What is this?" She was on her hands and knees, crawling toward me.

That view. Hot damn. The things I wanted to do to her when she was like that.

I cleared my throat and pushed the cooler and Bluetooth speaker I'd packed before jumping up with her.

"What did you do?" she asked, rubbing her hands together.

I shuffled back on the mattress and rearranged the pillows against the cab of the truck, giving us a comfortable place to sit. "Come and see, but be careful. We're not supposed to have food here."

A quick glance around to other cars showed there were several other people who weren't following that rule either, so I didn't feel too bad.

She dug into the cooler, pulling out small bottles of wine I'd thrown in along with a stemless wineglass, she handed me a beer. Since I was driving, I only brought a couple.

I pulled the radio app on my phone, set it to the right station and turned on the Bluetooth speaker. There were advertisements and trailers for upcoming movies and old favorites like *Back to The Future*, *Twister*, and *The Wizard of Oz* on the screen as we settled, snacked on crackers and cheese and summer sausage. We dug into containers of salads and other foods I brought, talking, laughing, sharing a few drinks.

"So how many times have you seen *The Hunger Games*?" I asked, twisting open a bottle of water.

"Only about fifty. But I'm excited to see it here. This is really neat."

Closer to the screen, people had set up lawn chairs and blankets. Kids tossed around footballs. A few threw frisbees. Parents wrangled toddlers on chubby legs as they roamed the area.

It was so damn *normal* it made me wonder what life would be like with someone like Brenna. Something normal and sweet and filled with a goodness I'd never thought myself capable of. Brenna made me want to be the guy to give her all the good things she should have always had.

If that wasn't love, I certainly didn't have a damn clue what it was.

We'd arrived early, giving us plenty of time to hang out and relax before it was dark enough for the movie to start and once the sun was close to setting, we set off to the concession stand and stocked up on popcorn, some cotton candy Brenna had eyed on the way and then I grabbed a couple cheeseburgers even though we still had food and drinks in the cooler.

Once we returned to the truck, Brenna pulled off a piece of cotton candy from the plume of sugar in her hand and popped it into her mouth.

She was irresistible. So damn sweet. She'd taste like sugar and candy. I crawled to her and opened my mouth, silently asking for some of her snack.

"No." She shook her head and dropped the bag of cotton candy to her side, sliding her hand to my neck. Brenna's fingertips putting pressure on my flesh was the only ignition switch I needed.

"No, what?" I asked, crawling over her, moving slowly.

"You don't want a taste of my candy."

"I don't?"

"No," she whispered and her voice was so husky, so much more confident and sexy than she'd been a few weeks ago. "I think you want a taste of me instead."

"Damn straight," I growled, and dove for her.

I covered her body with mine, slammed my mouth to hers, and spent the next two hours giving her an experience at the movie theater she'd never forget...even if we barely watched the actual movie.

"DO YOU WANT ANYTHING TO DRINK?" I tossed my keys to the kitchen counter and moved toward the fridge.

I'd gotten Brenna off with my hands during the movie, encouraging her to bite down onto my shoulder when she came to keep quiet. I'd have marks there for days. The girl could *bite* and it was hot as hell.

It'd been dangerous and stupid, making out with her like that in public but Brenna was so greedy, so responsive, it was unavoidable.

When it came to her, my self-control flew out the window.

But before the night continued in the way I wanted to take it, I needed a minute to calm down.

My dick had been hard for hours. Between her sitting next to me in the truck, her hands on me during the movie, I hadn't allowed her to do anything more than rub her palm over my hard dick through my shorts.

The last thing either of us needed was for me to get caught with my pants down in public.

But fuck, I was hard as stone. So damn needy my nerves felt alive for the first time, hotter than the excitement I got from playing football. I was feeling more demanding and less in control than I could remember.

This wasn't what it was like with other women. Making out with Brenna was *everything*.

But I really, really fucking wanted more and I hoped she was ready for it.

I wasn't planning on taking her virginity tonight, I was planning on giving her something I'd never given another.

I wanted to make love to Brenna. Not fuck. I wanted it slow, drawn-out all night long. I wanted to taste and touch every speck of her skin, bring her to orgasm over and over and over again. Slide into her until my dick was unable to get hard again.

I wanted to spend so many hours inside of her she was unable to get out of bed in the morning and then I wanted to do it all over again.

"I'm good," Brenna said and it took me a minute to remember what I asked her.

"Right." I chugged my water and nerves hit. So fucking strange.

I'd been with countless women. The steps with them were easy. Pick them up. Bring them home. Make them come. Send them on their way. The only switch up to that routine was when I went to her place instead, or sometimes the nearest hotel room.

Brenna required more time, more thought, and I didn't want to push anything. It was her call how far we went. Always.

What did I do now? Watch television? Take her straight to my bed? Take her on the kitchen counter?

So many options, but this had to be good for her.

A small burst of warmth pressed against my back and Brenna was resting her palm on me. Good God, I was so damn uptight that just her hand on me settled me.

"Connor?" Her neck was twisted and she didn't meet my gaze, instead, she was focused on a spot on my shoulder.

"Yeah?"

She lifted her fingers and curled them into my collar, pulling it down. A blush stained her cheeks and she rolled to her toes, kissing the bite marks she imprinted on me earlier. "Take me to your room."

The whisper was soft but needy. Almost begging.

Blood rushed straight south to below my waist and I groaned as she continued kissing the marks she'd left.

"Brenna," I groaned. "I want this to be good for you and I'm so damn uptight right now. I don't want to hurt you."

She laughed against my flesh and a mix of pleasure and pain spread over my shoulder, down to my arm.

Shit. Damn it. The emptied bottle of water still in my hand crushed and crackled as I gripped it harder.

"I think I know it might hurt, but we've done enough lately, haven't we? Isn't it time?"

The time was weeks ago when I first whisked her into the back room at Glitz. Thank God I'd pulled back then. Had that night ended differently, there was a chance I wouldn't have given her a second glimpse afterward.

I must have frowned at the thought, or shown some remorse for it because Brenna's hopeful smile turned down. "Unless, you don't want...."

Oh. I *wanted.*

"I want." I pressed my mouth to hers, turning her and picked her up so we were chest to chest. She wrapped her legs around me as I kissed her, carried her down the hall. We were in my room and at the edge of my bed before I stopped the kiss. "You'll tell me to stop or slow down if you don't like it."

"I won't." She clung to my shirt and pushed it up my abs. "I'll like it."

"You'll set the pace—"

Her hand slipped over my mouth, quieting me and when she grinned up at me, cheeks flushed and lips swollen from our kiss, she was the most beautiful woman I'd ever seen.

"Connor, thank you for wanting to be careful, but I'm *ready,* more so than I was weeks ago. I *want* this. I want *you.*"

Fuck. She was serious. Somehow, an asshole like me earned the heart of a sweet and innocent and kind girl. It felt better than any win on the football field.

She was also a woman who knew what she wanted and I had to trust her.

I sat back on my knees and ripped off my shirt, flinging it to the floor. Sliding off the bed, I stood at the end, my gaze solely focused on her as I unbuckled my shorts, shoved them down with my briefs.

Her tongue swiped her bottom lip. Her eyes glazed over. I moved to the dresser and turned on a lamp so I had more light in the room in order to see *everything*. I wasn't missing a moment of the first time I slid inside Brenna and claimed her in the most intimate way possible.

My dick was rock hard, proud and standing straight out. I wrapped my hand around it, stroking slowly, loving the way Brenna devoured me with her look, seemed to crave every single part of me.

It was so damn heady I was drunk on the way she looked at me, the way she wanted me.

"Come here," she whispered, her voice was gritty.

I went to her, stopping at my nightstand to grab some condoms. Only Satan himself could stop me and even then I'd fight to the death to get to her. Brenna was spread out on my bed and her hands went to her shorts. Her button popped open. I tossed the strip of foil packets onto the bed by her hair.

The zipper seemed like a scream and I stayed still, my gaze on her face, her mouth and her eyes as she wiggled out of those sexy as sin denim cut-offs. Her lace and satin panties almost as pale as the color of her skin. She sat up enough to reach behind her back, and then she was peeling off her tank top, slipping her matching bra straps off her shoulders.

I was wholly undone. Physically. Emotionally. Watching Brenna undress and bare herself to me in the most intimate way possible was as close to any spiritual experience I'd ever had.

My gaze slid over every inch of her body like a caress.

"You're staring at me." Her hand went to her stomach and she ran it over the soft, sensitive flesh of her abdomen, down farther, up to a breast. Good Lord, when did she become the seductress in all of this?

My hands flexed and curled. I was rock hard. Blood rushed through my veins fast and furious.

Sweetly, in a way only Brenna could be, she lifted her hand and wiggled her fingers. "Come here, Connor. It's okay."

How had she been the one to comfort me during this? Somehow she took the lead, and I allowed it as I fell between her spread thighs, my cock sliding through her folds, her drenched and *soaking and so hot* pussy.

My mouth fell to hers, slid across her mouth, and I teased her with my tongue, tiny little flicks of my tongue against the corner of her mouth. I teased her and tempted her. Reveled in the way she slid her body against mine. She rolled into me, soaking my dick and I took her mouth, chased her tongue with mine and she curled her hands to my shoulders.

"Connor."

I kept kissing her and it took effort, almost all I had as I rolled off of her and slid my fingers down to her sex where I eased one in and then two. "I need to make sure you're ready."

I fucked her slowly with my fingers, kissed her mouth, sucked on her nipples. She came quickly and easily. My ego soared with every cry she made, no longer forced to stay silent. Her body responded to me like it was meant to be mine. A prize I wanted to always treasure.

"Please," she said and curled up until she was on her elbows. Her shining hair was wet at her temples, draped over one shoulder, pooled onto the pillow behind her.

If only I had my phone to take a photo of her, just like this, undone from orgasms, glistening from exertion.

I picked up the foil packets and ripped one off and opened it. There would be time later to explore everything, to take my time, let her get me off with her hand or her mouth. I'd get to all of it before the sun rose.

Now, I needed to have her wrapped around me.

"Hurry," Brenna whimpered. Her hand had trailed down her stomach to her center, and then her fingers were at her clit, rubbing. Fuck. Maybe we'd get ourselves off later, too.

I rolled the condom down my length, squeezing my base harshly to stave off the rioting emotions flooding every inch of me and climbed over her.

"I'll go slow," I warned her, easing down and kissing her. "If it's too fast or hurts too much—"

"Shh, I know. You'll take care of me, I know that." And the way she said it was so honest. So open. I had to give her something.

"Always," I promised her and as her lips parted in shock, I pressed my lips to hers, pushing the tip of me to her opening.

Oh damn. She was so tight, snug around the head of my cock. Her stomach flexed beneath me, legs spread farther. "Relax," I murmured. "Let me in."

She rolled her hips and I slid in farther. She kissed me harshly, biting my lip as I continued so damn slowly, so overcome by the heat of her and the tightness.

So damn tight. Hot. Silky.

I could blow at any moment but I couldn't blow *this*. Not her first time.

"Are you with me?"

She nodded and her fingers curled into my ass, nails digging into my skin and holy shit that felt good. Fire licked down my spine as I eased in, pulled back, wetting my dick with her juices and sliding in farther.

It felt like it took forever and she gasped several times.

"Are you okay?"

"I feel...full. Oh God, Connor." Her limbs trembled.

My arms shook like I'd done five hundred push-ups.

My need for her was insane and it could have been minutes or hours before I was fully planted, hitting the end of her. She squirmed beneath me.

Groaned and whimpered.

I took her cries with my mouth, forcing myself to stay still. Any movement and I'd ruin all of it.

"Give me a minute." I shook from restraint, but my need grew. The need to *take* and *rut* mixed with the desire to go slow and love and be tender with her.

"Move," she whimpered, face shoved into my throat. Her hands slid up my slackened back, digging into muscles at my shoulder. My ribs, back down to my ass. "Please. It feels...so good."

Shit. I wanted to stay rooted deep in her forever.

I listened to Brenna and prayed like hell my craving to protect her would override my desire to thrust into her like a wild animal. I moved slowly, propped myself up on my elbows so I could slide one hand down and rub my thumb against her clit.

She clenched around me, letting out a sound full of vowels, completely guttural.

The sexiest sound to vibrate through the room. And then I was done for.

She ripped me apart and bared me open and somehow stitched me back together in a way I would never be the same after this. Would never *want* to go back to unknown women and emotionless sex.

I rolled my hips, played with her clit. I gritted my teeth as she tightened and pulsed around me and she clung to my biceps as I went harder. Faster. Sliding in and out of her until the room was filled with the scent of our sex, the sounds torn from our throats.

"Shit," I groaned. "So damn good, Brenna. You feel amazing."

"I'm close," she cried, nails digging into me. There wouldn't be a place on my body she didn't mark by the time we were done and it was so fucking satisfying I only went harder.

Deeper. I took my finger off her clit and grabbed her hips, adjusted our position so I could go deeper. Like I needed to find her soul. Or the parts of her that craved me as much as I needed her.

"Connor," she cried out, and she lost it. I took her over the edge and watched every etched expression on her face, the bite of her lip, the tightness around her eyes and shock on her face as she *came and came and came* and I drove her through it, increased my pace so I could finish and when I did, I shouted her name, fisted my hands into the sheets at her side and shoved so hard deep inside of her she cried out and pulsed around me again.

Holy fucking shit.

I would never recover from this night. Never recover if she walked away from me. We hadn't just had sex.

It was indescribable. And completely necessary for my life and my heart.

TWENTY-THREE

Brenna

I WOKE up before the sun rose, unable to fall back asleep. Connor slept next to me, his leg draped over me like a heated electric blanket, his breath soft and comforting at my neck.

God. This man. And what he did to me the night before. My muscles ached like I'd spent hours in the gym. *Everything* ached in a delicious way.

I would remember last night for the rest of my life and it was so much more than anything I could have expected. So much better than it would have been in the back room at Glitz with him holding me against the wall.

Although at the memory, I added that to *must try soon* list.

I closed my eyes and exhaled, slid out of bed as my stomach rumbled. Careful to be quiet to not wake Connor up, I grabbed the polo shirt he threw on the floor last night and shimmied into my panties. Tiptoeing out of his room, I was careful not to make a sound. He left for training camp in less than two days and had been practicing and working out hard and then even more so last night.

He needed his sleep and I had some overwhelming urge to take care of him. In the kitchen, I dug through my purse I'd dropped on the counter the night before and pulled out my phone charger. I'd come prepared to spend the night at his place and grabbed the toothbrush I'd packed along with a small toothpaste tube. Phone plugged in, a quick scan showed nothing important to return. A text from Gina with a raised eyebrow emoji and the only word **So** followed by a dozen question marks could definitely wait.

I brushed my teeth in the hallway bathroom and used the restroom, heading back to the kitchen where I dug through his fridge and pulled out eggs, some bacon. He had bread in a box out on the counter so I grabbed the butter and peanut butter from his pantry and as quietly as possible, dug through the cupboards until I found skillets and mixing bowls.

His condo wasn't large, surprisingly small and it still surprised me that someone with as much money as Connor, someone who could afford anything, chose such a simple place, decorated it even less.

Probably just bachelor life. But I also knew he'd come from very little. Maybe he recognized that it wasn't the *things* you surrounded yourself with that made you happy.

I only hoped I made the list of people in his life who enriched it.

Always.

He'd muttered it in my ear right before he took the most precious thing I had to give and more than saying it, he had meant it. His promise had reverberated down to the soles of my feet. I wanted to be that for him and give him everything I had, everything I possibly could.

Breakfast.

We'd start with bacon and eggs. I got to work on getting everything ready, humming quietly to radio tunes that replayed every hour on the hour, those obnoxious songs you heard so much you eventually had to fall in love with.

I was lost in making breakfast and the sounds in my mind and the memories every ache in my body pulled to my surface that when an arm slid from my back to my stomach I jumped and scream, spinning around so fast I slammed into the counter. Pain bloomed on my hip and radiated outward.

"Oh shit," Connor said, laughing at my freakout.

"I'm sorry. You scared me." My hand went to my chest. My heart was racing.

"Oh fuck." His humor vanished. Concern replaced it. "I'm so sorry, Brenna. I didn't mean—"

"It's okay. It wasn't *that*. I was lost in my head."

His eyes were focused on me. My face. Was I being honest? Mostly.

"Lost in your head about what?"

A flush slid across my chest and down to my fingertips.

He knew. Of course he knew. "About last night? The things we did. How I made you feel?"

"Yes." He stole my breath in seconds and made my stomach flutter with need even faster. "All of it."

I reached for him. Slid my hands down his arms. Tiny little moon-shaped scratches were on his biceps.

I'd *marked him*. I traced the marks. My bite from the movie theater on his shoulder and he gave me that time to inspect him, turning so I could see two thin scratches several inches long down his back.

"I scratched you."

"I fucking loved every minute of it." His gaze scorched me as he looked at me over his shoulder. Bacon popped and sizzled on the stove but it had nothing to do with the way he lit up my senses with a look. He spun and cupped my cheek. "Did you?"

"Every second." I kissed his palm and pulled his hand off my cheek, squeezing it. "I wanted to make you breakfast."

"I figured that when you weren't in bed when I woke and I smelled bacon. You didn't have to."

"I want to take care of you."

He brushed his lips over mine, a softness in his dark eyes that was so rare. So special because of its infrequency. "I want to take care of you, too."

I kissed him languidly. We had the entire day, and other than checking in with Shelly to ensure she didn't have work for me to do, I had nothing on my schedule.

We finished cooking breakfast together and ate at the kitchen counter, sexual tension swirling around us while I asked him about training camp, what it was like, the practices. He talked about his teammates, some more about his friend Malcolm, how he got started in owning Glitz.

But we were both passing the time, eating our food and not tasting it...requiring it only for fueling purposes.

As soon as the plates were loaded in the dishwasher, he grabbed me, lifted me up and put me on his kitchen counter. His hand went to my chest and he slowly guided me until I was lying on it. The counter cold on my flesh for only a minute before it warmed.

"What are you doing?"

His finger trailed down my stomach to my underwear, he hooked his finger to the side of my panties and pulled them to the side. His eyes stayed on my sex, pulsing for him. Already wet. I'd been since he first kissed me that morning.

"I'm still hungry and I didn't get to do this last night."

"Yes, you did...after that second time."

"That was only to tease and to play."

I slid my hands down my thighs. He was standing too far away to touch but he might as well have been on top of me for how much I *felt* him. "Then what's this?"

"This is for pleasure."

And then he proved to me how much he meant it and when he was done, me clawing at the counters, thrusting my pussy into his mouth, my thighs tensing around his shoulders, I dropped to my knees on the harsh floor and returned the same pleasure for him.

~

I MIGHT AS WELL HAVE STAYED HOME Sunday morning for as little as I focused on anything at the Farmer's Market. I usually made a list of fruits and vegetables I wanted, made mental notes of other tented proprietors where I wanted to stop.

I'd been there for hours and only managed to grab some peaches and tomatoes. I was certain I'd meandered past my favorite flower tent twice already and hadn't seen it either time.

I was floating on air, my head in the clouds. I spent the entire weekend with Connor, only coming out of bed for substance in the form of food and some drinks. We showered together, watched television in his bed together before turning to other more pleasurable activities.

He took me on my hands and knees. Taught me how to ride him until I came so loud I was sure the neighbors would pound on his walls or call the cops. We had sex on his couch. His living room floor. And my favorite, when I mentioned that first night at Glitz, he'd picked me up and made love to me so harshly and perfectly against the wall I broke a nail clawing at the drywall behind me as I came.

Good Lord. I was so thankful I hadn't given away my

virginity to bumbling, immature teenage boys in the backseat of a car like Gina had. I had this experience to remember for the rest of my life.

This man...one I didn't want to lose. I hadn't held on to my virginity for someone special, but damn...I was so glad I found one.

"Hey you!" a familiar voice called out. Shannon Powell was in front of me. Metal bangle bracelets jingled on her forearm as she raised her hands to her eyes, blocking the sun. "You look lost."

Odd. After the weekend with Connor, I felt *found*.

"Oh. I'm well...enjoying the weather I guess." It was a humid day and already well into the nineties. Nice lie, Brenna. I mentally kicked myself and Shannon snickered.

"Are you." It was more a statement than a question and I didn't answer. I couldn't really. She grabbed my hand and pulled me into her tent where three fans were on, cooling the air minimally. "Are you ready for training camp?"

The guys left early this morning. My dad was gone as well, but we still went to my mom's for dinner Sunday afternoons.

"I think the team will be great this year," I said. "At least that's what my dad says." Odd how the last few weeks I'd started paying so much closer attention to any mention of the Rough Riders. I could parrot back everything my dad said, something I never really paid attention to. And I wasn't fooling myself that it was because I was now invested as an employee.

It was straight-up Connor. Last night, I'd opened the playbook and quizzed him on some new plays he wanted to ensure he had memorized by the time camp came on Monday.

I admired his dedication, physically and mentally, he put into his love for the game.

"Sure it will." She shrugged and her hand went to her stomach, rubbing it as she made a face. "So what are you doing the next two weeks while the guys are gone?"

She dropped her hand and I forgot what I was going to ask her. "Um. I'll be working, getting ready for FanFest."

She looked at me like she wanted to pat my head and whisper *Bless Your Heart* in that condescending Southern way we all mastered by the time we were twelve. "Sure you will. I just meant your nights will be more open what with Connor gone."

I glanced around her tent on instinct. She had two employees who were happily discussing jewelry with customers and more than a handful of women eyed Shannon with disdain. Jealousy stamped on their faces like they couldn't believe the gorgeous woman in front of me was married to Oliver Powell.

"Um. What?" She knew? Of course she did. We hadn't done a great job hiding it the last time we ran into her.

"I think it's great. Connor needs someone sweet in his life, he's always so intense and grouchy."

"He still is," I replied before I could filter myself.

Shannon threw her head back and laughed. "Does your dad know?"

"No. I wanted to wait awhile I guess. It's the beginning of the season and I didn't want to screw anything up for him."

"I wouldn't worry about that." She shrugged and turned to help a customer her employee couldn't. "Your dad's a fair guy and the coaches love Connor. It'll all work out."

It was the first time I'd actually considered my dad not caring. Then I kicked it out of my mind. My dad respected Connor, but did he want him with his daughter? It wasn't his decision to make, but I'd spent half my life doing whatever I could so I didn't worry them. It was a difficult habit to break.

"We'll see," I muttered.

She finished helping the customer who walked away with three metal bracelets with the words *love hope faith* stamped on each one and came back to me, business card in her hand. "Text me later. My cell is on here. Some of the wives and girlfriends and I get together while the guys are gone. We get caught up on reality TV, drink wine...it's all rather stupid and immature."

"But fun." I took the card. "And I like immature."

"I need to get to work but you're not going to get lost again, are you?" she teased, a glimmer in her eyes like she knew why I was daydreaming.

"I'll be fine."

"Good. Then Wednesday we're getting together at Gage and Elizabeth's house. Bring your swimsuit if you want. We usually hang out in the pool or hot tub too."

"Sounds good. And thanks, Shannon. This is really nice of you."

"What can I say? I have a feeling we'll be seeing a lot more of each other soon."

TWENTY-FOUR

Brenna

"ARE you sure you don't want to come with me?"

Gina shook her head, lips pressed together with one foot propped on our coffee table. "No. I'm good here. Honest." She swiped another coat of nail polish on her toenails and blew gently. "Brandon's working later but might stop by."

In the last few weeks, Brandon hadn't ever spent the night at our apartment. At least not when I was there. I was surprised with Gina for finding someone so quickly. She probably thought I was more insane.

Leaving tonight without her felt strange though, and I knew why. It was rare over the years where I went out and Gina wasn't with me. She'd had a much more active social life but when I needed her company, she was always there.

"I feel like you've thrown me out of the nest," I blurted stupidly.

"What?" She huffed a laugh and turned, twisting the top to the nail polish back on. "What are you talking about?"

The look she gave me was as ridiculous as my statement.

"Never mind." I was in a weird place and couldn't put my finger on what it was or why exactly.

"Does this have to do with me not wanting to hang out with your new friends?"

"They're not my friends." I sounded defensive. I wasn't trying to be. "I just...I guess I don't go many places without you so it feels strange."

"It's normal, you know. For us to have different friends. And I'm not mad. School starts in a week or so and I already have reading to do. And Brandon."

"I know."

"Does this have to do with Connor?"

"No." Maybe. Partly? "I don't know. He's at training camp."

"And you're missing his huge dick already?"

"Shut up." I slapped her shoulder and she stepped back, smirking. "I mean...I don't blame you or anything."

"We haven't really talked, I guess. I mean we had this weekend and then he was gone and I knew I wouldn't get to see him or talk to him a lot." We'd talked since he left. He called me Sunday night while he unpacked in the dorm room he was sharing with Kolby, another starting running back. It was now Wednesday and I'd heard from him last night for about two minutes. Two minutes into the conversation he was sighing and apologizing for being so damn tired. I'd teased him about having my dad tell the coaches to take it easy on them and then we'd hung up.

Was this what other girls went through having a boyfriend? The constant *want* to be around them and the frustration when you couldn't. I didn't want to be like that, so needy and dependent on a man. I hadn't expected all the emotions to hit me so hard when we finally had sex, I kept so much to myself over the years I wasn't used to being vulnerable.

"I think I miss him."

Gina smiled the sweet kind smile a best friend could give. The kind that said she understood but was trying to hold back giving me a load of crap at the same time.

"We're going to grow and change, you know? We already have."

"I didn't think it would happen so quickly. We've been college graduates for less than three months. How did everything get twisted and complicated within a span of weeks?"

It terrified me and yet there was a buzz in my fingertips. It was energizing too. Like the start of a new school year. The dawn of a new season.

That's what this was. *You're in a new season.*

She hugged me then, wrapped me in her thin arms and the minty scent of her shampoo hit me. "I'll go to law school. You'll rock it at the job. We're both falling in love for the first time, and we'll make new friends. It's a good thing, honey. But you know I'll always be here for you."

"You're the best, you know that?"

"As long as you remember. None of these football wives have anything on me."

"They don't. You know too much." I'd meant it as a joke but it came out dark, maybe morbid.

Gina pulled back and lifted a brow. "Because I know where the bodies are buried?"

"Yes, those too." I wiped a stray tear off my cheek and shook my head. "Okay, I'm done being stupid. Have a good night. Tell Brandon I said hi."

"I will. We should all go get dinner some night. Maybe on one of Connor's days off when he gets back?"

"You got it."

I turned and left our apartment, grabbing a cloth grocery bag with wine and snacks on the way. Shannon had told me not to bring anything but the Southern girl in me couldn't show up to someone's home empty-handed.

～

SHANNON, Paige, and Elizabeth were some of the loudest and craziest but also sweetest women I'd had the pleasure of meeting in a long time. They reminded me of girl gangs you'd see in movies, without the villain who was passively aggressive bitchy to everyone. They were close, laughed easily, encouraged each other and included me in every conversation without hesitation.

I was so used to staying on the outside of most social circles I thought it'd be awkward when I arrived but Elizabeth scooped me into her house with a hug, easily taking the wine and food I brought and ushered me into the kitchen where Paige and Shannon were already standing around the counter, snacking on charcuterie and vegetables.

It wasn't only the fact that I hadn't had many friends over the years that made it awkward, but the fact I worked for the team. I didn't want them treating me differently. I was an assistant in the marketing department only, but would they be open about their lives and all the inner gossip details they knew with all of their husbands being on the team?

It took me about three point five seconds to learn they had nothing to hide.

"So," Paige said. "It's lovely to meet you. Feel free to drink up and leave your car here tonight. Shannon's our designated driver."

"You're not drinking?" How weird. She'd been the one to invite me.

"Apparently I got knocked up a couple months back," she said it with a smirk but her hand fell to her stomach.

My eyes dropped as fast as my jaw. "What? That's wonderful!"

"Oliver hasn't wanted to tell anyone yet, but these girls and their guys know. Keep it quiet until he decides to spill to the coaches?"

There wasn't a hint of concern I would spill or that she couldn't trust me. "Yeah of course!" I rushed to her and hugged her. "So two months? Means you're due..." I did a quick calculation. I'd become a pro at this with my siblings procreating like rabbits. "March?"

"Yes. Right after season ends which ends up working out perfectly even if it was a surprise."

"You weren't trying?"

Paige jumped in. "I told her Beaux and I were going to start trying and like everything else she does, she had to beat me."

Shannon snorted and wrapped her arm around her sister-in-law. "Yeah, that was my plan. Fool."

Paige scrunched her nose at Shannon and turned out of her hug. She took my hand and pulled me toward the wine already uncorked and breathing on the counter. "Come on, come on. We have drinks and food, a safe way home—"

"Or ten bedrooms y'all can crash in," Elizabeth said, winking at me and reaching for a bottle of red blend. "Mi casa es su casa."

Paige laughed. "That too. But most importantly, we have five different reality shows to get caught up on."

"Five?" I choked on my first sip of wine.

Shannon laughed and grabbed a handful of carrots. "We save them all for these two weeks when the guys are gone.

Gives us something ridiculously stupid to do." She raised her glass of water in the air. "Cheers to our Second Annual Bitchy Binge Watch Fest."

We all clinked glasses and it took approximately ten minutes for the giggles and stories to begin. They'd started with the earlier year's season of *The Bachelorette*, cursing at the jerky guy and ranking their favorites. I didn't bother telling them I watched it already and knew not only who the Bachelorette chose, but that they'd already broken up. But through it all, we only paid attention to half of the actual show, having too much fun talking and laughing and drinking.

We were halfway through the second episode and I was two glasses of wine in when Elizabeth leaned forward, popped a grape into her mouth, and wiggled her brows. "So, what *is* going on with you and Connor?"

I froze. Gaze slid to Shannon. She shrugged. "I can't keep a secret to save my life, not with these girls. Plus, I'm totally curious, too."

She was completely unapologetic and I twisted the stem of my wineglass between my fingers. He hadn't told me *I* couldn't say anything. And he loved his teammates. But this wasn't something I really wanted getting out before I could tell my own family. And with Dad gone for the next week and a half, there wasn't a lot of time to do that.

"We're seeing each other. Sort of."

Always. That word again. It flickered through my brain with Connor's deep, rumbly voice. We hadn't actually promised anything. Nothing concrete was said.

Three curious expressions gaped back at me, expecting more. But I wasn't used to spilling secrets and thoughts and dishing about love lives like everyone else did with ease. "I like him," I admitted. "A lot. And I think he feels the same." I stared at my wine and swirled it. Chewed on the inside of my cheek. "I don't have a lot of experience when it comes to guys though, and Connor, well...he's intense. I'm afraid of being swept up in his shadow, I guess."

"Oh girl," Elizabeth said. "I think we've all been there. These guys are larger than life."

"And bossy assholes," Shannon added. "Jerks."

"Protective though, too," Paige said, with a soft smile and then glared at Shannon. "And they're not *all* assholes or bossy. Some are really sweet."

She flipped up her hand. "Please. I don't need to know *anything* about how Beaux and you are."

Paige snickered and rolled her eyes, returning to me. "How'd you two meet, anyway? At work?"

A handful of memories of our first night together rushed through my mind. The dance floor. That look of his as he watched me dance from the balcony. Whisking me to the back room. It felt like forever ago and yesterday and my cheeks flushed. I took a sip of wine. How much could they really be trusted with? How much should I share?

"Glitz," I finally said and took a sip of wine. "My friend Gina and I went there a few weeks ago."

"And Connor picked you up *there?*"

I thought back to how I'd seen him, hands curled around the railing, gaze so intense once I felt it before I saw him. I remembered the way I smiled at him, how he nodded and then later, how he joined me. "Actually, I think I did the picking up that night."

Elizabeth snorted. "Thatta girl. That's the way to do it."

"How would you know?" Shannon asked. "You met your husband at a sex club, blindfolded I might add."

I spit out the sip of my wine I'd just taken into the palm of my hand. "What?"

Oh my gosh. The heat on my cheeks burned to the tips of my ears.

"Yeah," Elizabeth said. Glanced at the television like she too was remembering her first encounter with Gage. Her voice went liquid as she said, "That was a good night. A *really* good night. Besides." She tossed a grape at Shannon. "You first met Oliver at Glitz too...*and* made out with him at a team party."

"I just wanted his dick."

Paige made a choking sound. "I don't need to hear that."

I was dumbfounded at their blunt honesty and yet Paige kept quiet. Maybe it was because she was quieter than the others anyway. Maybe it was because she married Shannon's brother. "How'd you meet Beaux?"

"I was waiting tables at Ride 'Em Rough, you know the place?"

"Where the guys hang out."

"Yeah, Beaux said something stupid and I dumped a pitcher of water on his head."

"You did?" I laughed. From what I knew of Beaux he was everything the way Paige described him. Playful and fun. He was the quintessential nice next-door All-American guy with a smile for everyone.

"What can I say?" She shrugged and grabbed the remote, leaning back into her chair. "He can be a jerk, too."

We turned back to watch the show, and I did it smiling. I might not have shared a lot. Barely anything compared to them, but their openness showed me one thing, I could trust them when the time came and I needed friends to lean on.

TWENTY-FIVE

Connor

THERE WAS nothing fun about training camp. We showed up on Sunday night, ate in one of the dining halls on campus. Dozens of grown men crammed into a dorm building like we were eighteen all over again with a ten o'clock curfew, eight hours a day of working our asses off. Coaches deemed it necessary for team morale and intense practices right before preseason started, but fuck I was so sore. And the ice baths in the small private university weren't enough to stop the aches from overworked muscles.

"Goddamn, I'm getting old," Powell groaned, taking a seat across from me.

I made a sound of agreement and shoved another bite of food into my mouth.

We were staying on a college campus but the food was catered. We had our choices of a huge variety of meals from Italian and Mexican to Asian and good old comfort American cuisine all proportioned for our weight requirements and body needs. All we had to do was check a box and meals were made specifically tailored to us.

I was shoving down a stir-fry, quinoa and cauliflower rice instead of normal white rice, a mixture of steak and chicken and broccoli, all made to keep my body lean and allow for the most muscle growth.

What I wouldn't give for a damn juicy burger like Powell was inhaling.

Note: American cuisine for the rest of camp.

"Shannon said the girls had a great time last night."

"Doing what?" I didn't quite care about Shannon or the other player's wives. I'd spoken to Brenna once all week and felt like an ass about it, but I was throwing my all into this camp. I had to. My five-year contract ended this year and I was working my ass off to ensure I'd be able to get a new one. My agent told me there were other teams keeping an eye on me, but I wanted to stay in Raleigh. We had the potential to be one of the greatest teams and I wanted to be a part of it.

Plus there was Brenna. No way would she want to leave.

I only half-listened to Powell as he started talking. Something about Shannon, drinks and wine, but then I caught Brenna's name.

"What?" She hung out with his wife? How in the hell did that happen?

He had his burger in his hands, frozen right at his open mouth. "You didn't know she was hanging out with them? Have you talked to her at all?"

"Tuesday? For like five minutes. I've been so damn tired I almost fell asleep on the phone."

"Yeah, no shit, man. I might be getting too old for this crap."

He was thirty-seven. He *was* getting old, especially for his body to keep taking a beating as a tight end, but he was still one of the best.

"Serious?"

"Shannon spilled last night, so Brenna knows, but we found out Shannon's pregnant and it got me thinking. At my age, all this traveling, the beatings. Might be getting close to hanging up the cleats, you know?"

So much information to process. *Way* too much.

"You're having a kid?"

"Yeah, could you stop looking at me like I'm an alien when you ask that?"

"I'm not...it's not...wow, man. That's awesome."

I'd never considered having kids. Never thought I came from good enough stock to have anything fatherly inside of me. But knowing Shannon was pregnant, my mind immediately went to Brenna. Swollen with a part of *me* inside of her. Her sweetness and grace and sass and strength.

Fuck.

"Thinking about it now, aren't you?" He had a fork shoved toward my face and when I glared at him, he used that fork to spear a chunk of cauliflower.

"No." I needed a subject change. Fast. "So what was Brenna doing with them?"

"You want to know, call your girl."

"She's not my girl."

"You're a shit liar." He grinned and shoved his burger into his mouth.

Yeah, turned out I was.

I DIDN'T CALL Brenna after I ate dinner. I had evening workout and then an hour of meetings going over plays where we went over what we did wrong during that day (a whole hell of a lot, according to our coaches), what we did right (very fucking little).

By the time I returned to my room, I was wiped out, but I forced myself to shower, threw on a T-shirt and propped up all the pillows I could find on my tiny ass bed and picked up the phone.

I still didn't call her.

I pulled up my video messaging app, found her number, and hit the connect button. While it rang, I grabbed my earbuds and pushed them in so I could hear her better.

Just when I thought I was going to get a "can't connect" message on my phone, she connected. The screen went blurry and then she was there. Her strawberry blonde hair piled into a mop on top of her head, small wisps of hair curled around her ears, at her temples. One small section stuck straight out behind her ear.

"Hey," she said and held up a finger. "Give me a minute to get to my room."

Her image shook as she walked but she didn't walk fast enough before I heard Gina in the background. "If you're going to have phone sex, do it quietly!"

The last of her shout was muffled and Brenna scowled.

"Brandon...how about you keep your girl quiet?"

"On it, Brenna."

Finally, her door shut and when she grinned at me, I was already smiling wide. "Phone sex? Now there's an idea I hadn't thought of when I called."

But hell if it didn't sound like a good idea now that I was looking at her for the first time in days. Starved for her...her touch, her smile, the sweet sound of her voice.

"I miss you," I blurted without thought. Without anything hindering me. I'd been thinking of her for hours, what Powell and Shannon had. What half the guys on my team had. I'd never considered myself good enough for something like that, but if Brenna saw something good in me, perhaps I hadn't given myself enough credit.

"Well," she said softly, her voice almost a whisper. I'd surprised her. Good. I liked I could do that. Her phone shifted and then she was laying back against pillows with pink and gray flowers. "I miss you too. How's camp going?"

"Brutal." Every muscle screamed for a massage. "But good. New guys are coming along and the old guys already know what they need to do. No serious injuries in the off-season so as long as we stay healthy through pre-season, we're looking good."

All except Powell. Who might be retiring. I still didn't want to think about that. We had several other tight end options, but none as incredible as him. It'd throw us off for next year unless we traded.

"You look like you're concentrating on something," she said and I relaxed my features and forced a smile.

"Work shit. Just thinking about the season. It's all swimming in my head."

"You didn't have to call if you're busy."

"I wanted to talk to you. See you. Powell said you got together with Shannon the other night."

"Yeah. And Paige and Elizabeth. They were sweet."

"Heard you found out some info Powell hasn't shared with anyone."

"He told you?"

"Dinner tonight."

"Shannon's so excited." Her smile was happy enough to light up an entire stadium. "Grouchy and not feeling great, but happy and I think Paige might be even more excited about being an aunt."

"What'd you think about it?"

"Me?" Her head jerked back like I surprised her. Was I going here? Tonight?

Yeah.

"What about me?" she asked. "I'm thrilled for her. Babies are the best things in the world."

"You sound like you want some."

Her lips pulled to the side.

This was too soon. Too fast. What in the hell was I *doing*? I could have changed the subject. Maybe asked her to show me her tits. Start stroking my cock to see if she wanted to watch me, but something called in me to wait. To find out. To dig deeper.

"I mean." She shrugged eventually, still uncertain. Probably because I was being a creep. "I guess, I don't know. I love my family's kids and our huge family. But I don't always do well with uncertainty and it seems like becoming a mom is the most uncertain thing in the world."

"But you want them, don't you?"

"Yeah," she said, and she sounded resigned. Like maybe admitting it would push me away. "I think I do. Someday. I'm still so young." She hesitated for a moment and who could blame her. And I wasn't surprised when she blinked, refocused on me, and asked, "You? Do you want kids?"

"Never thought about it before in my life." The disappointment fell over her like someone had flipped a light switch. "Until recently," I said. "Very recently."

She could take what she wanted from that. And what she took was something sweet, vulnerable and shy. "Yeah?"

"Yeah, Brenna. In case you haven't figured it out yet, I really like you."

I love you. The words flew so quickly up my throat I barely bit them back. I hadn't spoken those words to anyone in my life outside my grandfather. They lodged in my throat as she blushed, her grin turned less shy and bigger.

"I like you, too, Connor Quinten. I think you're something pretty darn special."

God, I wanted to kiss her. Taste her. Lick her cunt until she had nails digging into my scalp.

I groaned and dropped a hand to my dick and Brenna's gaze followed the movement of my hand.

"Are you...?"

"Getting hard thinking about how much I wish I could kiss you right now, eat you until you scream, yeah Brenna. I'm getting off on that thought."

She shivered, visibly and wildly and licked her lips. "Show me," she said and it was so guttural, so damn wanton and needy, there was no way I could refuse.

Her phone wobbled and for a minute I caught the ceiling until she returned. The angle wasn't perfect, but in the few seconds she was gone, she'd ripped off her shirt and bra, propped the phone on something so she could use both of her hands and then her legs bent, knees spread and she dipped her hand beneath the waistband of a pair of black lace underwear.

"Holy shit," I grunted and stood. "Hold on."

I searched the room and found my playbook. The three-inch binder was the best I could find along with a stack of pillows I used to prop the phone up on the small desk. I stood in front of it, the phone angled so she could see everything from my face to my hand wrapped around my hard length.

"Wow," she breathed. "It almost looks bigger on the screen."

Hell. She made me laugh. I didn't know laughing and jacking off at the same time was possible until her. But then Brenna made everything better. Lighter. Happier. She bewitched me with her goodness and I didn't want to be un-spelled.

"Let me see you." My voice was gruff. Thick with need. "Take off your underwear."

A brief flash of hesitation slid across her and then she moved to her knees, wiggling. All I could see was the jiggle of her breasts, the clench of her stomach as she shimmied out of her underwear, showing me her bare, slick pussy.

"Holy shit, you're so damn sexy."

I still couldn't see her face, but I heard her moan as she cupped her breasts. Pushed them together. Someday I'd fuck them. Get a little dirty with her. Come all over them. She pinched her nipples, tugged on them and played with one tit while her other hand drifted lower.

"Sit down and spread your legs. I want to see your face. Watch what you do to yourself."

Was she rougher than I was? More gentle? Did she fuck herself with her fingers? Play with her own ass a little bit or did she keep it clean and sweet, only using her clit to get off?

The things I wanted to know about this woman were so damn raunchy I surprised myself.

I cupped my balls with one hand and stroked myself while she played with her clit. Two fingernails painted sky blue ran in circles around her clit. Occasionally she'd run them through her slit, gather moisture and it was all I could hear over the roar of my breath racing through my ears. The wet sounds she made.

"Tell me a fantasy," I groaned. She'd alluded to them and she might have been a virgin but she was so comfortable with sex she'd watched...or read...or had time to *think* about all the things she wanted. "You said once they weren't mine to have, but I want them." Fuck my balls were tight. I squeezed my base hard to stave off the shot of pleasure running through me.

"Do you think they're yours now?"

"I want everything you have."

My statement was so bold, so fierce due to my gritted teeth her gaze shot from my dick on the screen to me.

"You heard me. I want everything, angel. All of it. Your thoughts, your fears, your fantasies."

Jesus. Who knew I could get off being so damn mushy?

"I'll tell you, after," she panted. Through the tiny screen, her inner thighs were shaking. Hell yeah, she was close. I was right behind her.

"Make yourself come. I want to hear you scream."

TWENTY-SIX

Brenna

I CAME LIKE A ROCKET. I'd been so close. Ever since I first saw Connor's face on my screen with his incoming call, I wanted to do this for him. I wanted it for me. I wanted him to remember me and everything good we had and I wasn't sure why it was so damn important until he told me he wanted everything from me.

Handing it over to him would be so easy it wouldn't require any effort. A part of me realized I'd already given him everything I had, maybe not the words, but he definitely held my heart in his large, strong palm.

Where else would it be safe?

I came on a cry, teeth clenched together so I didn't scream. My eyes squeezed close and my body shuddered. "Connor," I moaned while I splintered and fractured and was put back together in a million shaky pieces.

"Right there," he grunted. "Angel."

I yanked my eyes open and watched as he came. Spurts of milk-white streams pulsed into his hand and his groan echoed through my room. Blocks of bricks appeared on his abs. The muscles on his hips and ribs contracted.

He was easily the most beautiful man in the world.

My mouth went dry at the sight of him and stayed there until he'd cleaned up, tugged on his briefs.

He swiped his hair off his forehead, phone shaking in his hand. "Hey," he said, laughing softly.

He was embarrassed? I didn't think it possible.

I barely gave him time to get settled and crossed my legs, leaned back against my pillows. "When I was a teenager, I used to have these handcuffs."

That grabbed his attention and his brows snapped together. "What?"

He knew. I'd told him. Being cuffed and taken. Held. Beaten.

I'd never told *anyone* this in my life. How messed up did it make me?

"Yeah." I picked at lint on my bed. I was still naked but didn't care. I was giving him so much more than my body. "So, I used to put them on, cuff my wrists together in front of me, and every time I did, I'd have this panic attack. A flashback."

"Brenna." He sounded tortured.

I kept going. Now that I started, I had to get it out. "Yeah, it was messed up. But I kept hoping one day that pain, that fear it'd go away if I kept trying. And one day, a few years ago back in college, I'd had too much to drink." I winked to lighten the mood. "And maybe read or watched something, well, erotic."

"Porn."

"Whatever." I rolled my eyes. "Do you want me to keep going?"

Connor had leaned forward. I couldn't see his arms but his

hands were in the screen, white-knuckled and clasped together. "I said I wanted everything from you. I meant it."

"Okay." Nerves bounced in my stomach. "Anyway, I closed my eyes that night to breathe through the panic. The paralyzing fear of being restrained, and I imagined something else... a better reason for being tied, cuffed...restrained."

"You got off thinking of being tied up?"

A cool breeze kicked on. The air conditioner. Nothing serious. It chilled me to my bones. God, I was so, so very messed up. I could barely swallow over the ball in my throat.

Connor leaned forward, pressed a fingertip to the screen like he was trying to touch me. "There's nothing wrong with some kink in the bedroom, angel."

"It's weird."

"Not if it helps you face your fears. You want that?"

I so desperately did. Talking about it turned me on, sent a throbbing to my sex. "Yeah. Maybe."

"We'll start slow," he said. He bit his bottom lip, a gesture so damn sexy as hell but something I hadn't seen him do. "Whenever you're ready. A knot you can get out of. Maybe at first you holding onto something. Or me holding onto you. We go at your pace."

That throb increased and I pressed my thighs together.

I love you.

It jumped so suddenly unbidden and without thought, I clamped my teeth together so it didn't fly out. It was too soon, right?

Way too fast. In the grand scheme of life, we barely knew each other. But in the short time we met, he'd become the guy I didn't *need* more than any other, he became the man I *wanted* with me more than anyone.

"Connor—"

It must have been written all over my face, this burgeoning love that came from nowhere, planted roots deep and quick, growing wildly.

"I know, angel. I know."

~

I SPUN a slow circle in place, head tilted back, gaping at everything I'd helped Shelly accomplish in a month of working for her.

"We did it!" I exclaimed. "This is incredible."

It was FanFest Day. The players arrived home from training camp last night. Connor called me as soon as he got in but I was still at work. Shelley and I stayed with the crew she'd hired to get everything ready until two o'clock in the morning and by the time I finally headed home, it was too late to text Connor if I could come to his house. He'd had a hard and rough two weeks. Younger players, faster players...he bitched about them with respect and maybe a hint of fear of losing his spot.

After that night, the rest of camp flew by. We talked more frequently. Not daily, but we somehow connected as often as we could. A text here. A phone call there. A few more video calls that didn't always end with us naked, but always smiling.

The three words I almost blurted out hadn't been spoken or alluded and yet there'd been a silent understanding that we *felt it.*

Everything else became a matter of time. Waiting to talk to my parents. My family. Introducing Connor to everyone as soon as I could at our next family dinner. Connor had always told me he'd take whatever he could get but I wanted everything from him.

I wanted everything for *us.*

Shelly walked to me and squeezed my hand. "Now we need to pray everything goes off without a hitch. My goodness, I should have taken an extra anxiety pill this morning."

Poor Shelly. She was so nervous and yet she'd planned the most amazing signings and events for the fans and players who would flood the stadium in a few short hours. Already outside, the streets were packed with fans sporting Rough Riders gear, a little girl in pigtails bouncing on her father's shoulders. Boys tossing footballs in the air. Live music. Beer. Lots of plastic beer cups were already littered on the ground.

There was an energetic hum in the air. Of hope. Excitement. Expectation for another season where the Rough Riders earned another Super Bowl. And while I'd never been a fan of football or cared too much, I was certainly highly invested now.

It was impossible not to become enthralled with the game, the love and excitement of it after spending so much time not only at work but around Shannon and Paige and Elizabeth. Gina had met us last weekend for a Saturday brunch where Shannon grumbled at her "virgin" mimosa, earning a snort from Gina.

And tonight, after all this was done and the practice was over and Connor was done doing his signing shift, we were going out to dinner and then back to his place.

I was counting down the hours until I could get my hands on him again. Until Connor could get his hands on *me*.

"Everything is set up and the players' buzzers are in their lockers. There's nothing else we need to do except enjoy the show and revel in your success."

The players would be buzzed ten minutes prior to their signing times. Some of them had it before practice, others after. It was the most efficient way we could figure out how to work it so we weren't chasing everyone down. For our part, Shelly and

I would be on the field, directing them anyway. During practice, I would watch from my parents' box.

She dropped her clipboard. Her entire checklist was scratched off. "You are awfully calm."

I bumped my shoulder into hers. "It's not my job on the line, and besides, I've nailed my part."

"Sassy young thing. In all honesty, you've done great work. When your father approached me about hiring you, I had some concerns."

Ouch. That stung, but who could blame her. "It's understandable."

"But you've worked hard and you've excelled at everything I've asked of you. Especially the last few days working long hours. You and the rest of the department have helped me and I really appreciate it. Your dedication especially."

Her praise melted over me and I beamed. "Thank you, Shelly. I promised I wouldn't let you down."

"And you haven't. Go home, get ready and I'll see you back here at four, okay?"

It was only noon. Despite working until the middle of the night, I'd met her at the stadium at eight this morning. I could use a nap, but adrenaline was racing through me, keeping me awake.

I only hoped it didn't crash later tonight.

GINA POUNCED on me as soon I walked into our apartment, her dark brown hair bouncing all over the place. "You'll never guess who stopped by."

"Chris Hemsworth?"

I mean, who else would make her so crazy.

"Hell no. If he was here, he'd be chained to my bed forever." Her hand curled around her chin. "Actually, I don't have anywhere to chain him to. I should figure something out, just in case."

Her gaze went glassy and I playfully shoved her to bring her back to the present. "Focus, gingersnap. Who stopped by?"

"Oh." She shook her head clearing away whatever fantasy she'd already pulled up. I should have known better than to mention Hemsworth. Bless her heart. "Connor. He dropped something off for you on the way to his practice."

"That's like twenty-minutes out of his way."

"Yes." She rolled her eyes and shoved me toward the bedroom. "What a hassle. A whole twenty minutes. Go. I want to see what it is too."

Connor was full of surprises. He'd taken it to a whole new level after our date to the drive-in, like he was trying to make up for a lifetime of me not having many. It was unnecessary, but a thrill went through me, straight to my fingertips as I caught sight of the wrapped boxed sitting neatly on my bed.

"Come on, come on." Behind me, Gina clapped, encouraging me on.

I almost kicked her out of the room. What in the world had he given me? It was a typical gift box you'd wrap clothes in for holidays and there wasn't a card on it, not that it was necessary since I knew it was from Connor. The teal and blue bow, Rough Riders colors, gave me a hint.

"All right, all right. Chill out, girl," I drawled to Gina.

I took off the bow, running the silk through my hands and I shoved it into my purse. Ever since we'd talked about tying me up some night, I hadn't stopped thinking about it. Perhaps that bow would work.

"I don't want to know what you did that for," Gina murmured, plopping down on my bed with a bounce.

I laughed and unwrapped the box. I had no plans to tell her anyway.

Lifting up the top, I found a small note card and beneath it something wrapped in teal tissue paper. I flipped over the card. *For now.*

"What's it say? What's it say?"

I flicked the card toward Gina and grabbed the package. It was heavy and soft and beneath it, another package with another note.

Gina grabbed that note before I could.

"Oooh, this one says, 'For later'."

"What?" She handed me the card and reached for the package. I slapped her hand. "Don't even think about it."

I unwrapped the top one. My pulse was fluttering. Now? Later? I had ideas and heat was making the top of my thighs throb as they raced through my mind.

"I knew it," I said, smiling. I held up the T-shirt, Rough Riders logo and name stamped across the chest and front of it. "He got me a shirt to wear today."

"Yeah, yeah, T-shirt. I want to see what's for later." She stressed the later part and I pulled the box away from her.

"Perhaps I should open this in private."

"Don't even think about it."

"This might cross the line of TMI."

"Honey, I've seen you naked over the years more times than he has in weeks. Trust me, I want to know what he's thinking."

"You're so weird."

"I know, I know." She plopped the last tissue wrapped gift into my lap. "Now open."

"Yes, my Lord," I drawled, but my fingers were itching to see what was inside. We were going out for dinner after FanFest, and then to his house, so this could be a dress or something for *later*.

I cut through the tape connecting the ends of the package together and then my jaw dropped. "Oh dear," I whispered.

"Wowzers," Gina said.

"Shut up." I opened the tissue paper and reached for two thin leather straps. Black. The rest was lace. Lingerie. He'd bought me the sexiest babydoll slip I'd ever seen. The small label read Agent Provocateur. "Holy crap, this had to cost a fortune."

"He wants you dressed in leather and lace and you're concerned about the price?"

I chuckled, tried to erase the weight on my chest. Holding it up, I swiveled to face my mirror. It was beautiful. Embroidered lace to cover my breasts with a plunging neckline in the middle of them. A sheer, silky black fabric that would fall to just below my ass.

"You forgot these," Gina said. A thong so dainty it could be ripped apart with the smallest tug hung from her index finger.

I snatched it from her. "Give me those."

She laughed and climbed off the bed. "Well, I think I've seen enough and might need to go see Brandon and get a quickie in between his clients tonight. This has me hot and bothered and feeling very, very odd imagining you in it."

"Oh my goodness you're a freak."

She smacked her lips to my cheek. "That's why you love me." Pointing at the lingerie I was still holding up, she continued, "And maybe a little of that freaky is rubbing off on you, huh?"

"I think it's something else rubbing off on me."

"Gah!" She slammed her hands to her ears and fled my room. "Too much! Too much!"

"You asked for it!" I shouted back and once she was gone, I turned back to the mirror.

Holy crap this was sexy and sweet. That throb at the top of

my thighs spread somewhere else so much more pleasing and beneath the clothes I was wearing, my nipples pebbled, pressed to my bra. My cheeks were already flushed.

What in the world did Connor have planned for *later*?

I couldn't wait to find out.

Connor

BRENNA WAS distraction in the sexiest form. She'd had me hard, cursing myself for giving her the gifts before practice instead of waiting until later since before practice started when she'd sauntered up to me, looking all professional with an iPad in hand, but wearing the T-shirt I bought for her, tied in a knot, skinny white jeans on that clung to her skin, holes in the jeans at her thigh and knees, frayed at the ankles.

She spoke with the players, reminded us of our times for the signings and events before and after practice. Checked to make sure we all had the pagers she insisted we wore as soon as practice was done for those of us signing later and as she walked past me, acting like I was the same to her as every other player on the field she whispered, "I'm wearing another part of your present now, too."

She walked away, ass swinging in that sexy saunter women

had, leaving my dick hard in my athletic cup, jaw dropping to the turf.

I barely managed to focus on the practice. Thank God for muscle memory that allowed me to pull off every drill without anyone realizing I was imagining that sexy black thong, the thin string on her hips, between the cheeks of her ass. I was going to tear it off her later for teasing me so badly. It was all I thought about while I practiced, tried to forget about it afterward when I jumped in the shower.

The last thing I needed was a hard-on in the team shower.

And I did my best to ignore her while I signed helmets and miniature footballs, posters and jerseys and T-shirts for fans afterward.

I had my picture taken with hundreds of kids, ignored the occasional groping from their moms or single women, blushing like a virgin when an eighty-year-old grabbed my ass and exclaimed, "Oh Lordy, you make me feel like I'm twenty all over again."

It garnered laughter and photos and hollers from the waiting line behind her and I engaged her, giving her a quick kiss on her wrinkled cheek before sending her on her way.

Women, man. They thought men were full of sex talk when they were around each other, but from my experience, women could be ten times raunchier than I would ever imagine.

Now, I was done, walking through the line to sign the last few items from fans I couldn't get to, but there was an urgency to it.

I wanted to get Brenna fed and then back to my place so I could ravage her all night long.

Finally done, I hurried back to the locker room and pulled my phone out of my pocket on the way.

I'm done. Grabbing bag from locker room. Meet you in the parking lot?

Reception sucked inside the stadium and it took forever for the message to send. I spent a few minutes getting waylaid in the locker room with the remaining guys who also had late signings, said goodbye to Beaux and was halfway down the hallway toward the underground parking ramp for players when the text reply finally came in.

Already here and waiting for you.

I was in the locker room with the speed I could run a 40-yard dash. She was there, waiting for me. Dressed in the shirt I gave her and wearing the thong I couldn't wait to tear off her. I found her at the trunk of my car, leaning against it and not seeming nervous at all at being found with me.

"I told my dad I want to talk to him Sunday," she said, pushing off the trunk. "That okay with you?"

"Anything you want, angel," and then I was in front of her, slamming my mouth to hers, the craving I had for her clawing at me, aching to get free, to get clothes off us and get her turned and flipped over my trunk so I could *take and take and take everything*. I groaned against her mouth and pulled back. "Shit. How hungry are you?"

She laughed, placed her hand to my cheek. Thumb ran along my jaw. "I'm starving. Feed me and fill me with caffeine or I'll pass out before we're back at your place."

"Can't have that then, can we?"

"Not unless you want to listen to me snore all night."

"No way. There are a lot of other sounds I want to hear you make first."

She shivered visibly before me and licked her lips. I unlocked the car doors and popped the trunk. "Get in the car before I start making you scream now."

She laughed like I was kidding. I wasn't. I hadn't had her

body in my hands in weeks and this was the first time I'd seen her since before I left training camp. And I hadn't even said hello to her properly, just went straight to innuendo and sexual promises.

Stop being an asshole and calm the hell down.

I inhaled a deep breath and then five more until I felt settled enough.

Sliding into my driver's seat, I turned to Brenna. She was already turned in my direction, brows furrowed. "You okay?"

"Yeah, feeling like a dick because I didn't even say hello to you."

She huffed and leaned forward. "Hey Connor. It's so good to see you again." There was a mocking tone to her voice that made me grin.

"Hey, angel. You're more beautiful than ever and I missed you." I cupped her cheek and drew her to me, kissing her and ensured I kept it tender and soft. There'd be time for me to be domineering later.

When I fulfilled that fantasy of her tied up. I hadn't been able to kick it out of my mind and I hoped from the lingerie I left her earlier that tonight would be more *intense* than anything we'd done before.

"I missed you, too," she whispered. Her lips lifted to a grin against mine and then her stomach rumbled. "Seriously though, feed me." Her hand fell to her stomach. "I've been running on crackers and cheese all day and I'm starving."

"Anything you want." I pulled back and started the car. "I'll give you anything you want."

"Will you feed me a huge cheeseburger with bacon and fries and maybe a salad and some chocolate cake for dessert?"

Jesus. The girl could *eat* apparently.

"I know just the place."

Most of the team was headed to Ride 'Em Rough, but I

didn't want to go there. It'd be packed with fans and loud and wouldn't give us a quiet moment to get caught up. Plus, there was still the chance her family or coaches would show and I didn't want anything awkward ruining the moment for us tonight.

"Have you ever been to Big Papa's?" It was a bar that served the biggest and largest burgers I'd ever seen.

"Yes." The one word sounded like an orgasm and her stomach rumbled again. "And apparently it sounds amazing."

This woman. She was losing her nerves around me the more time we spent together and somehow the two weeks we'd spent apart, having only phone conversations had brought us closer together. Odd how that worked, but I liked it more than I thought I would.

WAS it wrong to think a woman was gorgeous when she shoved a bite of a fried mozzarella burger with extra bacon into her mouth? The burger was so thick, Brenna smashed it with her palm, some of the mozzarella cheese squirting to the side. I'd been mesmerized by it, in a strange, maybe creepy way but there was something seeing her so unashamed about her hunger and enjoyment of food that was attractive.

The noise around us carried on, but we were tucked into a corner table. I sat with my back to the restaurant to minimize the odds of getting recognized. And really, there was nothing I wanted to see more than Brenna.

We spent most of the night talking about camp, how the practice went. The FanFest night had been crazy and every time I complimented her on it, she brushed it off as Shelly's idea.

"I was the assistant, doing what I was told. It was Shelly who thought of all the new activities."

"Whoever it was, I doubt it would have run so smoothly without all your efforts."

"You're sweet," she said and bit into her burger again. Watching her eat was almost as good as sex with the way she closed her eyes like ecstasy had hit her. Her moan alone reminded me of the sounds she made me when I teased and bit her nipples.

I cleared my throat, banishing the thoughts from my mind and tucked into my own sandwich. No large fatty burger for me unfortunately but the grilled chicken with buffalo sauce was still delicious. The massive pile of onion rings next to it was my indulgence for the week. We had the weekend off, reporting back for practice on Monday before our first preseason game on Saturday, but I wasn't worried.

I doubted I'd play in the first game anyway for more than a snap or two. All of our off-season training was done, and in the last two weeks at camp, I had no doubt I'd proven myself worthy of an extension.

As long as I didn't end up injured at some point during the season, I had no more worries about anything.

"You mentioned your family dinner on Sunday. You ready to tell your dad?"

I'd stunned her with the change in subject and it took a minute for her to respond. Part of that was because of the massive bite she took right before I spoke.

She wiped the corners of her mouth with a napkin unnecessarily and nodded. "Yeah, I think so. That okay with you?"

"Had he found out about us at the beginning, no, I wouldn't want him to know. But your dad's a fair man. He always has been and more than being a fair man, I think he's a good man. He has my respect. I have no problems with him knowing about us, or being the overprotective father you say he is and grilling me about my intentions for you."

She giggled. "That's probably exactly what my dad would say to you." She dropped her voice and sounded nothing like her old man. "Tell me Quinten, what exactly are your intentions with my daughter?"

I tossed an onion ring at her. "If you think he sounds like that, you need to get your ears checked."

She stuck out her tongue and popped the onion ring I threw at her that had landed on her plate. "I don't like hiding things from them and my sister and sister-in-law have already asked me why I've been acting so weird lately."

"Weird?"

"Yeah, maybe a little more daydreamy than usual?"

"Hard to stop thinking about me?"

I meant it as a joke but she blinked slowly and her voice went to that soft sound that shot straight to my dick. "Something like that."

Yeah. I liked hearing that. Almost as much as I liked her.

"You almost ready to get out of here?"

She glanced at the remaining food on her plate. A small amount of fries and one bite left of her burger but she'd sunk back into her chair, groaning with her hand on her stomach. "I don't think I can eat another bite."

"Still want dessert?"

"Ugh. No more mention of food. Maybe later."

"All right, let's get out of here then. I have my own dessert in mind."

She chuckled, shaking her head. Someday she'd stop getting shocked by the shit that came out of my mouth.

She sipped her iced tea while I finished my own meal and paid the check.

I stood from my chair and wrapped my hand around the back of hers. "You ready?"

She grinned at me and then her gaze slid to where I'd been, mouth tightening into a smile that took me a moment to place. Fake.

"Excuse me."

I shifted to a woman dressed in a denim skirt that hid almost nothing, a top that showed almost everything, hair out to *there* and lips the color of a fire truck. "Are you Connor Quinten?"

Crap. My hand slid from Brenna's chair to between her shoulders. "I am."

She shoved a napkin and a pen in front of me. "I'm a huge fan of the Rough Riders. Can I get your autograph?"

A quick scan told me others noticed. A table of women similarly dressed to the woman in front of me were fluffing their hair, shimmying down their tanks to expose as much as possible. Jesus. Didn't they see I was with a woman?

"Sure." I gave her a smile as plastic as the woman's faux tits and scribbled my name and jersey number onto the napkin. "Have a good night."

I was intent on getting out of there as soon as possible before mayhem broke out. It wasn't uncommon to get noticed, but I'd hoped I wouldn't.

I didn't even mind it sometimes, but tonight was different. I had plans for later and hadn't seen nearly enough of my angel in two weeks.

We should have ordered in was my thought right before the rest of the fan's friends gathered their nerves and sashayed straight to us. We'd been sitting in a corner and they managed to block us in.

Double shit.

"Can we have autographs too?"

They didn't give me a chance to say no before more napkins, a notebook, a small calendar were shoved almost straight into my body.

"You okay?" I asked Brenna, looking down as I took one of the pens. She'd tensed beneath my hand and nodded.

"Yup. Go ahead."

I glanced at her quickly. She wasn't annoyed. There was something else going on behind her green eyes that danced around the restaurant. But hell, she saw it before I did.

The *crowd* of people now moving toward us.

"Hey, can you ladies back up some, please? Give me some space." They didn't listen and their energy was contagious.

I couldn't move past them into a larger space without shoving them out of the way and their volume increased with the excitement and size of attention we'd gathered.

Brenna's hand curled into the back of my shirt and she pressed tight to me. "I need air," she whispered and while it was more to herself, I heard it like a gong.

"We'll get out of here," I said, and signed the items, stepping toward the women who didn't seem in any hurry to leave. "Please," I gritted out. I wasn't past being a dick if I had to be. Brenna was my priority.

Behind me, Brenna counted. Slowly. Softly. Her hand on my back started shaking and her nails dug into my skin through my shirt.

I flinched from the sting and pushed forward again. "Thank you all for coming and wishing us a good season. If you'll excuse me and give me space, I'll sign everything I can on my way out."

But being polite wasn't working. Behind the women who still hadn't left but somehow managed to maneuver even closer, pushing me back instead of forward, there was a group of guys, not much younger than me, beers raised in the air and chanting "Rough Riders! Rough Riders! Super Bowl! Super Bowl."

"Come on." Screw the autographs. Phones were out, recording everything and I'd probably end up on some Athletes Behaving Badly social media site but who gave a shit. I paid people good money to clean that up for me.

I wrapped my arm around Brenna's back and held her to my chest. I shoved into the women who scrambled backward. "Hey!" One of them wobbled on heels but her friends caught her.

The men who started a now restaurant-wide chant didn't move as we came closer.

"Who's the jersey jumper, Quinten?"

"Fuck off," I growled. That I wouldn't tolerate. At all.

One held up a phone and snapped a pic, getting right in Brenna's face. She dug her face into my chest like she was trying to burrow inside.

"Move. Now." It wasn't often fans got out of control. Most were polite, but it was a late night probably filled with alcohol and fueled by a herd mentality. The restaurant was losing its mind and near the front door, I saw parents ushering out several small children like they saw the storm brewing as vividly as me.

Too bad I was so far away from that damn door.

Someone tripped, bumped into me, and I reached out to grab them. Doing so though forced me to untangle from Brenna and as I did, one of the chant-starters grabbed her.

"Hey honey, I bet I can do for you when Quinten passes you on."

"Hey!" I shouted and reached for her. But Brenna had frozen in his grip, her eyes wide. Her face was pale and she wasn't moving. Wasn't saying anything.

"Brenna!" I called to her, but the crowd separated us. One

of the men touched her hair, and I elbowed whoever was next to me, eliciting a scream from a female.

Goddamn it.

I pushed through the growing crowd to the men who *were still fucking touching her.* And then they let go. Brenna spun in a slow circle, blinking, but it was like she didn't see anything.

Her eyes rolled back into her head.

"Brenna!" I yelled, finally reaching her, but her legs folded like paper and I caught her right before her head smacked to the cement floor.

TWENTY-EIGHT

Brenna

I WAS awake but not alert. This strange, so strange comatose feeling of being aware of the world around me but unable to respond.

I couldn't remember how I got to Connor's car, but I came to as he turned a corner, almost throwing me into his lap. He was rushing through the streets, intent on taking me to the hospital but I'd stopped him.

"Home," I'd said over and over. "Home home home."

I wanted to go *home*.

He took me to my apartment. It was my home. Not what I meant, but I struggled to find any other words to tell him, so instead I stayed quiet while he carried me up the floors to my apartment, dug my keys out of my purse and flew open the door so harshly I was vaguely aware of the bang and crash as it closed behind us.

Gina had run from her room. "What the hell?" She'd

shouted, surprised at our entrance and when Connor started walking toward my room, Gina followed.

"What the hell, Connor?"

From her bedroom door, Brandon's face peeked out and he swore, closing the door.

Connor had me laid in the bed and faced Gina. "I don't know what the fuck just happened. We were at dinner. Fans recognized me and I can't even explain how fucking insane they went. Shit." He scrubbed his hair. From my view of his back, he was breathing heavy. I remembered that. The first fan who'd walked up, glared at me and then dismissed me in the span of a breath.

There had been some men. Touching me. One tugged on my hair. One said something. Maybe the same man. Everything was so cloudy. Swirled together and I couldn't place what was reality and what had been my fears of what *could* happen.

"I didn't know what to do, Gina. She passed out. I saw her fucking crumple to the floor and—"

His breath hitched and I laid there on my bed, half sitting, watching Gina hug him unable to tell him it was okay. I was fine. It happened sometimes. Not often. Hadn't for a while. I'd be fine after sleep.

Everything I wanted to say lodged in my throat and Gina glanced at me and cringed.

"She'll be okay," she said, and she knew I would be. Thank God for Gina. "It's happened before."

"The fuck?" His strong hands shoved into his hair again.

"Her therapist said it's a protective way she used to stay sane during her...you know."

"Fucking hell," he muttered and his head dropped to stare at his sandals.

"Home," I said and it sounded more like a croak. My throat

hurt like I'd been screaming for hours and I cringed, rolled so I faced the wall. "Home."

"Her mom," I heard Gina say. "She wanted her home."

Their voices traveled from underwater. Close but quiet, rumbly but so distant. I closed my eyes to ignore them.

Gina was right and she was wrong. I wanted my parents. My *home*. I wanted them to go away. And I definitely, would never be *fine*.

Pretending otherwise was what had gotten me into this in the first place.

"Fuck. Fuck. She said home and I brought her here."

"It's okay. You stay with her. You don't have to talk. But she won't want to be alone either. And maybe don't touch her until she moves first. I'll go call her parents."

"They don't—"

Gina's voice took on a strange tone. "Connor, they'll be thankful you were with her. It's happened before when she was alone. Give them some credit."

He swore again and the room went silent. Outside my room, I heard Gina's voice drift away.

I closed my eyes and tried to do the same, but when I did memories I'd long since tried to forget were bright as reality. I popped my eyes open and stared at my wall. Bright white walls were better than what I'd see if I closed them again.

"I'm here, angel," Connor said. I heard something scrape against carpet. My chair, I guessed. "And I'm not going anywhere. You're safe, and I'm so damn sorry."

I was sorry too.

Sorry that I tried to be normal even when I now knew how impossible it was.

Fighting for freedom had been a mistake.

Perhaps the constraints of the safety I'd made of my life was better for me after all.

~

I WOKE to darkness and the press of warmth on my forehead. I peeled my eyes open. Gracious. Had I scrubbed them with sandpaper? They cracked as I opened them searching for light. Before they opened fully, I caught the scent of perfume. It was sweet, lilac and lavender and so very, very familiar to me.

"Mom?" I croaked.

"You're okay." It was her hand at my forehead holding a wet, warm cloth to it. "I'm here." She gingerly took my hand and placed it on the washcloth. "Hold this, sweetie. I have some water for you."

I blinked and my mom's profile came into view. Was it just earlier I saw her at the practice, waving to me from my spot on the field before I met her and my dad in their box? She'd been wearing cream dress pants and a teal shirt, a long, silky bow tied at her neck and draping down. She wasn't wearing that now and her makeup was gone. Hair pulled back at the sides and top and clipped at the back. She had on a long sleeve grey shirt, so simple but cute cut-outs for her thumbs. Black leggings.

"What time is it?"

"Shh. Don't speak yet." She held a cup with a straw close to my mouth and I took it, sipping down the cool liquid. "You're okay and I'm here. Both your dad and I are."

Dad. I'd wanted to talk to him earlier. Or was it yesterday? I *hated* these moments when I lost time. The memories would return followed by the embarrassment. The rush of humiliation that it had happened again. When was the last time? Months. More than. My sophomore year of college when Gina had convinced me to go to a frat party at a nearby co-ed university. But the lights, the darkness, the press of bodies and the sweaty stench.

That wasn't what happened this time. I felt it. It was

different.

Almost something worse.

I drank until my throat was soothed and shifted, sitting up in my bed. I was in my apartment. How did I get here?

"What happened?" I asked again and dropped the washcloth into my mom's hands.

Her smile was strained, eyes rimmed with red.

"What time is it?" *When is it?* Sometimes I blacked out for days. Sometimes minutes or hours. When I was sixteen, I once lost a week all because a car backfired on the street.

"It's two in the morning, sweetie. But you don't need to stress. Relax and everything will come back."

"Friday? No, I mean, Saturday?"

She nodded and leaned in, clasping my hand with both of hers. "I'm going to go talk to your dad, okay? He'll want to know you're awake. But I'm here and Gina and..." She brushed the hair off my forehead. "Well, we're all here for you okay?"

"Yeah." I drank more water and closed my eyes. "I want to go home."

Stupid. I was twenty-three years old and needed my mommy and daddy something fierce. My bed was too small. The room too dark.

"We'll do whatever you want," she said and stood, kissing my forehead. "Whatever you think is best. I'll be back."

She flicked on a lamp on my desk on her way out, illuminating the room in the way she knew to do. Not too bright. Not too dark. Not now. I needed the light.

My door pushed open while I tried to remember everything about the day but it stayed at the blurred edges of my mind. Dancing, turning figures and things I couldn't place. A creak and then a deep voice. "Hey, you're awake."

My eyes flew open. Connor.

Oh God. Had he seen this? He was at training camp. No...

he was back. If it was Saturday, yesterday was Friday. FanFest.

Oh God. We'd had dinner.

My lips parted. I didn't know what to say.

"Your mom said you're awake and I wanted to see you." He moved to me slowly like I was a wounded animal. Not too far off. I couldn't bring myself to look at him.

"I'm sorry," I said although why I was apologizing didn't make sense.

"Don't be sorry. Your mom and Gina said it was a panic attack?"

Not so much an attack so much as I checked out. Fled the scene in the only way I could. My therapist once described it as my fight or flight instinct kicking in but instead of running or actually *fleeing* I disappeared another way.

"You were there," I said and as his eyes widened, I explained. "I don't...I don't always remember everything. But we were at dinner."

"Yeah." He sat on the chair next to me. Too close.

I scooted back and by his flinch he caught it.

I didn't want to hurt him. But I wasn't thinking of him. Or us or whatever we were.

My throat ached like I'd been punched. Maybe swallowed razor blades. I drank more water, but it wasn't enough.

"Did you bring me here?"

"You collapsed at the restaurant. Fans went apeshit and I couldn't get to you in time. Jesus fuck, Brenna, I was scared as hell when..." He shook his head, those strong fingers shoved into his hair and he dropped his head. Elbows hit the bed and his back shook. "Fucking scared as hell. Are you okay?"

He barely lifted his head.

I gave him a sad smile. "I think we both know that I'm far from okay. Or normal."

"You're perfect," he said and his lips quirked. "I meant are you hurt, or, I don't know...I don't know what to do here, Brenna but I'm so glad to see you talking. When I brought you here, you wouldn't speak. Fuck, Gina talked me down from calling an ambulance I was so scared for you."

"I'll be okay." I tapped my water glass. "You should go though."

"I'm not leaving. I'll do anything you ask, angel, but please...let me be here for you."

There was no way to explain it to him. I'd coast by like a zombie for weeks. It didn't matter how I tried to move on from the episodes, it always took time. More therapy sessions to sort through it. This wasn't *normal,* but I handled it the only way I could.

By going home.

"I'll be with my parents for a while," I said. And how stupid and pathetic did that make me? But even now my small bed was too hard. Too itchy. The comforter not right. Nothing made sense unless I was there.

"I'll come and see you."

He might. For a while. But what about next time? Or the time after that? What would he do if I lost time for weeks and was confused and slept all day?

He'd tire eventually of how needy I was. How withdrawn. Being normal wasn't for me. Neither was stability.

"I don't want you to," I said and I stared at my water because my heart hurt almost as much as my throat, like I was ripping it out of my chest.

Thinking I could handle the stress of a life with him was insanity. I hadn't been careful. I hadn't realized the risks. Whatever happened tonight, it proved one thing.

I was much better wrapped in safety and comfort and then wildness and freedom.

"Brenna. Let's talk about this later. Don't push me away.

Not now."

A shadow and then a figure was at my door, my dad pushing it open farther. "Hey, darlin'."

"Dad." My chin trembled and I lost it. Right there. Sometimes I needed my damn daddy, but I fought against losing it in front of Connor.

I was humiliated enough.

He came into my room and squeezed my shoulder. "You doin' okay?"

I nodded, but we both knew I wasn't. I was sniffing away tears and stared at my lap to avoid Connor's deep, intense gaze I felt on me, wanting to be there for me. Wanting to help. Wanting to fix it.

But I wasn't someone who could be fixed. I could be managed. How long until he grew tired of it?

I loved him enough to want more than this for him. He'd never take me out in public again without fear and worry and the memory of whatever fully happened tonight darkening him. Forcing him to be someone different.

"Can you give us a minute?" I asked my dad, looking at him before going back to my lap.

"Yeah. Whatever you need. But your mom and I are here for you. Always. Whatever it is."

Always.

"I know." I sniffed and breathed in his cologne. Spicy and manly. So vastly different than my mom's sweet and calming perfume but familiar all the same.

He clasped his hand to Connor's shoulder as he left, murmured something I didn't catch but had Connor nodding.

When we had privacy again, I forced myself to meet Connor's gaze. "Thank you for bringing me here. For taking care of me."

"I don't need thanks for that, Brenna."

He needed free of it.

"Did you tell my parents? About us?"

He leaned forward, seemed to want to reach for me but instead clasped his hands together and set them both close to my hip. I didn't reach for them. "I told them everything. I told them what happened. I told them we were dating." He cleared his throat, debated, and kept his dark eyes on me as he lowered his voice and said, "I told them I loved you. Loved you in a way that will never go away. Please, don't tell me to go now."

I'd wanted to hear it. I'd felt it. I felt it from him and I'd known it blossoming in my own soul for him. And God, it was beautiful.

Beautiful and deadly. Falling in love with me would change him and not for the best.

My chin shook and tears fell. I brushed them away *hating* I couldn't give that back to him. Not now.

He pleaded me with his eyes so silent and strong while his shoulders were tight and his back hunched forward, trying to get as close as possible to me without pushing me away.

I'd already done that myself.

"I can't be with you, Connor. I'm sorry. I should have known this would happen. Should have prepared you but I wanted to enjoy what we had."

"You did enjoy it. And I know you feel the same even if you're scared to say it right now."

God, how I loved him. As much as I loved sunsets and crisp sweet wine and laughing with Gina and going out with the player's wives and thinking over the last few weeks that I could be somebody different.

"I will kill you in pieces," I said, choking over the words. "Your worry for me will take over everything and you'll be stifled by it. I know you. You're more protective than my own parents and you're such a good man. I can't take that from you.

I can't give you *normal*, Connor, and you deserve someone whole and healthy. I don't think...no, I know that will never be me."

"I don't care."

He would. At some point. He'd care down the road, maybe years, maybe if we had kids and I lost it with them. He'd care when I ran back to my parents instead of leaning on him. Oh, he'd care then.

"I don't want this. I want you to go." I tried to steel my spine for his rebuttal. Erase the emotions running rampant through my veins down to my soul and straight to my heart with piercing pain.

Connor simply tilted his head. Grinned like I was a puppy. Leaned forward and bravely took my hand, bringing it to his mouth. He kissed my knuckles. Ran his thumb along my palm. My inner wrist.

I couldn't do anything to stop the shiver from his touch. Oh so beautifully deadly. To both of us.

"I will never stop loving you. Or fighting to convince you you're wrong on this. But tonight, I'll give you the space you want."

"You've always said you'd give me anything I asked for."

He kissed my palm, curled my fingers into a fist like he was forcing me to hold on to it. Then he stood. "I will. Anything but this."

And then he turned and left the room, leaving my door open on his way out and it was only moments later when my mom came in, wiping beneath her eyes and whispered, "He's so much sweeter than I ever thought he'd be."

"Mom."

"I know, I know. Don't meddle." She grinned and turned toward my closet, pulling out a suitcase. "Now, what do you need packed?"

TWENTY-NINE

Connor

IT'D BEEN A WEEK. A week since Brenna kicked me out of her bedroom.

A week since her father pulled me into her small kitchen, arms crossed over his chest, a look on his face I'd seen once—that look of utter disappointment. He'd asked me to tell him everything and before I filtered anything, I did. I told him about meeting her at Glitz before the party at his house. I told him about the last few weeks. I laid my heart bare to the man who held my career in his hands and whose daughter held the rest of me in hers. I apologized profusely for putting her in a situation I couldn't have predicted and didn't protect her from and when I was done, David looked at his shoes, slippers because it was so late and he was in such a hurry to get to his daughter he hadn't bothered thinking of what he was wearing.

Lifting his head, he simply said, "Give her some time."

That was it. He gave me a few minutes with her when her mom came out and that was all I had with Brenna in the last week before she packed up most of her things and went back home with her parents, closing herself off to me.

It hurt more than it should have that she didn't turn to me. That she *still* hadn't turned to me. I couldn't stop thinking about her.

She didn't return my calls or my texts. I stopped by her parents' house, risked her father's wrath because I still didn't know where he stood with us being together. Every time, her mom answered the door, a pitiful look on her face as I rocked on my heels.

"I'm sorry, Connor. She doesn't want to see you."

I meant every word I said to her that night. Every word I said to her father. It might not have been the best time to tell her I loved her. In the scheme of things, it was probably the worst.

I also meant it when I told her I'd give her space, I'd give her anything...but I would not give her a life without the two of us together. She was meant for me in a way I felt deep in the marrow of my bones and there was no way I was walking away without a fight.

Practice was over, our last practice before the first preseason game tomorrow night. I would only play a handful of snaps if even that. Physically I was ready. Mentally, I hoped I was benched. It was the first game in my career since my grandfather slipped pads over my shoulder at the age of eight, my first Pop Warner football jamboree that I had ever thought of *not* wanting to play football. But Brenna consumed every waking moment.

How could I have changed that night? Why didn't she tell me how bad things could get? When did shit go so sideways?

I was lost in all of it, still beating myself up when I stepped out of the locker room and David Kemper was resting against the hall on the other side.

His expression was unreadable. A dangerous sign for me.

He pushed off the wall and gestured with his head. "Come have lunch with me."

He started walking and I had no choice to follow. It wasn't a suggestion but a command and he was still my boss.

"Yes, Sir."

"David, Connor. You haven't called me sir in five years and you don't need to start now."

I wasn't sure whether to take that as a good sign or not, so I followed, my workout bag flung over my shoulder. He kept walking to the parking garage, beeped the locks on his silver Range Rover and popped the trunk. "Throw your stuff in the back. I'm starving."

"Okay." Was it wrong I had a flash of him throwing me in the back as well? Perhaps taking me somewhere to bury me? "How's Brenna?"

"Lunch first, son. Get in."

He clicked the button to close the back hatch and I climbed into the passenger seat. His mood was ominous and strained. David wasn't a man prone to shouting or anger. He encouraged his team like the ultimate cheerleader and he was as invested as any pro owner I knew. The man *loved* his sports and his players and his family and most definitely not in that order.

Scrubbing my hands down my athletic pants, I forced myself to relax. Going to lunch with David meant any number of things and we didn't speak while he whipped out of the garage, drove through downtown streets and pulled up in front of a brewery.

"Beer?" I asked.

"Been a stressful week. Have what you need, I won't tell Coach. This isn't a work-related meal."

I never knew the man could be so cryptic but at least that meant he wasn't kicking me off the team before the season started. A small burst of hope ignited in me as I replayed his words. This was about Brenna, and at least someone came to me about it.

"Right," I muttered and climbed out of the SUV.

We found a table inside, the restaurant surprisingly slow for it being summer and a Friday. Two tables were filled on the outdoor patio where the customers also brought their dogs. The animals were lying at the owner's feet, tongues lolling out of their mouths.

David ordered a flight of their summer selections while I stuck to a lager. Normally I didn't drink before games but all things considered, I'd had more than my share this week.

Our beers came and we ordered our food. The whole time, pins and needles pricked at my nerves. David needed to start sharing or I was going to assume the worst. Did she leave again? Go somewhere to hide?

It was quite possibly the worst-case scenario, but I'd find her. I had millions in a bank account accumulating interest and I'd use it all if I had to.

He took a sip of beer, gaze on the row of screens above the bar to our side. "You don't know what it does to a man to not have any idea where his baby girl is, Connor."

Shit. We were starting there. "You're right. I don't."

"A full week. We had no clue. Was she alive? Getting raped? I gotta tell ya, the thoughts that ran through my mind while she was taken and even after she returned before she started talking. Worst few months of my life and the evil thoughts I had were something I couldn't imagine ever thinking. Things I wanted to do to the men who took her, the ones who were going to buy her. All of them deserved a death worse than they got. I would have tortured them if I were able to get my hands on them. My pure anger alone would have let me rip limbs from their bodies."

He took a drink. I stayed silent. Even now his voice was the same kind tone he always had but edged with a darkness I'd only felt when Brenna told me what happened.

"How is she?" I asked. I'd take his memories and his fears and his anger, but Brenna was all I cared about.

"Sad," he said and finally turned to me. "And I think I'm once again helpless. Seems to me, there's nothing I can do to get rid of that for her, only one person can." He arched a brow and tried a different beer even though he'd only had a few sips of the first.

"Can't help her if she won't see me, David. I've tried. She ignores every call and text. Kassy won't let me inside. I'm giving her the space she asked for but I don't like it."

He leaned back in his booth and spun the small glass in his hands in a circle on the table. "I'll be honest with you. I think you're either brave or stupid for getting involved with my daughter. It's risky for you."

I could have apologized for all of it. I wouldn't. I loved her too much and it was that moment when I thought *fuck it*. If loving Brenna cost me my job with the Rough Riders, I'd risk it.

I'd risk everything for her.

"To be more honest," he continued, and his gaze met mine. Green eyes that reminded me of Brenna were narrowed on me. Tension lined the edges of them. Stubble on his cheeks telling me hadn't shaved in a while. "I didn't think you were the man for her. Not that first day you were at her place. Not the day after when she spent most of it staring at a wall in her room."

"I love your daughter." It hurt he didn't think that much of me. He'd never alluded to that but sitting across from him, I saw it. He didn't think I was man enough and that fucking stung.

"I didn't say I don't think it now," he continued like I hadn't said anything. Like I wasn't giving him everything I had. Frustration bubbled beneath my skin like an itch I couldn't reach. I took a large swig of my beer.

"Why am I here, David?"

"I want my daughter back. I want her healthy and whole and frankly, thinking back over the last month, the only time I've seen a glimpse of the little girl she used to be...was I think attributed to you."

"I don't understand."

"Because you haven't spent thirteen years watching this girl, this sweet little girl who danced and laughed and played pranks on people and was smart as a whip but sassier than anything you ever saw lose herself daily. You haven't watched her fight for life and to get past what happened to her. You haven't seen her fall to the depths of despair where you had her hospitalized for suicidal thoughts for *years*, Connor. And I'm only telling you this because we all saw it the last few weeks. Her sister, her brothers. We've all seen something different with her and we figured it was a man. We figured it was something...and we were right." He leaned forward and pushed his beer out of the way, dropped his voice. "I think the reason she was truly lighthearted and playful for the last few weeks was because of *you*. And if you give her that, if you can sit here right now and tell me you'll spend every moment you have with her trying to give her that, then you've got my respect. You have my permission if it means anything to you. But what I need from you is to start trying harder to get her to see you."

"I'm worried if I push her too hard, she'll run the other direction."

"Possibly." He frowned and reached into his back pocket, pulled out a folded piece of paper. "I guess we'll see."

He slid the paper across the table. I didn't hide how desperately I wanted it and snatched it up.

It was thick card stock, not paper, and once I unfolded it, bright-colored balloons grabbed my attention first before the words *Happy Birthday* snagged it next.

It was a birthday invitation for her niece. Next Friday night.

I'd fight the Devil himself to ensure I could make it.

"You want me to show up?"

"I'm giving you a chance. Don't blow it."

THE HOUSE WAS MAYHEM. The adrenaline assaulting my senses was worse. Another week without hearing from Brenna, but I'd scaled back in anticipation of tonight. I still texted her, but I didn't call and I didn't stop by. I texted her about my day and practice. I texted her when I saw Shannon. I texted her every stupid little thought I had. My entire text string to her was an endless story of my boring as hell life, spilled out like a journal for her to read. I didn't even know if she had her phone on and received them.

I still had no idea what to say when I saw her. I suppose I'd let her lead the way with that when she saw me.

David didn't tell her I was coming. He called me twice during the week and gave me an update which was really nothing. "Still sad. But thinking about heading back to her apartment soon."

Which meant she was feeling better in one way at least.

"You made it."

I turned toward the voice, only to see her oldest brother Aiden. His hands were loose at his sides, but his posture depicted anything other than someone who was relaxed. No, he looked like he wanted to shove his fist into my face for the hell of it.

"I did."

"You hurt my sister and I'll take you out at the knees."

I tried to brush it off. I assumed I'd have a whole group of overprotective Kempers on my ass as soon as I stepped through these doors but as the oldest, I figured Aiden would be the worst. "You take out my knees, that ruins my career...your dad's season."

He didn't hesitate. "Brenna's more important."

I stepped toward him and then leaned closer. "Yeah. She is. Where is she?"

"Still upstairs. She'll be down soon. Our sister Eva took her some wine a few minutes ago. She doesn't do well with noise after these...episodes."

"Good to know. Anything else I should know besides the physical threats to my safety?"

He sneered and then shook his head. "No. The rest you'll have to learn for yourself, by taking care of her the way she deserves."

"Understood." I slapped his shoulder and moved past him. I wanted a drink before I saw her too and given David's love of scotch and beer there had to be a supply around somewhere.

"Connor, you made it." Kassy found me and headed straight to me, a worried smile on her face and lining her eyes. "I'm glad you're here. How are you?"

I leaned down and kissed her cheek, gave her a hug. "Thanks for having me and I wouldn't miss it."

"Good, good." She patted my cheek and smiled. "Beer is

out back where the guys and games are. Kids are well, every-where." She flipped a towel in the air as two small boys raced between us, shooting Nerf Guns and screaming, "You're dead now, sucka!"

"That's Kollin and Beckett," she said and came back to me. "She'll be happy to see you, I promise, even if she doesn't first realize it."

I held up a bag I'd forgotten I brought. I wasn't exactly sure what a girl turning twelve was into but thankfully I'd gone to Paige and Shannon. Now I had a gift bag filled with books and nail polish and a half-dozen hair accessories.

"Where would you like me to put this?"

Kassy smiled again. And damn it felt good to have at least Brenna's family on my side, Aiden's threats aside. "There's a table out back. You know the way?"

"Of course." She took off when she heard more screams from kids and I made my way to the back porch. Outside, dozens of kids, mostly girls who were probably Sophie's friends, jumped and swam in the pool. I wasn't sure which one of the thirty-some girls were Sophie but the gift table was easy to find. Presents piled a mile high and an ungodly amount of pink and purple everywhere made it easy.

"Connor!" I lifted my hand at David's shout. "What would you like to drink?"

Something stronger than beer would be incredible, but I held back. "Whatever is cold, David, thanks." I dropped off the present and met him with a handshake and backslap before he gave me my drink. Around him were his other son Tanner and son-in-law, Sam, who bounced a baby on his lap. I'd met everyone several times over the years but this was the first time conversation didn't come easy. They all stared at me like I was their Hail Mary play. The seriousness of why I was here landed in my gut like a brick.

I wasn't invited because they liked me with Brenna and wanted us together. They expected me to be the one to heal their hurting family member.

It was a role I'd take seriously, but what in the hell would happen if I failed?

THIRTY

Brenna

I FELT him before I saw him. No wonder why Eva acted so strange upstairs earlier. She'd brought me a glass of wine while I finished curling my hair and refused to leave. It was her words that startled me the most.

"Here." She'd thrust the glass onto the counter in front of me. "You might need this."

I looked at her like she'd grown three heads but listened.

Now that I was stepping onto the patio, that same sensation I got every time he was near came back in full force at the back of my neck.

"Go on," Eva whispered behind me. Her hand was at my back and she shoved me over the threshold and I almost fell back into her when I finally saw him.

Connor.

Talking to my dad and Tanner and Sam. Aiden was by the

pool but his head swung in my direction then to Connor's when he saw me.

He was here.

Why was he here? And who let him in?

The last two weeks had been painful. Once I got over my embarrassment of what happened, I regretted the way I treated Connor. I regretted the things I said to him most of all, mostly because I hadn't actually meant them.

I loved him.

But how could I love someone the way they deserved when I wasn't healthy myself? I spent hours in therapy over the last few weeks and ironically, our main conversations weren't about what happened, what triggered me or what made this episode so bad, they were about Connor.

How I felt with him. How he scared me...how him *loving* me scared me.

I turned off my phone after the first few days and hadn't turned it back on. Gina called my parents' house phone when she needed me, but I couldn't read Connor's texts. I didn't know if he was still trying, but a week ago he'd stopped trying to see me.

Had he already decided I wasn't worth the effort? I couldn't blame him. He'd given me enough chances. I'd walked away from him enough.

Connor was a man who should have a woman who would have the strength to handle everything his life brought and despite how much I cared for him, I didn't have that, no matter how much I wanted it.

I whipped around and stared down my sister. "Did you know he was coming?"

"Dad talked to him."

Great. I was an adult who still had Daddy fighting her battles. How pathetic.

"Eva," I whispered, but she stepped toward me, forcing me backward and onto the patio where Connor was so close. "Are you kidding me?"

This wasn't the time or the place. It was Sophia's birthday for crying out loud.

"Nope," she said.

"Brenna."

That voice. I knew it in my sleep. I *heard* it in my sleep. Daily. Nightly. Connor was everywhere the last two weeks as I tried to forget him, but nothing helped, and now he was here because of my family.

I didn't know who to run from first.

My eyes closed and I inhaled a shaky breath. "You shouldn't be here."

"I couldn't stay away anymore."

I opened my eyes only to find Eva gone in front of me. Connor was to my side. I could skip back inside and lock the door behind me and barricade myself in my room until he left, but good Lord it was time to stop acting like a scared little girl all the damn time.

"Can we talk?" he asked. "In private?"

If it would get him out of there, it'd be for the best. My heart was already waffling, softening toward him and flip-flopping all over the place.

Without replying, I headed back inside to my dad's office. It was the only place the grandkids knew they weren't allowed to enter, so it'd be quiet and free from Nerf Bullets and fart jokes or the sporadic wrestling match.

He followed me and when we reached the office, he didn't bother closing the door. He also didn't block it. I shouldn't have been surprised. He'd learned a lot about me in a short amount of time. I wished more of it were good.

"Why are you here?" I asked.

He stepped toward me slowly. Two steps closer and he stopped. We were far enough apart we couldn't touch. I still felt him everywhere. "Because I love you, and I'm not sure what you're afraid of when it comes to me, or if you're embarrassed, but I'm here to prove to you there's no reason for either. Not with me."

If only it were simple.

"I think that night proved to me I'm not the woman you'll need."

His hands curled into fists and relaxed. He settled them on his hips before letting them fall to his side. Was he...nervous? "I think I'm old enough to know what I need and want, angel."

Angel. I'd missed that.

"Connor." I sighed his name. My fight was leaving me with every second I was close to him. I couldn't help it. My gaze wandered. His black hair. That marble cut jaw with no hint of a beard. In an age where beards and scruff were everywhere, always seeing him so cleanly shaven made him that much hotter. And those eyes, burning with something indiscernible and aimed at me ripped straight to my core. My soul.

He was all man. Cocky and arrogant with a side of rude when we first met, but he was so much more than that.

"You'll change," I said, gathering what little strength I had left. "You'll become someone different with me. You'll be worried about me when we go out. You might even stop going out. I know you, Connor, and it's one of the reasons why I love you, but I don't want that for you."

His hands were at my cheeks before I realized what I confessed.

"Say it again." He was warm and strong. Tender. His cologne was spicy but sweet, perfect for him.

"I shouldn't have said that."

"You should have. You should have said it when you first

felt it. Or later. Or maybe when I said it. Or texted it to me. Breanna, I love you in that forever way, for better or worse, in sickness and health." He leaned down until our noses were almost touching and oh how I wanted to melt into him and his touch and forget the reasons why this wouldn't work.

"You love me," he said. "And I love you. That's all that matters here. The rest we'll figure out. And as far as changing, that's what love *does*. It will change us for the better. We'll grow together."

"I don't know if I'm strong enough for that."

"Then you'll lean on me when you're weak and I'll hold you up."

I sniffed away tears and he wiped them away with his thumbs. "I think you'd give me so much more than I could ever give you back."

His head fell forward until he was resting against mine and then his shoulders shook as he laughed. "Angel, if you think I'm giving you more than you give me, you haven't been paying attention. I didn't even know my heart *worked* until I met you. You've given me hope I can be a good man. That I can have a woman who won't leave like my mom, and someone who will someday give me babies and boring nights at home and laughter when things are shit. I don't *care* how long it takes to show that's what you give me, but I'm in this, for the long haul. I just need you with me."

"Everything's a mess. From how we met. To who I am." My throat hitched over a sob. "I don't know how to be normal."

"Fuck normal, Brenna. I just want you." His fingers pressed to my cheeks, his voice went gritty. "I only want you. You don't need to be afraid of me, I promise you."

He gave me hope. He made it sound so easy. "You and me against the world, huh?"

"No. You and me, your family, your friends, Gina...we're all here. We always will be."

For the first time, I touched him. My hands went to his wrists, curled around them and squeezed. "I've made a mess of this."

"Tell me you love me again, let me kiss you, and you're forgiven."

I laughed, shook my head against his. "You make everything seem so easy."

"Falling in love with you was the easiest thing I've done. I imagine loving you every day will be even easier."

He meant it. He meant every rumbled word he spoke with a confident fierceness I couldn't resist.

It could end up being a horrible mistake. It could end up being the biggest and best risk I ever took.

And for the first time in my life, I went with the risk.

I jumped in with both feet and looked Connor straight in the eyes.

"I love you, Connor. Forgive me?"

"Already done," he growled, and then his mouth slammed to mine and we kissed until we were at risk of doing very bad things in my father's office. Until I was breathless and filled with him. Until our lips were swollen and we were both out of breath.

I kissed him until my sister walked into the room, cleared her throat, and loudly declared, "If y'all are done making out now, there's a party going on out back where you're supposed to be."

Connor pulled back from me, grinning down at me and there was nothing in those dark blue eyes of his except absolute adoration. He held out his hand for me. "You ready to party?"

I took his hand in mine and made the leap of my life. "I'm ready for everything."

Brenna

SEVERAL MONTHS later

A KNOCK HIT my bedroom door, but I already knew who it was. Connor was taking me out tonight and he'd already texted he was on his way. I assumed Gina let him in when I didn't hear the buzzer to our apartment go off.

"It's open," I called out, threading an earring through my ear. It was a small diamond stud. Connor gave them to me a couple of weeks ago for Valentine's Day. When I first saw the box, I almost passed out. An engagement?

It was too soon, wasn't it? And then I'd opened it and been disappointed.

Connor had laughed at my expression, ran a finger around the base of my left hand's ring finger and promised me something better than the beautiful earrings he gifted me that night. "Soon. Very soon."

"Shit, you keep getting more beautiful."

My gaze in the mirror's reflection slid to him in my doorway. My jaw dropped and my hand shook, making it difficult to put the back of the earring on. "You are...wow..."

I saw him in suits every weekend he left for the stadium or for the airport to catch his plane for an away game. His beauty hadn't diminished at all and over the months he only grew more attractive, not only his body. But the more I spent time with him, the further in love I fell.

Connor might have been bossy and cocky and arrogant when we first met but I now knew that was only a skin-deep facade he portrayed to keep people out of his personal business. But once he let me in, all the walls crumbled and I came to know and love the core of him. His protectiveness, his strength in body, mind and spirit. His love for me knew no bounds. He'd become my greatest encourager. My fiercest protector.

Connor was the love of my life, and one I would kill to keep in my life forever.

Turned out, trusting him to be the man I needed was as easy as breathing. Loving him was the most natural thing in the world. He felt the same way about me because he told me daily, through his words and his actions.

Months ago, I'd walked in fear, and Connor spent every day, every moment together, showing me how absolutely unnecessary my fear had been.

At first, we took several steps back. We spent time with my family. Dinners with friends. Slowly, we went out in groups. Quiet parks and movies and all the places people who dated hung out and then we spent time alone. Some days I felt ridiculous at how slow we moved. It was weeks after our reconciliation, after I returned the words he wanted to hear so badly we were intimate again.

And even then, we moved slower. I hadn't been certain the physical had rushed me forward into a spot where my last blackout was the reason, but Connor wasn't going to risk it.

It had worried me at first and when I told him, he laughed in my face, kissed me harshly and wrapped me in a hug. "I want you every damn moment of the day, but we're doing this my way. Slowly. Safely. I want to earn your trust before we go there, prove to you I love you as much as my words say. We'll have the rest of forever to be wrapped in each other physically, so stop worrying."

And that was that. We took everything step by step and I think his crazy schedule with the season starting and the team playing *incredible* helped.

We were both busy. I worked on carving out a social life and group for myself. I took him to a therapy appointment he insisted on attending.

He came to family dinners when he could which were changed to Monday nights on home game weekends only during the season.

We spent Thanksgiving in a cozy cabin in the mountains, the two of us secluded and made love until he had to get home to prepare for Sunday's game. We shared Christmas morning together and then the afternoon with my family. The night screaming at the television watching college football bowl games.

We rang in the New Year privately, turning in early for an away game to Kansas City he had to fly out to the next day.

And then I celebrated with him on the field of the Miami Gardens Stadium the night they won the Super Bowl again. Confetti falling, screams making the field vibrate from the noise level. My mom and family around me. Connor never out of touch. The experiences we shared together, the situations we found ourselves in, I'd only had one episode during some random fireworks over St. Patrick's Day. But even that wasn't bad. Lasted minutes and when I came to, it was Connor I curled into and embraced.

Somewhere along the way, he'd become my *home*.

And I was happy. So damn stinking happy that as the memories flooded me, I turned to Connor and winked. "Do we have to go out for dinner?"

I trailed a finger down the buttons of his dress shirt and tugged on his tie.

"Yeah." His hand wrapped around mine and he kissed my fingertip. "We have reservations and I have a surprise for you."

"More surprises?"

He surprised me so often with gifts and a trip right after the season to Jamaica that my life with Connor was really one large surprise and yet stable and safe at the same time. I was far past questioning how that worked, it did, and that was the only important thing.

"All right then," I pouted and picked up my blue clutch from my bed. "I'm ready."

Gina and Brandon were curled on the couch as we left. "See you later," she called out and it was hard to see her around all the packed boxes. I was moving out next week and I was slowly packing all of my things.

It was the end of an era of Gina and me together, but it was time to move on and grow. Brandon was moving in, although his clothes and he himself were already there. They were just waiting for me to finish packing so my room could become their office for Gina's studying and Brandon's tattoo artwork.

They were as different as Connor and me. I supposed opposites definitely did attract.

We walked into the high-end steakhouse and wine bar in

downtown Raleigh hand in hand and were immediately sat at a table near a wood-burning fireplace. I grew up in a family with money, so exorbitance and decadence wasn't anything new in my life, but it still surprised me the way Connor threw around his money when we went out. The best restaurants. The quietest tables.

Sometimes he rented out entire restaurants for us alone.

We sat down and our waiter was at our table almost immediately. He was close to our age, tall and lean with perfect done and gelled blonde hair but it wasn't his face or his body that grabbed my attention, it was the bucket of ice and champagne he held in his hands.

"Good evening, Mr. Quinten," he greeted us and turned to me. "Miss. We hope you enjoy your evening with us tonight."

Connor wasn't nearly as surprised as I was when the waiter popped the cork of the Dom Perignon. I realized. He was full of surprises but this was over the top even for him.

"Thank you," he told the waiter and once he left us to peruse the menu, I turned to Connor.

"Are we celebrating something?"

He dipped his chin, urging me to take my glass. "I hope so." He clinked our glasses together and took a sip.

"You do?" Curiosity quickened my heart rate. "What is it?"

Connor was quiet for a moment, but as he opened his mouth to speak, my phone went off.

"I'm sorry," I said, digging into my purse. His phone rang then too and both of us looked at each other.

It was instinct and I didn't have to look at my phone to know. "Shannon," I said.

He had already pulled his phone out of his suit coat pocket. "Yup. She's in labor."

I checked my cell phone and saw the same message. A

massive group text to the team wives I was now included on. Other ones from Paige.

The baby's coming! The baby's coming! Holy crap I'm going to be an aunt!

I laughed at her text. "We should be there."

"We should." He made no effort to stand and his hesitancy gave me pause.

"What is it?"

"Nothing." He tossed his napkin onto the table and then took a quick sip of his champagne. "Nothing at all."

We left, him explaining what happened to the hostess on our way out and he paid for the champagne.

WE WERE AT THE HOSPITAL, surrounded by Gage and Elizabeth, Paige and Beaux, Kolby and his daughter and various other players with their wives. The men were large enough they took up almost the entire room and I felt horrible for the other people who were waiting. There was barely any room left once all of Oliver and Shannon's friends showed up.

My own parents beat us to the hospital.

We'd been there for hours. Connor had long since removed his suit and tie, untucked his shirt and a nurse had told us that Shannon was progressing quickly and we should have news soon.

It wasn't until relief rushed through the room with that declaration that I remembered the dinner we didn't have.

The champagne Connor bought.

"Hey," I said, walking up to him. He was talking with Gage but as I walked up to him, he turned his full attention to me.

"Hey angel," he muttered and kissed my temple. "You okay?"

"Yeah, but I just remembered dinner earlier. You said we hoped to celebrate something."

He'd already signed another contract with the Rough Riders. That was a no-brainer when he ended the season as the second best running back in the league, the most touchdowns made on the team. I was damn proud of my man.

He glanced around the room. "You know...I think this might be better anyway."

He grabbed my hand and dragged me into the middle of the waiting room and pointed to the floor. "Stay here."

"What are you—" Before I finished, he moved to his suit coat, dug something out of it and walked back to me. His hand was curled around something.

"Hey!" he shouted and everyone in the room quieted. "I got something to say."

"Whoop!" Beaux cheered. "Speech! Speech!"

"Shut up." I laughed at Connor and Beaux and then that laugh disappeared when Connor turned his attention to me. He didn't wear a single hint of humor.

His expression was heavy. So beautiful my heart ached as I looked at him. Watching him blink slowly. His shoulders heaved with a deep breath. "I wanted this to be private, and I don't want to steal Shannon and Oliver's night, but there's something I'm dying to say to you and now, with everyone we love in the same room, I don't want to wait anymore."

"Okay...."

I glanced around. Near the windows, my parents stood. My dad had his arm wrapped around my mom's back and she leaned into his shoulder. Tears made her eyes look glassy and all of a sudden it happened...

Connor dropped to his knee in front of me.

My mom gasped.

A cheer went up again.

Someone cried.

"I've had this ring in my dresser since before I bought you those earrings you're wearing. In fact, I've had this ring since Christmas, but I wanted to wait. Give you time."

"I didn't need it," I blurted. On his knee in front of me, hand out, a closed box in his palm, he went blurry. "Oh God. Are you doing this in a hospital?"

"I love you, Brenna Marie Kemper. I didn't know what love was until you. I didn't know I was capable of it and I certainly didn't think I was capable of giving that to someone else. But you have made me a better man, a stronger man and I'm so thankful for you every single day. So, in front of our friends, your parents, and everyone we love the most...will you do the honor of becoming my wife? Having a family with me? Making babies and raising them with me?"

"Yes!" I cried and I dropped to my knees before he could stand. I threw my arms around him and kissed him, as the entire waiting room went up into a roar. We kissed. Sloppily and happily and it was beautiful. The most beautiful moment of my life until he popped open the box and slid an enormous, emerald cut ring onto my finger and kissed me again.

Soon, we were yanked apart. My dad pulled me in for a hug and my mom did the same. We were passed around with hugs and slaps on the backs and handshakes.

And finally, when Oliver walked into the room, watched us celebrating, we grew even louder when he threw his hands up in the air and shouted, "A girl! I have a healthy, beautiful girl!"

We cheered again. We waited until we could see the baby and then Shannon cried and hugged me while I apologized for getting engaged while she was in labor. She slapped the back of my head and told me to forget about it which only made me cry harder.

The rush of energy and happiness turned to sleepiness and

exhaustion, Connor and I went to his home...soon to be our home...and we celebrated.

We celebrated every beautiful moment of how we'd met, what we'd been through, and what we'd face together.

Forever. *Always.*

DID you love Cocky Player and want to read more from Stacey Lynn?

CLICK HERE to sign up for my newsletter and receive information about all upcoming releases as well as sales and other exclusive content. Plus, as a thank you, you'll receive a FREE E-Book of mine.

WANT to be the first to know about upcoming sales?
    Follow me on BookBub!

WANT to ensure you never miss a new release?
    Follow me on Amazon.

Thank You

HUGE THANK you to Hilary and all of Social Butterfly PR for throwing your full enthusiasm and support behind each and every book I write. I have loved working with all of you and can't wait to see what's ahead! Hilary, I miss you most of all. ;-)

Ellie and Virginia, as always, thanks for putting up with my mess and spit-shining each manuscript until it sparkles.

Shannon, you're the best. Always. Forever. Your talent is astounding and I'm thankful I can call you a friend.

Special, enormous thank you to my family who is always here, cheering me on and being so patient when I'm in my office. Your support is everything to me and I love you all with all of my heart.

To my Sweeties! I love you ladies and your excitement for my books! Special thanks to you this time for coming up with Brenna's name for me. It fits her perfectly.

To all the bloggers who devote their time and passion into reading books, book tours, release events, leaving reviews, promoting and pimping – you are all rockstars! Thank you for all the love over the years.

And last but definitely not least – to you the reader. I'm blown away with every release how much you adore my books. You have made my dream a reality and I hope I can cheer you on with yours.

Other Books by Stacey Lynn

LOVE In The Heartland
Captivated By You
This Time Around
Long Road Home
Before We Fell

THE ROUGH RIDERS Series
Dirty Player
Filthy Player
Wicked Player

CRAZY LOVE SERIES
Fake Wife
Knocked Up
28 Dates
Weekend Fling – coming soon!

THE LUMINOUS SERIES
Dominate Me
Crave Me
Long For Me

THE FIRESIDE SERIES
His to Love
His to Protect
His to Cherish

His to Seduce

TANGLED Love Series
Entice

Embrace

Enflame

JUST ONE SERIES
Just One Song

Just One Week

Just One Regret

Just One Moment

THE NORDIC LORDS Series
Point of Return

Point of Redemption

Point of Freedom

Point of Surrender

STANDALONES
Remembering Us

Don't Lie To Me

Try Me – A Don't Lie To Me Novella

www.ingramcontent.com/pod-product-compliance
Lightning Source LLC
Chambersburg PA
CBHW020100310726
48970CB00002B/405